Old Wounds:
A Nick Shelby Case
and Other Crime Stories

Tom Batt

Dedicated to my family for supporting my creative ambitions.

Siren

The city was silent. Lights twinkled in the dark like the stars in the night sky. The window sill wasn't exactly comfortable, but it allowed Devlin to relax as she admired the view. She drew on a cigarette blowing the billowing smoke out the open window, the soft wind taking it away. As she pulled the burning stub from her full lips, her blood-stained hand was shaking, a charm bracelet slipping down her arm. Although she was skinny and wore nothing more than lingerie, she was immune to the cold. Her mind was on other things. Her eyes were glazed over, blood dripping from her face. She flicked the cigarette butt out of the window and slipped off the sill with ease. As she made her way across the studio apartment she glanced over at the carnage she was responsible for only a few moments ago. His head was almost gone and what remained was unidentifiable. His naked body was drenched in blood and soaking the silk bed sheets beneath. A spray of pure red up the headboard and wall. Devlin entered the bathroom, flicking on the bright light. She stared into the mirror and thought back to how she got here.

Devlin sat at the bar of a busy club, the synth-pop competing with the many voices chatting away. She was sipping at a glass of wine staring longingly at a photograph of Roxy and herself, happier times. She stroked the glossy image with a gentle finger, memories flooding her brain. Days spent together shopping, dinners out, every moment together was a gift. Her mind drifted from one to the next, a subtle smile growing on her face. Her cheerful reflections faded away when she remembered it all ended on one particular night.

There was a strong chill in the air. Devlin and Roxy were waiting on the street corner in provocative clothing trying their best to keep warm. Clients were always harder to come by in the winter months. As they hugged themselves, rubbing their arms, a car pulled up beside them. Roxy wasted no time approaching the vehicle and leaning in through the window to talk to the hidden driver. Devlin watched impatiently before Roxy turned to her and smiled. She pulled the passenger door open and the internal light lit up the face of the driver. Devlin got a short, but clear look at the sinister man before he disappeared back into darkness as Roxy climbed in and slammed the door shut. She didn't know it at the time, but as the car drove away that would be the last time she saw Roxy.

Several days of stress and worry followed. The police were no help and Devlin was beginning to lose all hope. She didn't have the energy to leave the house, eating food and sleeping were impossible. She spent many hours of the day staring at the front door of their small apartment hoping she would step through and all would be okay again. That moment never came and she realised it never would when she flicked on the news one morning. They were reporting the discovery of a body, a young girl severely beaten and dumped in a field. Devlin's fingers gripped the arms of the chair as she watched with bated breath. As the photograph of Roxy flashed up on screen, Devlin felt her entire body relax in despair. Tears welled in her eyes as she slumped forward onto the floor. Her blood-curdling scream echoed around the room.

She was back in the bar, still staring at the photograph. She glanced down at the charm bracelet around her wrist. It belonged to Roxy. Among her personal effects given to Devlin as her only next of kin. Something to remember her by at least. She heard his voice at first ordering a rum and coke, soft and soothing, nothing like what she had imagined. As she turned to look at him, she almost froze with fear when she saw his face. Strong features with kind eyes and a charming smile, the complete opposite to the night she saw him in the low light of the car. Could this really be the same man? Of course it was, she knew it was, but doubt sometimes sets in even when you're sure. He caught her staring at him and offered a gentle smile and a wink of the eye. Her heart was racing, but she had to maintain her cool. She returned the friendliness and slipped off her stool. Taking her small handbag, she glided over to him oozing sex appeal.

Devlin was back in the bathroom washing the blood from her hands. She scrubbed them furiously to remove every last trace. She splashed some of the water over her face to remove the red staining clinging to her skin. Each drop a reminder of what she had done cast aside as if to erase the crime. As she stared into the mirror, her dark eyes reflected back at her, upon the face of a demon she no longer recognised. She reached up and pulled a black wig from her head to reveal golden blonde hair with pink streaks through it. There was the girl she knew. Suddenly, nausea overcame her and she turned to the nearby toilet. The vomit burned her throat. She had not eaten in a while, so it was mostly bile laced with vodka and coke.

Devlin collected her small handbag from the bedroom and returned to the cold bathroom with anticipation. She sat down on the toilet lid and removed a small tin from her bag, flipping the lid open to reveal her "survival kit". It consisted of a syringe, rubber tube, spoon, lighter, and a small plastic bag of white powder. Soon the needle pierced her skin with ease, the rubber tube tight around her arm helping locate a protruding vein. As she slowly squeezed the plunger, the liquid rushed into her body sending a chill of elation throughout. She drew the needle from her arm dropping it to the floor, then pulled the rubber tube loose to allow the flow to reach every part of her. She sat back against the cistern and let it take hold.

Just as she had expected, it didn't take much to persuade him to take her back to his. Within half an hour, they were entering his lavishly decorated studio apartment. As he made his way to the kitchen to fix them both a drink, Devlin analysed the decor. Modern furniture neatly placed, shelves lined with antiquities and artistic photographs of nude women on the walls. He returned with two large glasses of red wine, passing one to her. They clinked glasses and both took a sip, staring into each other's eyes. He with passion and her with retribution. He gestured for her to sit on the white leather couch. She sank into it as it creaked beneath her. They placed their glasses on the coffee table and he threw an arm over the back of the sofa, a charming smile on his face. She could see in his eyes he wanted her and she would let him think the same of her. She leaned toward him, hinting at him to do the same. They kissed passionately, their lips pressed tightly. His venturing hand reached out to cup her breast. She pulled from his lips and smacked his hand away playfully. The tease excited him. Devlin collected her handbag and, slowly standing so he could see every curve in her body, made her way to the bathroom and disappeared inside.

He knew the protocol. It was something he had experienced many times before and he wasted no time getting to the king-sized bed at the other end of the apartment. He sat down on the edge of the silk sheets and leaned over the bedside table where a small mirror holding several lines of cocaine waited. Taking a rolled up bank note, he snorted a couple of lines with relish before hurriedly ripping his clothes off. Devlin stood on the cold tiled floor looking at herself in the mirror. She took several deep breaths before slipping her leather jacket from her shoulders. She then unzipped the pink cocktail dress hugging her slender body and let it slide to the floor. The black lingerie, stockings and suspenders leaving very little to the imagination. One last breath and she felt ready. She had waited so long for this moment and now it was finally here. She couldn't back out now. She had to do it for Roxy.

Devlin collected her handbag and exited the bathroom. She found him lying on the bed in his underwear, hands behind his head, waiting in anticipation. She slinked over toward him and placed her handbag down on the shag carpeted floor. She caught sight of the lines of cocaine and felt the need for some boost in confidence. She bent over ensuring her plump rear was shoved in his face and snorted a line. She felt the rush through her veins and the power it gave her.

He extended his grasping hand to take hold of her right arse-cheek, but she pulled it back from his reach and slapped his hand away. He grinned devilishly.

Devlin spotted a couple of ties hanging alongside a suit on the wardrobe handle. She whipped them off and smirked as she climbed on top of him, legs straddled, and bound his hands to the bed frame. He found it hard to contain his excitement and she could feel it. He watched as she kissed his hairy chest delicately, then shifting her focus to his piercing blue eyes reached up and gently teased his eyelids down. She continued to kiss his chest as her hand searched the nearby handbag. She lifted a rusting hammer from its containment and slowly raised it above her head. He couldn't help but take a peek, but found himself looking up at the hammer high above him. The metal glistened in the light. His eyes widened with shock as the heavy steel head crashed down into his face. His nose broke immediately caving in to the cavity of his skull. Devlin proceeded to raise the hammer and bring it down four more times until there was nothing recognisable about him. The amount of blood was immense, redecorating the walls and drenching Devlin's hands and face. Bits of bone and flesh scattered like jetsam. Exhausted, she stared at the mess before her, hands shaking, breathing heavy. Her grip on the tool released, letting it drop to the floor with a thud. She climbed off his corpse and took a packet of cigarettes from her handbag, struggling to light one with nerve shredded fingers. She made her way over to the window.

As the heroin's power wore off, Devlin opened her eyes and remembered where she was. She sat up on the toilet lid and looked around with glazed vision. For a moment, it seemed like it had all been a dream. She picked up the crumpled cocktail dress and slipped it over her hips, zipping it up tight. She then threw on the leather jacket and collected her handbag before stepping out to view her carnage again. Devlin couldn't help but stare at the hideous sight once more. A sense of relief washed over her. She picked up the stained hammer from the blood soaked carpet and wiped it down with the bedsheet. She placed it back inside her handbag and slung the strap over her shoulder. Her eye was drawn to a brown leather wallet sitting on the bedside table. As it flipped open, a large wad of notes wedged inside revealed themselves. She plucked them out and shoved them into her pocket, tossing the wallet back onto the table. She then headed for the front door and quietly pulled it open, taking one last look back at the scene before ducking out into the darkness.

Days passed and she still struggled to sleep. The action she took that night didn't give her the sense of closure she hoped it would. Revenge was not what she had been led to believe. It stuck like a thorn in her side. She found herself sitting up late watching television every night, hoping the relief would eventually come, but it didn't. Then one day something she saw on the news made sure that sweet emotion would never come. Police were reporting they had arrested a notorious serial killer. He had been arrested attempting to murder another girl and subsequently confessed to several others, one of which was Roxy. Devlin had killed the wrong man.

Old Wounds: A Nick Shelby Case

The pain in my chest spread and tightened. It wasn't like that of a bullet, which I had first-hand experience of, but it hurt just as much. A broken heart can bring down the tallest of men like an imploding skyscraper and now this stunningly beautiful woman I called my fiancée was pushing the detonator. I watched in horror and despair as she opened the front door, glanced over her shoulder to look at me one last time and then disappeared from my life forever without explanation.

I awoke in a daze and found myself sat in my rundown '47 Chevy Stylemaster. I looked around with tired eyes to get my bearings. I've been having that dream a lot. It's been three weeks since Louise left, but her goodbye is still fresh in my head, like it only happened yesterday. As I was nursing my emotional pain, something up ahead caught my attention and I suddenly remembered why I was here, parked in a filthy alleyway outside a Los Angeles apartment building at one o'clock in the morning.

On the second floor, a seventeen year old girl approached the window to draw the curtains closed. She was wearing a man's shirt covering her modesty where it mattered. I snatched up my camera with long-zoom lens and began snapping away with reckless abandon. Before you get the wrong impression, let me explain; I don't get off on this kind of thing. I'm a private investigator and have been hired to track down this girl and provide proof of her actions and whereabouts. It's not my forte and I don't enjoy it, but it pays the bills. I watched as a tall shirtless man in his twenties stepped up behind her and wrapped his arms around her skinny waist. He kissed her neck passionately. She liked it. It was the same old story. Teen girl is seduced by older man then runs away from home to live with him. These tales never end well. And I would be a catalyst in that tragic end. I took a few more pictures of them together before she drew the curtains to hide the world from their love. I checked the images on the preview screen, I'm no Ansel Adams, but I was happy with the quality. I started the engine and crawled the car out of the alleyway.

I do a lot of my business at Paulie's Diner Downtown; meeting clients, pouring over investigatory material for clues and of course, eating. It was the early hours of the following morning and pancakes were on the menu. I was sat in my favourite booth opposite a distressed Mr Richmond, my latest client and the man who asked me to track down his seventeen year old daughter. He was dressed in a scraggy suit with ruffled hair analysing my latest photography work. With each picture, he became more and more irritated. I see that as evidence I've done my job well.

'You're daughter is staying in a cheap apartment in Inglewood. It seems she's got herself a roommate,' I told him, as if the pictures didn't make that clear enough.

He looked up at me with strained eyes, they were bloodshot. I could feel he was on the verge of exploding with anger and trashing the joint.

'What's the address?' he asked.

'Now, Mr Richmond, you only asked me to find her, make sure she was okay. Giving you the address doesn't strike me as a smart decision, given the circumstances. You have the look of someone planning to do something irrational.' I hoped my words would get through to him, but they had the opposite effect.

'What I do with the information is my business, Mr Shelby. I'm paying you to serve my interests. If my interests change, that is no concern of yours. I'm willing to pay extra.'

He reached into his inside jacket pocket and pulled out a wad of notes wrapped in a money clip. He placed it down on the table in front of me like he was tempting a lion with meat. I took it in my hand and counted through it. There must have been at least two hundred bucks. I considered his offer for a moment and then the words spilled from my mouth.

'1404 Lime Street. Apartment 2C.'

Mr Richmond hastily gathered together the photos on the table and slipped them back into a large envelope I used to transport them. He stood up and towered over me asserting his dominance.

'I appreciate your professionalism and discretion, Mr Shelby.'

I didn't know what to say so I just nodded. He then turned and rushed toward the diner exit like he'd just robbed the joint. I leaned back in my chair still looking at the money on the table. I was sure I'd done the right thing giving him the address, his daughter is seventeen after all and still his legal responsibility, but there was something in his eyes that worried me. In the meantime, that extra two hundred dollars would keep a roof over my head and food in my stomach for another month, so no matter what you think, in my eyes, it was worth it.

When I arrived home later that day, I found a small piece of paper sitting on the welcome mat. This was not unusual. I'd had my fair share of death threats over the years. I unfolded it to discover it was a note that read, "Nick, please visit me at my family's home. It's important, Stephanie." Stephanie? Why would she be contacting me? No doubt it was regarding Louise, but what? I should explain, Stephanie is Louise's older sister, raised the same, but a lot more cynical about life. I remember the first time Louise took me to meet her family, which is to say her sister and mother. I never found out what happened to her father, I guess he was never in the picture. Her family lived in a large white house up in the Hollywood Hills. It was a warm summer's day, the city had been suffering an extreme heat wave and I'll never forget the drive over was insufferable, like travelling via sauna. We pulled up outside the house that afternoon. She led me up the garden path toward the large double front doors. She was giddy with excitement pulling me by my hand.

'I can't wait for them to meet you. They're going to love you,' she said with more enthusiasm than a child on Christmas Day.

'Will you calm down?' I laughed back.

Louise rang the doorbell, not the dull monotonous tone you normally hear but a beautiful melody calling the residents to the front door. A Hispanic maid named Maria greeted us with such politeness. Having not come from money myself, this was all new to me. We stepped into the large entrance hall with grand staircase winding up. Polished marble flooring, pillars straight out of ancient Greece, expensive artwork on the walls. Was this for real? Maria informed us that Louise's Mother and sister were out on the veranda. I didn't even know what a veranda was until she led us out a set of patio doors at the rear of the house. Louise's mother, Jemima, was sat at a garden table knitting what looked like a scarf. Stephanie lounged on a deck chair reading a book. She looked a lot like Louise, maybe not as attractive, but that was nothing to do with genetics, just a lack of effort on her part. Jemima looked over the rim of her thick glasses at us and smiled.

'Hello, Louise dear,' she called out. Louise pulled me closer to them.

'Mother, Stephanie. I'd like to introduce you to Nick Shelby.'

I approached Jemima and extended a hand to shake. 'It's a pleasure to meet you, Ma'am,' I said with more politeness than I thought I had.

'And you, Nick. Please, call me Jem.'

She placed her hand in mine and I could tell she was a woman of tradition. I raised it gently to my lips and kissed her knuckles. I gave her my most charming smile.

'If you insist, Jem,' I followed up with. She blushed struggling to look me in the eye. I knew then and there I had the mother on side. Next was the sister.

Stephanie reluctantly put down her book and stood up to approach me. She extended a hand to shake and I was about to give her the same courtesy as her mother, but she snatched her hand from my grip.

'I'll save you the effort. That's not going to impress me,' she said with a snarky attitude. Before the moment got awkward, Louise interjected.

'I have some exciting news for you both. We're getting married!' Louise announced as she flashed the engagement ring on her finger, the diamond sparkling in the sunlight.

Jemima was now on her feet rushing toward Louise with arms open wide.

'Oh, that is wonderful news, dear. I'm so happy for you.'

As Jemima embraced Louise with a loving hug and kissed her on the cheek, Stephanie was staring daggers at me. I wasn't sure what I'd done, but Stephanie clearly didn't like me.

Jemima was getting a closer look at the ring lifting her glasses revealing her short sightedness.

'Isn't it beautiful?' Louise asked her.

'It certainly is, dear,' Jemima assured.

'What do you think, Stephanie?' Louise asked as she swung her arm around for Stephanie to get a better look.

'It's pretty,' she replied with only the briefest of glances. 'Could I speak to you alone, dear sister?'

Louise followed Stephanie into the house. I saw them enter a dining room through the window and a heated conversation broke out between them. I was trying to read their lips, a skill I'd developed over the years, but Jemima distracted me.

'What line of work are you in, Nick?'

I tried answering whilst also keeping an eye on the sisters, but it was proving difficult and I could see Jemima wanted my full attention. I couldn't risk upsetting the mother now that I had her in the palm of my hand.

'I used to be a detective with the LAPD, but I've recently started my own private investigations company.'

'Oh, how fascinating,' I think she said, because at this point I saw Stephanie place a reassuring hand on Louise's shoulder, but she slapped it away and stormed out of the room. Louise reappeared on the veranda clearly not happy.

'Come on, I think it's time we left,' she called over to me.

'So soon? But you just arrived,' Jemima protested with disappointment.

'We have a wedding to organise.'

As Louise said this, she gave Stephanie a dirty look you'd have to be blind not to see. Louise grabbed my hand and pulled me toward the patio doors. I looked over my shoulder toward Jemima and Stephanie and waved.

'It was nice meeting you,' I said, my voice no doubt fading as I entered the house. I did enquire as to what the heated conversation was about between them, but Louise never revealed anything.

I was now standing outside that very house again. All that seemed so long ago. I didn't think I'd ever come here again after she left, but here I was, on the sister's request of all people.

A sorrowful looking Maria answered the door. I smiled with a greeting, but she was clearly in mourning about something. She said she'd been expecting me and sent me through to the living room where Miss Stephanie would be waiting. As I entered the living room, I found Jemima sat in a wing back chair by the fire. She held a handkerchief to her eyes, red from tears. I frowned with concern and was about to speak when Stephanie jumped up from a nearby couch and rushed over to me. I froze, half expecting her to throw a fist in my face, but she wrapped her arms around me tightly.

'Oh, Nick,' she said.

'What is it?' I asked, becoming more and more anxious. Stephanie released her grip on me and looked deep into my eyes. I could see she had been crying also, but the tears had been recently wiped away.

'Terrible news. Absolutely terrible,' her voice wobbled on the verge of crying again.

'What's going on?' I was desperate to know.

Stephanie glanced over at her mother staring into the fire.

'Let's go through to the study,' she suggested.

She led me into a room I suspected was rarely used. Everything was placed neatly and didn't have the feeling of life. Perhaps this was their father's room and was kept as it was after his departure. She asked me to close the door, which I did. I was becoming impatient and confronted her, keen to know why I had been summoned and why everyone was upset.

'You should take a seat,' she told me.

'I'd rather stand, if it's all the same.'

'Very well. This morning, Maria returned home from the market with a copy of a Mexican newspaper. Something she does all the time. Only this time, when she sat down to read it, she let out a terrible scream.'

Stephanie approached a large ornate desk in the corner of the room and picked up a newspaper. She flipped open to a specific page and laid it back down on the desk. She then took a step back and gestured for me to look. I cautiously approached, a part of me knowing what to expect. The first thing I saw was the photograph of Louise. Her full lips, thin nose, beautiful eyes and flowing dark hair. Next to it the headline read "Mujer Americana Encontrada Muerta." I'm not fluent in Spanish, but I knew just enough to tell the words 'Americana', 'Muerta' plus the image of Louise weren't painting a pretty picture.

'She's dead! My sister is dead,' Stephanie cried, tears beginning to stream down her cheeks. I picked up the newspaper for a closer look at the article for more information.

'It says she was shot in the face. Who would do something like that?' Stephanie asked.

Something about the article caught my attention and my poor Spanish came in handy again.

'It says here the victim's name is Lucy Stevens,' I pointed out to Stephanie.

'That's the name they found in her passport. We've tried contacting the Mexican authorities to tell them, but they're no help. I just don't understand, why would Louise be in Mexico with a fake passport? And why would someone kill her?'

I was thinking the same thing.

'Maybe you could find out,' Stephanie followed up with. I'd be lying if I said I wasn't expecting her to ask, but I hoped she wouldn't.

'I don't know,' I said, shaking my head. I put down the newspaper as a metaphorical way of saying I don't want any part of this, but Stephanie placed a hand on my arm and squeezed.

'Please. You're a private investigator, right? This is what you do.'

'You don't understand. I'm trying to move on with my life. I don't want to open old wounds,' I explained, knowing full well no matter what I said it wouldn't fly. When a woman wants help, she'll get it, eventually.

'But surely you still want to know why she left so abruptly without an explanation. We all do. If you could find out why she was there, it may become clear, you may even find closure. Maybe she was in trouble, she had no choice. There's a whole host of possibilities. Don't you want to know why?'

'Of course I want to know. But something like this could just make the whole deal ten times worse. More complicated. Just confuse me more,' I stressed.

'But you won't know until you start asking those questions. Please, Nick. For my mother at least.' She stared at me with puppy dog eyes. My one weakness, something Louise always used. I exhaled with frustration. It took more persuading than I expected, but I knew she was right. Of course, I wanted to know why Louise left without reason, but what if I don't like that reason. It's like when I'm asked to find a missing person, chances are I'll find them dead and I wonder what would the families prefer, to never find them and maintain hope they're still alive, or find them and know they're dead? Sometimes no answer is better than a bad one. I watched the overhead gantry sign reading "Mexico Border, 1/2 Mile" fly over my head as I drove my Chevy down the highway.

A honeymoon in Mexico, that was our plan. I'll never forget the way her eyes lit up like Christmas tree lights when she opened the ring box and stared at the huge rock gleaming back at her.

'For real? No kidding?' she asked in disbelief.

I smiled and assured her it was genuine. I took the ring out and slipped it on the finger of her left hand. She immediately raised it up to her face to see how it looked, rotating her hand to make it sparkle in the light.

'It's so beautiful, and it fits like a charm.'

'And we'll take a honeymoon down in Mexico,' I told her.

She was so happy, the joy pouring from her eyes. She kissed me before returning her focus back to the ring. She couldn't wait to tell her mother and sister.

'They're going to be so thrilled,' she claimed. 'We have so much to think about, so much to arrange.'

'I was assuming a small ceremony with a few close friends and family.'

She wasn't happy with that idea, wanting to aim a little higher than my expectations and I was ready to give her whatever her heart desired. If she wanted the sun beaming, I would part the clouds. Then she said something that made me pause for thought.

'I can't believe it. I'm going to be Mrs Nick Shelby. And I was starting to think I'd never get engaged again.'

Again? Did she say again? I questioned these words, but she was quick to have an answer.

'Oh no, I meant at all. I was starting to think I'd never get engaged at all. This giddiness is affecting my speech. I thought I'd be a spinster my whole life, but then you came along and changed everything for the better. How can I ever thank you.'

'I can think of one way,' I replied with a seductive grin. I leaned in and kissed her, completely forgetting about her Freudian slip. In hindsight, I should have probed more, maybe there was something there to discover, but I was in love and not exactly thinking straight.

Well, Louise, we both made it south of the border eventually, just not the way I imagined.

I arrived in the town of Ensenada, Mexico around midday. First port of call was the local "federales" station. I knew they probably wouldn't be much help and they wouldn't want me sticking my nose in, but it's always worth a shot at the start of any new investigation. Plus I wanted them to know I was in town, just in case. After speaking to the desk sergeant and explaining my business, I was escorted to the office of Captain Alejandro Diaz. It's strange, no matter what city, what country, all police stations feel the same.

Captain Diaz was a large heavy-set man with thick moustache and thick eyebrows to match. He seemed to have a permanent frown, either that or he was perturbed by my presence. Another gringo disturbing his peace.

'You must be Shelby,' he said with a hand extended to shake. He had large hands and as I shook it, he squeezed tightly to let me know he was the alpha male here. 'I am told you are here regarding the murder of the young American lady.'

I told him I was and he offered me a seat. I sat in a small uncomfortable wooden chair while he reclined in a soft leather armchair behind his desk.

'What exactly can I do for you?' he asked staring me down from his higher position.

'I was wondering if you could tell me the progress of the investigation.'

'Well, it is early days yet, but we have substantial man-power doing everything they can to bring this crime to a conclusion.'

'I'd like to offer my services. I've been asked by the victim's family to look into it. As a close acquaintance of the deceased, I feel I can be of some use to you.

Diaz gave a sigh and shook his head.

'That won't be necessary. We are quite capable of doing our job. We don't need another American sticking his nose in where it's not wanted. I'm sure you appreciate that.'

I was a little surprised, I thought it would be a lot longer before he commented on my nationality and what it represented for many foreigners, especially down south. I decided to let it pass. This man hadn't yet thrown me out of his office so I thought I would gather as much information as possible.

'Do you have any leads?' I asked, knowing he probably didn't and if that was the case, I would at least embarrass the man.

'There is only so much I can discuss with you. Specific details must remain confidential,' he said with an air of irritation in his voice.

'So you don't have any leads?' I pushed.

'That is not what I said.'

Diaz was getting frustrated, I could see it in his face. I knew I wasn't going to get anything from him so I lost my temper and decided to push his buttons instead.

'It's okay, Captain. I used to be a police detective myself. I know the look of a man with no clue.'

Diaz was taken aback by this audacity to insult a police Captain in his very own office, a gringo, nonetheless. 'You don't have to play big and tall with me. You can say if you're stumped. I wouldn't expect anything more,' I continued, unable to control myself now.

'Do not insult my intelligence!' he bellowed jumping up from his comfortable seat.

'I would if you had any.'

'How dare you? Get out of my office before I have you thrown into jail.'

I didn't need telling twice. I stood up and headed for the door, but as I pulled it open, I couldn't leave without having the last word.

'Tell me this, Captain. Are you aware the passport you found is a fake? You don't even have the correct name for your victim. Next time, you should listen to the grieving family trying to help.'

I stepped out slamming the door behind me. Not the best start to the investigation and I'd probably made life more difficult for myself in town, but it felt good to vent some pent up frustration I was feeling since Louise left. Don't get me wrong, I'll always have respect for the law, but what I can't stand is arrogant men too proud to accept help. Solving a crime is about justice, not glory. And I can tell Captain Diaz has no interest in justice, just a fat pay cheque at the end of the month.

Not long after leaving the police station, I noticed two plain clothes officers tailing me in my car. How did I know they were police? You develop a sixth sense for these things especially having been one myself. Also, they weren't exactly keeping their distance, making every turn I did. Diaz must have sent them to watch me. I knew I wouldn't be able to investigate freely with them sticking to me like leeches so I had to lose them. I pulled over outside a convenience store, they did likewise the other side of the road a little ways back and kept their eye on me. I entered the store with a casual demeanour to make it appear as though I was going in for a snack or beverage. Once inside, the store clerk was kind enough to guide me toward a back door where I exited into a large alleyway, made my way to an adjacent street and hailed a cab the rest of the way. Simple, but effective.

The house Louise's body was found in was small and rundown in a dodgy area of town. Way below her standards of living. God knows what she was doing here. Police tape was stretched across the locked front door. I took out my trusty lock-pick set and began working on the keyhole with precision. A few seconds later, I had the door open and I ducked under the tape to enter. I walked cautiously around the sparsely decorated room. Forensics had clearly been and collected all they found, but I didn't trust their instincts and expected to find something they'd missed. There was minimal furniture dotted around, no pictures or ornaments to provide character or make the place feel like home, save for a picture of Jesus in the living room. This was not a place to live. It felt more like a place to hide out or a place to bring someone to kill. It didn't look like anybody had lived here for a while. My initial thought was, Louise was brought here to be murdered.

In the bedroom was a pool of dried blood on the carpeted floor. I crouched beside it and ran my fingers along the stain. Even now, staring at her blood, I can't believe she's really dead. If only we could get back that time together.

We met back home in Los Angeles. I was driving along Vine Street early one morning on my way home from a stake out when she collapsed onto the road in front of me. Despite my tiredness, my reactions remained sharp and I slammed on my brakes before it was too late. Passers-by were screaming in shock as I climbed out and ran over to see if she was okay. She was conscious, but faint.

'Are you okay?' I asked.

'What happened?' she replied, looking up at me dazed and confused.

'You collapsed in front of my car. I almost flattened you. Come on, let's get you sat down somewhere.'

I took her to Paulie's diner which was nearby. As she sat down in my favourite booth, I noticed blood on the back of her head and shouted for Paulie to grab me a flannel. I went behind the counter and filled a glass with water. Paulie doesn't mind me helping myself on the odd occasion, I am his best customer after all. As I placed the glass down in front of her, she was still trying to get her bearings. Paulie, a short, dumpy Italian-American man appeared with a damp flannel and enquired as to her status. I sensed it was more the fact he didn't want someone dying in his diner than real concern for her wellbeing.

'She'll be fine. It's just a slight cut. I'll keep an eye on her,' I told him as I placed the flannel against the back of her head. Satisfied he wouldn't be needing to call a coroner, he made his way back behind the counter. I took her hand and placed it over the flannel gesturing her to hold it in place herself. I then sat opposite her to check her eyes were focusing okay.

'How are you feeling?'

'Like I've taken a baseball bat to the head,' she replied.

I laughed, relieved she was able to find humour in her situation. No lasting brain damage at least.

'I'm not surprised. You went down pretty hard. Is that a regular occurrence for you? Or was it you saw me coming and were just trying to get my attention?' I showed the pearly whites and she smiled back at me.

'I guess I should be grateful to your quick reflexes.'

'I'll say. You caught me on a good day.'

'I'm Louise Danvers.'

'Nick Shelby. So, Louise Danvers, is there a reason you're passing out in the street?'

'I haven't felt very well lately. I guess it all just got too much for me at that moment.'

'Well, let's hope it's nothing that can't be fixed.'

We stared into each other's eyes in silence and felt a spark between us. Love really does happen in the strangest of ways.

I pulled myself from my daydream and refocused my attention on the blood stain before me. I shook my head and then began searching the room. I opened drawers and cupboards, but they were all empty. No surprise there. My eye was caught by a small corner of paper sticking out from under a drawer unit. I reached down and slid it out. No matter how thorough police search, they always miss something. I flipped it over to reveal a polaroid photograph of Louise and a dark haired man with five o'clock shadow and devilish eyes. Something about the man in this photograph didn't sit right with me. Never mind he and Louise looked cosy together, but there was a glint in his eyes that gave me concern.

I visited nearby neighbours to see if anyone had seen or heard anything strange around the house over the last few weeks. Most weren't willing to speak to me, but one did give me something useful. She told me Louise had been living there with a man. I reached into my pocket and showed her the photograph I'd found and enquired if the man she was living with was the man in the photograph. She confirmed it was and that she had seen them together a few times.

20

'Did they seem normal to you?' I asked.

'Normal?' she replied with confusion.

'Did she seem happy to be with him? As though she wanted to be with him?'

'Si, I suppose.'

'You didn't hear any arguments or physical abuse? Fighting?'

'No, Senor.'

'After the murder, did you see the man leave?'

Before she could answer my final question, the sound of a baby crying emanated from the house and she excused herself slamming the door in my face. I stood there for a moment thinking. *Who were you with, Louise? And did he kill you? If so, why?*

When I got back to my car, the police officers had gone. No doubt they got bored of waiting, clocked onto my ruse and went looking for me. Before heading back north to tell Stephanie my findings, I stopped by a bar. For some, alcohol dulls the senses. For me, it opens up parts of my brain that lay dormant sober. A shot of whiskey usually helps, but this time I just can't think. I stared at the photograph of Louise and the mysterious man and ordered another shot.

Stephanie met me at Paulie's in my favourite booth. I offered to buy her a cup of coffee, but she refused, keen to hear the progress of my investigation. I told her I had a possible suspect and showed her the photograph. I explained I thought he may have killed her, but I didn't know who he was or what motive he had. Seconds after looking at the picture, she shook her head.

'That's not possible,' she claimed.

'Why not?'

'This is Michael Ferzetti. Louise and he were engaged until he died about a year ago.'

'He's dead?' I said in surprise at this revelation.

Stephanie assured me Ferzetti had passed on, but couldn't explain how a witness saw him only a few weeks ago.

'They must be mistaken,' she claimed. 'Michael died in that motel fire in Silver Lake. Don't you remember it? It was all over the news.'

I did remember it. A national tragedy, no survivors. Motel fire regulations were under the microscope after that one.

'Louise was really broken up about it. She really loved him. That's why we had an argument the day she told us you were to be married. It was only a few months after his death. I just wanted her to be sure she was ready.'

'I had no idea about her past relationship. She never talked about it.'

'Once she met you, she saw it as a way to forget about him. She didn't want to talk about it.'

Stephanie asked if I'd found out anything else, but I had to disappoint her. The man in the photograph felt like a sure lead, but knowing the guy was dead put me back to square one.

'Thank you for doing this, Nick. I know it must be hard and all, but I really appreciate it.'

She stood, kissed me on the cheek and left. I sat and considered everything I'd learned, there had to be something more to this. Either that witness was seeing a ghost, or this guy wasn't really dead. Either way, I was determined to find out. I called out to Paulie and asked him if he had anything stronger to drink behind the counter. Silly question, I knew he had.

I visited the Los Angeles Public Library and had the librarian hunt the microfilm archives for newspaper articles related to the Silver Lake motel fire. An hour later, they brought me several results and I got to work feeding them through the reading machine. The first headline read, "Motel Fire Kills Seven, Police Suspect Arson." Scanning the article, I came across some key points such as; the seven people who died, they were unable to be identified visually due to severe burns. I selected the next microfilm, the headline read, "Motel Fire Investigation Still Ongoing, Police Bring In Expert To Identify Victims." It seemed with traditional methods of

22

identification impossible, the cops had utilised the help of a dental forensic expert to help put a name to a body via dental records. I tried the next result with the headline, "Motel Fire Victims Named." It didn't take long to find his name among the list of victims. There it was in black and white, Michael Ferzetti, dead. Then again, it wouldn't be the first time someone had faked their own death.

I needed to know more about the case, information I couldn't get from the media. I stopped by a local bar I know to be the haunt of my old colleague Mickey McConnell. Sure enough he was there nursing a cup of coffee and reading the newspaper. Physically trim and bald headed, he was one of the finest officers I had the pleasure of knowing and I was sure he would be able to help. When he saw me sit down next to him, he looked over and smiled. Mickey didn't normally smile unless he was in an exceptionally good mood. Good news for me.

'Nick Shelby. What brings you to my side of the tracks?' he said patting me on the back.

'I was just passing through the neighbourhood, thought I'd stop in and see if my favourite lawman would be here sipping his black coffee and reading his horoscope.'

'I'm that predictable?' he laughed.

'There's nothing wrong with being predictable. Gives people a sense of ease. A sense of assuredness. You're trustworthy.'

Mickey frowned at my overuse of compliments. This was unlike me.

'Why do I have this uneasy feeling you're about to ask something of me?'

'Because I create a sense of unease in people?' I smirked.

He wasn't liking my stab at humour and insisted I spit out what I came to say. I asked him to give me access to the files related to the Silver Lake motel fire that occurred, specifically the victims. He did not like my request. After all, I wasn't a cop anymore, I gave up that kind of privilege. If caught, we could both get into a lot of trouble. I knew I had to make it clear there was a personal interest in it for me. Mickey had a heart, I just had to penetrate it.

'Please, Mickey. Louise was found murdered in Mexico and I think it's connected. I wouldn't ask if I wasn't desperate,' I said giving him my best puppy dog eyes.

Mickey was taken aback by the news of Louise's death, I guess he hadn't heard. He liked Louise. He would always say, "Why can't I meet someone like her?" I explained her family had asked me to look into her death and that so far my only lead was that fire and that if he did this, I'd owe him more than one.

'From my recollection, you already owe me fifty, but I'm working the late shift tonight. If you come by the station around ten o'clock, I'll see what I can do.'

I thanked Mickey with a firm friendly handshake and slid off my barstool. He asked me to join him for a coffee, but I suggested a rain-check. I hadn't slept for nearly twenty four hours and needed forty winks if I was going to be out late again tonight.

I stood in the main lobby of the police station looking around with a nostalgic mind as I waited for Mickey. It was like coming home and I wondered why I ever left. I caught a glimpse of a missing persons poster on a pin-board and took a closer look. It was a face and a name I knew. Randall Colter. Fellow P.I. and barfly. I wondered what happened to him. If the cops didn't find him soon, I was sure his folks would come knocking at my door one day. Mickey appeared at a set of double doors and called me through. I guess he was waiting for the coast to be clear, it had gone ten and I was starting to think he'd changed his mind.

'You had any progress on the Colter case?' I asked trying to make conversation as we walked down the long corridor.

'No, nothing. It's like the guy just disappeared into thin air. He was a friend of yours, right?'

'We'd been known to share the odd bar and make small talk. I wouldn't exactly call him a friend.'

Mickey led me through another door into a large room filled with shelves. Each shelf was filled with boxes related to each case, numbered and catalogued for future reference. He moved down one of the aisles scanning the case numbers on each box until he found the correct one and slid it out. He dumped it in my arms.

'There you go.'

'Aren't you going to help?' I asked hopefully.

'You got to be kidding. I got my own shit to worry about. Make sure you put it back exactly how you found it. This is still an open case.'

I told Mickey I knew the drill and he left the room. I carried the weighty box over to a small table and gently placed it down. Flipping open the lid, I was a little stunned to see so much paper work. This was going to take a lot longer than I expected. I pulled out the first file and began flicking through the documents. I came across the first victim, July Templeton. When a life is collated into one of these folders, it's easy to forget they're real people. All of a sudden their death becomes the most significant thing about them. Half an hour later, I found the report on Michael Ferzetti. I sat down at the table and flipped through the file pausing as I reached a set of gruesome photographs detailing every part of his burned corpse. Jesus, no wonder they had trouble identifying the victims. Judging by the crispness of the body, that fire burned for a long time. I found the coroner's report and the confirmation of identity. It had been signed by a Doctor Victor Lensham. I pulled a small notepad and pen from my pocket and copied the name down. If anybody knew if Ferzetti was really dead or alive, it would be this guy.

Lensham's home was a modest little one-story house in Wilshire. It didn't take long to discover his address. It's amazing what you can find out from the phone operators with a little sweet talking. Lensham was a short man of around five foot, balding and thick glasses I'm surprised his nose could hold the weight of. I introduced myself and explained the reason I was there. That was a mistake. Lensham refused to discuss the case and tried to slam the door in my face, luckily my foot was preventing that option. I reasoned with him again offering to keep it short and with full discretion, but that didn't fly. So, I pulled out my Ace and threatened to investigate the details of his last employment and the real reason he was dismissed. Rumours had been circling the medical world for a while now and I thought maybe it was time to turn that hearsay into fact. He knew blackmail when he saw it, lucky for him, I only wanted information. He offered five minutes of his time and that was all I needed to confirm a few things.

His house was well-decorated, clearly a man with good taste. I offered my compliments to his interior designer, but he was not appreciative, insisting I get on with it. I sat down on the leather couch and took out my notepad and pen. Victor eased himself down onto an armchair, but he did not look comfortable.

'Michael Ferzetti was one of the confirmed victims.'

'Was he? I don't remember all their names,' he replied in a thick German accent.

A clear lie. I remember the names of all the victims I've ever encountered. It's not something that leaves you. I decided to give him the benefit of the doubt and continued my line of questioning.

'Do you remember if Michael Ferzetti paid you to claim he was killed in that fire?'

I knew it was a long shot question, but it was my current theory and a quick confirmation would blow this thing wide open. Lensham feigned confusion badly. I backed up my theory hoping it would rattle him.

'I ask because I think he's still alive. You deposited ten thousand dollars into your bank account the day after you announced the victim's IDs. That's a lot of money to come into in one go. I think he paid you for the false identification.'

'I don't know what you're talking about. I think you should leave!' he shouted, jumping up from his seat and pointing toward the door. I stood up so I could tower over him and apply some pressure.

I knew it wouldn't take much, but just enough intimidation and he'd be singing like a canary.

'Do your neighbours know the sort of thing you're into? That could make life hell if they were to find out.'

He started to cower, stepping back and lowering his arm. Time for some good cop.

'I'm not looking to bring you down, Doctor. Right now, I couldn't give a shit about you. I'm investigating a murder and I think Ferzetti may have been involved. So, is he really dead?'

Lensham sat back down and hung his head.

'No. He's not dead. Not long after I was assigned to the case, I received a visit from a mysterious man.'

Lensham regaled his story. He'd returned home one night to find someone sat in his living room shadowed in darkness. Lensham questioned who the person was, but they merely told him not to be afraid, they weren't there to hurt him they just needed something from him. They were aware he'd been assigned the motel fire case and that he'd been tasked with identifying the bodies. Room number twelve was registered to a Michael Ferzetti. They claimed the body found within that room was not Ferzetti, however, they wanted Lensham to positively identify it as him. When Lensham asked why, they told him it wasn't any of his concern, but that he would be paid ten thousand dollars in cash upon announcing Ferzetti as a victim. Lensham agreed and the shadowy figure stood and left the house via the back door. As I hastily scribbled all this down in my notepad, Lensham was still talking.

'I'm proud of my work and perform to the best of my ability, but I also have mounting debts and I needed the money. So, I did as he asked.'

'You never saw the mysterious man's face?' I asked, a little confused as to how someone can be in a room and yet not one defining feature stand out in the low light. Lensham shook his head.

'It must have been Ferzetti. Who else could it be?'

My thinking exactly. Only Ferzetti would have something to gain from faking his own death so it made sense that Ferzetti would be the one to visit the doctor. Now the question remained, why did he want to be dead?

'You won't tell the police what I did, will you?' Lensham whispered forlorn and ashamed.

'Not directly, but if the truth happens to find its way to them, I can't say I'm sorry,' I replied, not really caring one way or the other at this moment. I stood and was about to head for the door when Lensham rushed around me to prevent my departure.

'Wait, there was something else. If it helps my case,' he said with desperation.

'It can't hurt to try.'

'A few days after announcing the victims, I received another visit from two men. They wanted to make sure I hadn't made a mistake identifying Michael Ferzetti's body. Like they wanted to be reassured of his death.'

'And what did you tell them?'

'I told them my report was accurate. Ferzetti was in no doubt one of the victims. I couldn't tell them the truth.'

'Who were they?'

'I don't know. They never said. Although, I remember one of them had a large scar on his cheek, in the shape of a C.'

This sounded interesting. I had a feeling I knew who he was referring to, but I needed confirmation.

'On his left cheek?'

'Yes. Do you know him?'

I was sure I did. Not many people with a 'C' shaped scar on their left cheek and I happened to know one of them. This little mystery was getting more and more complicated, but I knew if I could find Ferzetti, it could clear this whole mess up.

I awoke the next morning with the sun bleeding through the curtains onto my face. I opened one eye to see what was disturbing my slumber and held up my hand to shield me from the warmth. The blood dripped from my palm onto the bedsheet. Both my eyes opened wide, shocked at the sight of my hand covered in crimson. I looked over at the form lying next to me under the duvet. I pulled back the cotton blanket to reveal Louise's butchered body drenched in blood, soaking into the bedsheets. My breathing increased as the panic set in and then I was truly awake. Sweat dripped from my forehead. I looked down at the bed next to me, nobody there. Ever since I started digging around Louise's murder, the dreams had been getting worse. Before, it was just heartbreak, now it felt like she was haunting me.

The Green Room is a classy joint serving elegant cuisine at extortionate prices or if you just want a light refreshment a small bar is prepared to wet your whistle, which is exactly where I headed, ordering a neat whiskey. The place was quiet, only a few patrons sat at tables eating. As I was scanning the room, I spotted two heavy set men in a booth drinking espresso coffee. Tony and Lou, two peas in a pod. You don't see one without the other. You also don't see Tony without his trademark 'C' shaped scar across his left cheek. They say Tony got the scar from fighting three guys at once, putting all in the hospital. I know he got it from a woman after she caught him cheating…with her brother. It didn't take long for Tony to notice me. He garnered Lou's attention to my presence and they both walked over, not looking too happy to see me.

'Morning, fellas. It's been a long time,' I said, trying to ease any tension.

'You were told not to come back here, Shelby,' Tony replied trying to stare me down.

'Come on, boys. I'm just enjoying a quiet drink by myself,' I lied.

'Well, you need to enjoy that quiet drink by yourself at another establishment. Mr Bank doesn't want you causing trouble here again,' Lou chimed in.

I promised them I wasn't there to cause any trouble, but they weren't having it. Tony grabbed my arm and yanked me from the barstool. I managed to keep my balance and pulled myself free from his grip.

'I want to see your boss,' I told them.

'Impossible. Mr Bank is busy,' Lou said reaching out for my arm again. I took a step back so all he could grab was air.

'Tell him it's regarding the death of Michael Ferzetti.' Tony and Lou paused and looked at each other. 'He might want to hear what I have to say,' I continued, knowing I had their attention now.

Several seconds later, I was sat in Dalton Bank's large office in front of a walnut desk. Tony and Lou stood behind me ready to pounce if I stepped out of line. Dalton Bank is the local mob boss, although these days they prefer to be known as "entrepreneurs of unconventional means". I've had my fair share of run ins with him which means I'm taking a big risk just being here, but if Bank has an interest in Ferzetti's death, I want to know why. A door to a private bathroom opened and Bank stepped into the room filling it with his presence. A tall and slim man with stern face and goatee, he was wearing an expensive three-piece suit. I should also mention he has a glass eye that gives him a sinister appearance. Nobody knows how he lost the eye, there are many rumours from him being shot in the eye to it being gouged out by a rival. I like to think it was something insignificant and mundane like accidentally poking himself in the eye with a cocktail stick. It made him seem less intimidating that way and made me feel more comfortable sitting before him. He sat down opposite me and stared for a moment, burning holes in my face.

'Nick Shelby. Otherwise known as the boil on my ass. I understand you want to talk to me?' he said with a raspy voice.

I told him I had a few questions that needed answering and he made a snide comment about my profession, but he was willing to listen to what I had to say.

'What's your relationship with Michael Ferzetti?' I asked.

'Never heard of him.'

'Come on, Dalton. Don't play games. The only reason I have an audience with you is because I mentioned his name to your goons.'

'Is that right?' Dalton said glancing up at Tony and Lou behind me and staring daggers at them. I didn't look around to see their reaction, but I'm guessing their faces were red.

'Why are you asking questions about Michael Ferzetti? As I hear, he's dead,' Dalton asked with a wry smile.

'And why were you so interested in his death?'

'Excuse me?'

'You sent your two cronies to interrogate the forensic doctor assigned to the case. That couldn't have just been a common courtesy. What stock do you have in this?'

'I don't like your tone!'

'And I don't like your stink!' I shouted, lifting up off my seat. Tony and Lou placed a hand on each of my shoulders and sat me back down. 'Listen, I'm not trying to cause trouble with you, Dalton. I'm investigating the death of a dear friend and I think he was involved. I'm asking any questions I can. Surely you can understand that. Was he working for you?'

Dalton flipped open a cigar box on the desk and took out a dark Cuban. He sniffed it before placing it between his teeth and lighting it with a diamond encrusted zippo. As he exhaled the smoke, he leaned back in his chair.

'I gave him a job here as a bartender.'

Dalton went on to explain how he hired Michael to work at The Green Room. He was a good employee, worked hard, was never late, popular with the clientele. A few weeks later, Dalton entered his office to find the safe door ajar and that it had been relieved of its contents. Michael hasn't shown up for work and Dalton instantly knows it was him. The classic get a job while you case the joint and wait for your moment to strike. Dalton asked his men to track him down, but Tony and Lou aren't exactly the best at finding those who don't want to be found. They're more the guys you call when you've found the mark and you need someone to rough them up. Dalton, instead, hired a private investigator, Randall Colter. Colter found Michael staying at the motel in Silver Lake and called Dalton to give him the good news. Colter offered to bring him in, but Dalton wanted to be positive he had the money before making any rash moves. He told Colter to break into the motel room and search for the money. Dalton never heard back from Colter.

'My first thought was Ferzetti caught Colter and killed him, but the next thing I hear, Ferzetti is dead. Killed in that motel fire. I sent Tony and Lou to question the forensic expert. I wanted to make sure there were no mistakes in identifying the body. Many have tried to escape my wrath by faking their own deaths. And Colter? Who knows what happened to him? Maybe he stole the money after finding it, but I've had several people try and find him and nothing.'

'So, you haven't seen Ferzetti since?'

Dalton looked at me like I was delusional.

'Of course not, he's dead! Are you not listening?'

I stared back at Dalton with a raised eyebrow. He knew exactly what I was thinking. He leaned in.

'Are you suggesting he's still alive?' he asked curiously.

'Yeah, I think he's alive. He paid off the forensic doctor to claim his body was found in that fire, but it wasn't his body. Most likely, it was Colter's. But I think you already knew that. I think you found out Ferzetti was still alive, hiding down in Mexico and you sent someone to kill him, except it went wrong and they killed the girl he was with by mistake.'

It was only a theory and I felt nervous accusing someone like Bank without evidence, but I was getting desperate and making assumptions could be the key.

'You've got it all wrong, Shelby. I had no idea he was still alive and I certainly didn't send anybody to kill him. Let alone kill some girl.'

'I don't believe you,' I said, even though I did believe him, but I needed to be sure.

'I don't care if you don't, but if I had sent someone to kill him, he'd be dead, for real. My guys don't make mistakes. But if you're right and he is still alive, well then, we have unfinished business. I don't know who this girl is you mentioned, but I can see you want to know who killed her. I can see it in your eyes, she obviously meant something to you, but it had nothing to do with me. I'd say, Ferzetti is the obvious suspect. I think you know that. Now, is there anything else I can do for you because I'm a busy man and I have somewhere to be?'

He was convincing. I'd never seen Dalton speak so passionately before. He's the type of guy that stays quiet if he's guilty. I told him if I thought of anything else I would be in touch. He asked, if I ever found Ferzetti still breathing that I should give him a courtesy call. I left still none the wiser as to who killed Louise.

I arrived back at my apartment frustrated and angry. This is what happens when you immerse yourself in a world of liars. The truth becomes an elusive ghost you hope at some point shows itself. I stormed over to a drinks cabinet and poured myself a large glass of whiskey. As I took a sip, I heard her voice behind me.

'I thought you'd quit drinking,' she said.

I turned to see her soft face lit only by the moonlight. Her big blue eyes glistening beneath delicate eyelashes. Her red full lips parted into a smile to show her pure white teeth. It was Louise. The glass slipped from my fingers and smashed onto the floor spilling its delicious contents across the floorboards.

I couldn't believe it. There she was, standing right in front of me. This wasn't a dream, no illusion, no trick. Just flesh and blood before my very eyes. She slowly walked toward me, a calming outstretched hand leading her.

'Don't worry, I'm not a ghost. I'm really here,' she whispered.

'How?' I shook my head in disbelief.

'That dead girl they found, it wasn't me. I guess the cops put two and two together and made five after discovering my passport. Lazy police work if you ask me.'

The corner of her mouth curled up hoping I would buy into her humour. I wasn't in any mood to laugh or smile. I needed answers.

'Who was she?'

'I don't know. Just someone in the wrong place at the wrong time.'

'You killed her?'

Her eyes widened and she shook her head erratically. She took another step closer to me. I took a step back.

'God no, I didn't kill her.'

'Did Michael?'

She ceased her movements, surprised at my question.

'You know about Michael?'

'I think you better start from the beginning.'

She dropped her head, staring down at the floor momentarily and then nodded in agreement. She looked up at me then glanced over at the drinks cabinet.

'Pour me a drink first. It's been a long journey.'

I poured her a glass of whiskey and passed it to her. She downed it in one and stared into the empty glass as she gathered her thoughts.

'I guess you could say Michael was my first love. I remember the first time we met so vividly. I was working at my family's dress shop when he came in and said he saw something in the window he liked. When I asked him what it was, he said me. I couldn't believe it, nobody had ever approached me like that before. He said he thought I was the most beautiful woman he'd ever seen and wanted to take me out to dinner. I wasn't sure at first, my mother had always warned me of confident men, they're only ever after one thing, but something about him made me think he was different. So I agreed to go out with him. We ended up seeing each other for a few months. I'd never met someone so charming, yet kind and gentle. Every moment I was around him I didn't want it to end. I just wanted it to last forever.

'And then one night, he pulled a ring box from his pocket and flipped open the lid to reveal a stunning ring. He wanted to marry me. He wanted to make sure it would last forever. I couldn't imagine how my life could get any better. I was in heaven. But then a few days later, it all came crashing down. My sister showed me the article in the newspaper about the motel fire and Michael's name was there with all the other victims. I cried for days. I couldn't eat, I couldn't sleep. I didn't know what to do. His was the first funeral I'd ever been to. Nobody else came, just me, my mother and sister standing by his graveside. And then you came along and I started to think life could be good again.'

She looked up at me and smiled. She walked up beside me and poured herself another glass of whiskey. This time she just sipped until the words began to flow again.

'I was at work, just tidying as I always do before closing. That place couldn't get any cleaner, but I just enjoyed it. I heard the bell of the front door and I was about to tell the late customer we're closing when I saw it was Michael. I only got a glimpse of him before I fainted. I'm not a spiritual person, but right there and then I was ready to believe in the afterlife. Much like I'm sure you were when you saw me. When I came round I was sat on a chair and he was handing me a glass of water. He explained how he'd faked his own death because some people were after him. He didn't want to leave, but he had to and he couldn't tell anyone as it may risk their lives. And then he said he wanted me to go back with him, to Mexico. He had just bought a small house for us and wanted to start a new life out there. I told him I couldn't, I had my job, my mother, my sister.'

'Me,' I added.

'He already knew about you. He was very insistent I go with him. He told me if I didn't go with him then he would hurt you, maybe even kill you. He didn't give me any choice. I didn't want anything to happen to you. He wouldn't even let me say goodbye to you, but I needed to say something. I couldn't tell you why I was going or who with, but I had to say goodbye at least.'

Louise made her way over to my bed and perched herself on the edge. She picked at a loose thread on her skirt, severing it and let it fall in slow motion to the floor.

'Keep talking,' I said, keen to know where this tale would lead.

'He had someone make me a fake passport so that we wouldn't be followed. I was hoping it wouldn't work. That the authorities would know they were fake and I'd be brought back to you. Three days later, we passed through the border checkpoint with no issue.

'It was a nice house, considering. It had everything a girl could need, but it wasn't home. I kept thinking about you and how much I missed you.'

'So where does the dead girl come in?'

'We'd been out for something to eat one night. We were walking back to the house when Michael noticed the front door was slightly ajar. He knew he'd locked it, so naturally, we were concerned. I followed him inside as he cautiously entered. I don't think I'd ever seen him so nervous. We heard a noise in one of the bedrooms and Michael began to panic. He opened a cloakroom and took out a double-barrelled shotgun. Right then, I knew it wasn't going to end well. I tried to hold him back before he did something stupid, but he shrugged me off and ventured further into the house. He crept into the bedroom and saw the girl. Michael just reacted. He aimed the gun and pulled the trigger. Just like that. No hesitation. I can still hear her body hitting the floor. He said she was there to kill him, but I don't think that was the case. She had my jewellery in the palm of her hand. I think she was just homeless, looking for something to sell. He grabbed my arm and pulled me out of the house saying we had to leave. We spent the next couple of days on the road hopping between motels. He had become paranoid and erratic and it was scaring me. He killed that girl in cold blood. I knew I couldn't stay with this man any longer. I was scared for my own life. I needed to get away. While he slept in an armchair, that shotgun clutched tightly in his arms, I snuck out of the motel room. I managed to sneak back across the border and came straight here. To you.'

She looked over at me, the tears welling in her eyes glistened in the light like diamonds. She wiped them away and smiled looking for reassurance. Reassurance I didn't know I could give her.

'So Michael is still in Mexico?' I asked.

'Maybe, unless he moved onto Peru. That was his plan.'

She was drawn to a record player by the window. I watched as she slinked over to it and selected a record from the rack beneath. She eased the vinyl from its sleeve and placed it gently down on the turntable, then swung the needle into action. The music filled the room with its vibrations. She looked over at me and smiled.

'Our song.'

She tiptoed toward me with her eyes closed listening to the tune. I felt her soft hands rest on my chest. I looked down at her five foot six frame and found her staring back at me through those big, beautiful eyes.

'Is there something wrong? You don't believe me, do you?' she asked.

'Right now, I don't know what to believe. I've been getting so many stories from so many people. I need to think it through.'

'Maybe this will help.'

Her hand reached round the back of my neck and pulled my head down closer to hers. She pressed her lips up against mine. I'd dreamed of this for so long and now it was happening I wasn't sure I wanted it. I pulled away and pushed her back from me lest I be tempted again.

'No, I can't. I need some time,' I told her.

Her head dropped in disappointment. She gave a subtle hint of a nod.

'I understand,' she replied with a whisper.

'We should get some sleep. You can have the bed, I'll take the couch.'

I pulled the needle from the record and the scratch became a signal for the end of the conversation. She shuffled over to the bed and sulked. I stood there a moment staring at her. Her forlorn appearance cutting me deep. I was caught in two minds. On the one hand I was happy to see her again, alive and well. But something about her story...I just didn't know if I could trust her anymore.

The next morning, I awoke to the sound of kitchen utensils clattering. I sat up on the couch and peered over the back to find Louise frying bacon. She must have heard my rustling as she looked over her shoulder at me and smiled.

'Morning. I thought I'd make breakfast. Bacon and egg okay?' she said.

Cooking breakfast? Did she think we could just pick up where we left off? I pulled back the thin blanket that failed to keep me warm all night and got to my feet.

'You didn't have to,' I replied, rubbing my eyes.

'I wanted to. I don't mean to sound rude, but it doesn't look like you've been eating properly since I left.'

I furrowed my brow at this insensitive remark. Did she really not understand why I hadn't been eating properly? I saw the penny drop in her eyes and she turned away ashamed.

'Sorry,' she said with remorse.

I ran the tap of the sink in the kitchen and splashed the cold refreshing water over my face. It's something of a morning ritual for me. Nothing wakes you up like it. Louise threw in some small talk while I was trying to gather my thoughts and prepare myself for the day. She asked if I slept well. I told her the couch was far from comfortable and she followed up with telling me I should have joined her in the bed. I explained that wasn't a good idea and I saw the disappointment grow in her face. What was wrong with me? I'd been given a second chance and I was acting like it's the end of the world.

She dished up the bacon and scrambled eggs onto a couple of mismatching plates and carried them over to a small dining table I was sitting at sipping a cup of hot black coffee. I stared at the food in front of me. God damnit! It felt like she'd never left. I could feel myself getting sucked back into this world of happy lives. I couldn't put myself into a vulnerable position. I had to keep a distance. At least until I was sure everything was genuine.

'Eat up, before it gets cold,' she said waiting for me to take my first bite.

I cut a piece of bacon and placed it in my mouth. It was delicious. Perfectly cooked with a slight crunch. She asked me how it was and I couldn't lie. This pleased her.

'So, I don't know if you have any plans today, but if not I was hoping we could spend the day together. Just you and I,' she said in between chewing.

'Don't you think it would be better to visit your mother and sister first? Let them know you're still alive. Your mother hasn't been taking it well.'

'Oh my God, you're right,' she replied placing a hand on her forehead. 'I should go see them. But maybe, after, we could spend the rest of the day together?'

'We'll see.'

We then ate in silence. I don't know what she was thinking, but my mind was racing a mile a minute.

We arrived outside Louise's family home just after ten in the morning. She took a long deep breath before pressing on the doorbell. That welcoming tune reminded me of my last visit here and now I was stood next to the person whose death I was sent to investigate. Maria answered the door and as soon as she clocked Louise she let out an ear-splitting scream. She lunged forward wrapping her arms around the poor girl squeezing her tight.

When we finally made it inside the house, Maria charged into the living room calling for Mrs Danvers who was still sat by the fire. Stephanie appeared first to see what the problem was and froze in disbelief when she saw me with Louise walking beside.

'Oh my God, Louise!' she cried loud enough that Jemima heard causing her to peer round the wing of her arm chair. Jemima was an older woman and so naturally slow, but she'd never moved quicker than she did when she saw her long-thought dead daughter standing before her like an angel sent back from heaven. When Jemima took hold of Louise, I didn't think she was ever going to let go.

I left the family to bask in their miracle and sat out on the veranda watching the birds. There's nothing more peaceful than watching the wildlife go about their business. How simple they have it compared to us. Stephanie came out to join me sitting on the sun lounger side-saddle.

'Are you okay?' she asked.

'I don't know. It's just a lot to take in.'

'It certainly is. A part of me thinks this is all a dream and at any moment I'm going to wake up.'

'Or it's a nightmare,' I snapped back without making eye contact.

There was a momentary pause as she frowned at me.

'You're not happy to see her alive?'

'Of course, I'm happy she's alive, but…'

'You don't believe her story, do you? That he forced her to leave? You think she went willingly.'

'Something like that.'

'Well, it wouldn't be the first time she's lied. Then again, what she's told us does make sense. I always had a feeling Michael wasn't completely what he portrayed, that he had a dark side and was capable of the things she said he did. I'm sure she loves you, Nick. Try not to let it eat away at you. We've got Louise back, something we never thought possible. It should be a happy occasion.'

'I don't feel like celebrating. Not yet, anyway.'

Louise managed to pry herself from Jemima's embrace and we said our goodbyes. Louise assured them she would be back the following day.

We headed back to my place where I had plans to interrogate Louise more and cross examine her story. I got more than I bargained for, however. We entered via the front door and before Louise could close it behind her, Michael pushed his way into the room with a snub-nosed revolver clenched in his hand. He slammed the door shut and Louise rushed over to me like Little Red Riding Hood needing protection from the Big Bad Wolf. She clutched at my arm.

'Hey, babe,' he said with a devilish grin on his tired looking face. His eyes were red from lack of sleep and his shaggy beard was unkempt. He'd clearly been sleeping rough the last few days.

'Michael, what are you doing here?' Louise cried.

She was shaking with fear. I wanted to look down to see if this was all just a performance, but I didn't want to take my eyes off the gun.

'Isn't it obvious? I came for you. I don't know why you left, but whatever I did, I'm sorry. I've chartered us a plane at Burbank. To Peru, just like we always wanted. We leave in an hour.'

'I'm sorry, Michael. I can't go with you. I'm frightened,' she replied squeezing my arm tighter.

'Frightened? You've got nothing to be frightened of. I would never hurt you.'

'You need to go,' I interrupted, still not taking my eyes off the gun.

Michael's attention switched to me and he scowled like he was trying to burn a hole in me. The pulled up collar of his raincoat was beginning to sag.

'You must be Nick. The private dick. I've heard all about you.'

'I could say the same about you and I'm not impressed.'

Michael glanced at Louise pressing herself against me.

'What did she tell you? That I kidnapped her? Took her from you against her will?'

'Something like that.'

'She's lying,' he smirked. 'You may not be happy to hear it, but she came willingly. I didn't even have to persuade her. As soon as she saw me, it was like a moth to a flame. She knew she had a second chance to be with me and she took it.'

'He's lying, Nick. Don't listen to him,' Louise protested.

I looked down at her and stared deep into her eyes. They were filling with tears.

'Is he?' I asked. 'You said it yourself, he was your first love and you had a second chance. I know how that feels. I wonder, did you ever love me or was I just there to help you forget him?'

'Don't say that,' she said, the tears now streaming down her cheek. She looked away releasing her grip on me and I knew I had her number.

'I don't think he believes you, babe,' Michael added. 'You never were good at lying.'

Michael was right, but he was also a piece of shit I wanted out of my apartment.

'You should leave, before it's too late,' I warned him.

'I'm not going anywhere without her.'

'They know you're alive, Michael. Dalton Bank knows and he will find you,' I was now talking through gritted teeth trying to strengthen the threat.

'Now who's lying?' he said with a hint of a smile.

'I'm trying to help you. If you go now, you may have enough time to flee to any country you wish. If you don't, you'll never see the light of day again.'

'Correction. You'll never see the light of day if you don't back off.'

Michael cocked the gun and was now aiming it at my head. I'd been in situations like this before, a gun in my face is nothing new, but I couldn't risk a stray bullet hitting Louise. I stepped in front of her, talking to keep Michael distracted.

'I wouldn't be the first private investigator you've killed.'

He didn't see what I was getting at, so I filled in the details for him.

'The motel fire. The body found in your room. After you stole money from Dalton, you hid it in the motel room. When you went back, you were in for a surprise. Randall Colter was there and he was searching the place. Maybe you thought he was there to kill you as well, so you killed him first. Then you set the room on fire in the hope the body would be unidentifiable. You murdered several other people in the process. The list is long Michael, what's one more name?'

'I didn't mean for those other people to get killed in the fire. If the motel had followed fire regulations, they would have been fine.'

'And Colter?'

'I didn't know he was a P.I. He had a gun, I just assumed…I was protecting myself. Like anyone would.'

'That man was a friend of mine. His body is buried in your grave and his family have no idea.'

'Don't you understand? I had to do what I did. I knew it was only a matter of time before Bank discovered I'd stolen from him. I thought if he believed I was dead, I'd be okay. And it worked. I was free. Seeing Louise crying by my grave though, that broke my heart, but it had to be done. I couldn't tell her or she'd be in danger as well. I knew one day though I would come back for her. She means more to me than anything and I would travel to the ends of the world to make her happy. So you need to step aside, before I put a bullet in your brain because I'm not leaving without her.'

Louise crept round from behind me to look Michael in the eye.

'I'm not going with you, Michael. I don't want to,' she said through trembling voice.

'Don't mess with me, Louise. Do you realise what I'm risking coming back here?'

'I didn't ask you to come back.'

'What? I love you, Louise.'

'I don't feel the same anymore.'

I could hear Michael's heart shattering inside his chest, but he shook his head refusing to accept her claim.

'No, I don't believe you. You do love me,' he insisted.

'I don't know you anymore. You've killed people, Michael. You're not the same man I once knew.'

'I am the same. I'll prove that to you. Just please, come with me. We can start a new life. Start afresh.'

Louise was done talking. She merely shook her head. Michael's hand began shaking with rage.

'Fine, if I can't have you, no one can,' he threatened.

He raised the gun at Louise. I was about to lunge forward, but I was worried my reaction would startle him into firing. The situation had to remain calm when a gun was involved, no sudden movements. Louise didn't seem scared.

'You're not going to shoot me, Michael,' she said confidently.

Michael stared into her puppy dog eyes. His gun hand still shaking. He released his finger from the trigger and lowered his arm.

'No, I couldn't. But I can shoot him.'

The gun lifted again, but this time in my direction.

'Michael, no!' Louise called out.

'Then come with me,' Michael said, extending an open palm toward her expecting her hand to rest upon it. She looked over at me with loving eyes.

'I won't let him hurt you,' she said, reaching out for him. She took his hand and he pulled her toward him keeping a firm grip.

'Things will get better, babe. I promise you,' he said before his eyes shifted over to me. 'No hard feelings?'

Michael opened the door and pushed Louise through it. She put up a bit of a fight watching me as she crossed the threshold. I knew I couldn't let him take her with him. Things may not be the same between us, but she was in danger around him. I took a step toward them, but Michael saw me approach and raised the gun. Louise could see he was about to pull the trigger and pulled on his arm.

'No!' she screamed.

Too late. The loud bang was deafening in the small room. I flinched and then felt the piercing warmth in my chest. My legs buckled and I hit the floor hard. I heard Louise call out my name and then silence.

A couple of minutes later, I came round and sat up. There was pain in my chest, but to my surprise, it wasn't fatal. Reaching up inside my shirt, I could feel the entry wound in my shoulder. A few inches lower and I would have been a goner and luckily it came out the other side. I may still be alive, but I don't let someone shoot me and get away with it. Michael was going to have a farewell party. I rushed over to the phone and picked up the receiver hastily dialling.

I arrived at the airfield a few moments after them. They'd had an altercation on the journey whereby Louise having failed to reason with Michael reacted poorly and grabbed the steering wheel. The car span out, Michael dropped the gun and they almost crashed. Michael got the car back in control slamming on the brakes, but Louise now had the gun in her hand pointing the barrel directly at Michael's chest. She couldn't kill him though, there still remained some love in her heart. Michael snatched the gun from her and cracked her over the head with the butt lest she try anything stupid again. This incident gave me time to gain some ground. As I pulled up alongside them by the plane, Michael was wrestling Louise from the car. He didn't get far before Dalton Bank stepped off the waiting Beechcraft Model 18 to inform Michael he wouldn't be flying anywhere.

'You look good for a dead man, Michael,' Dalton said revelling in this surprise.

Michael froze in his tracks. He pulled the gun from his pocket and was about to aim it at Dalton when a shake of Dalton's head made him think otherwise.

'I wouldn't advise that, Michael. It won't end well for you. Put the gun down,' he said with authority.

Michael dropped the gun on the ground and smirked.

'I don't suppose I'd get out of here alive, would I?' he said in defeat.

Dalton merely shook his head to confirm Michael's assumption. Louise broke free from Michael's grasp and ran toward me. She clattered into me so hard I almost stumbled. She clutched on for dear life as she watched Michael and Dalton. Michael turned and looked over at us. Meanwhile, Dalton gestured over to a nearby car beckoning it to come closer. The black Mercedes glided up the runway and pulled up alongside Michael, blocking his path to the plane. Dalton walked round and opened the rear door.

'Now, Mr Ferzetti, if you wouldn't mind getting into the car. We have a lot to discuss.'

Michael pulled his attention away from me and Louise, curious as to what might be in the car.

'What are you going to do to me?' he asked, the fear palpable.

Dalton didn't say. He simply reiterated his instruction and Michael complied after one last glimpse at Louise. We watched as

Dalton climbed in with him and the door slammed shut. They drove off and we were left standing in the middle of a cold runway. Louise looked up at me.

'What will they do to him?' she asked.

'I don't care.'

'And where does this leave us?'

'It leaves us right here. You go your way, I go mine,' I said coldly.

'But I still love you,' she protested placing her hands on my chest.

'Yeah, but sometimes that's not enough.'

I removed her hands from me and pushed her back. She didn't try and fight me, she just let it happen. I got into my Chevy, started the engine and drove off. I couldn't resist one last look at her in the rear-view mirror and caught her give a subtle saddening wave, but it meant nothing to me. This rollercoaster of emotions had finished its ride and I was ready to get off and throw up in the nearest trashcan. No matter how hard we tried, things would never be like they were. She was different to me now. That was the last time I ever saw her.

An Unexpected Encounter in Spitalfields

George did not like the fact he was in the pub in the middle of the day, but he didn't have much of a choice. Since losing his job at the docks, he'd struggled to find work elsewhere, not much need for a man with his limited skills. After several weeks of sitting at home questioning his worth, his wife and he became concerned by the mounting bills they needed to pay. They had burnt through the last of their savings to keep the house warm and they needed an income quickly.

Mary suggested the idea first. Well, she'd have to, it was an idea that would never cross George's mind in a million years. He disregarded it as nonsense, but he could see in her eyes she was serious. He couldn't quite believe she would sink to that level. Surely things were not that bad. There must be other options. She explained it would be the quickest way to bring in the money, at least until he found work. George pondered the idea for several days, at the same time hunting for a job so that they didn't have to go through with it. Unfortunately, no job was found, but the landlord of their small one room abode did not hesitate to show himself when the rent was due. He gave them one more week to pay, otherwise, they would be out on the street. George relented and agreed with Mary they should at least try it. And so now three weeks later, rent and bills paid in full, George comes to the pub during the day while Mary stays home and entertains gentlemen as London's latest woman of easy virtue.

Everyone local knew the situation the couple had opted for, especially those in the Dog and Bone pub. Most of the men who frequented it had either come from Mary or were heading out to visit her. George couldn't bear it. Often there would be times he overheard patrons discussing their tryst with his dear wife. On his way to the Dog and Bone, he would purchase a copy of the London Daily Post and bury his head in it while he sipped at a pint. It was a welcome distraction from the incessant sniggering and gawping.

'They're saying he's a doctor,' a gruff voice said.

A small timid man in his forties with thinning tussled hair and bags under his sad eyes, George looked up from his newspaper to see the pub landlord staring at him vigorously cleaning a glass.

'What?' George replied, confused by the comment.

'The ripper,' the landlord said gesturing with a nod toward the front of George's newspaper.

George folded back the page to read the headline, "Jack the Ripper Claims 5th Victim. Woman Brutally Hacked to Death."

'Scotland Yard are saying he may be a doctor because of the way he cuts up the bodies. Seems to know what he's doing. The Lord Mayor is also offering a five-hundred pound reward for his capture,' the landlord continued as he picked up another glass to polish.

George nodded in acknowledgment before returning to the article he was reading about the Great Sheep Panic in Oxfordshire. Experts were stumped as to how it happened, but they had their theories. Before George could learn what those theories were, he was interrupted again by a voice he despised.

'Alright, Georgie-boy? How ya been? Still looking for work?'

The voice emanated from Bill Pickford, the local loudmouth. Tall and commanding with a flat-cap hiding his baldness, he filled every room he entered with his bravado. Growing up, Bill was the school bully and George was the regular butt of his jokes. Over the years, Bill had all the luck, while George scraped through life. Suffice to say, George hated Bill and couldn't stand being in his presence. Unfortunately for George, he had nowhere else to go and he also had half a pint of bitter left.

'Of course I'm still looking for work,' George snapped back. 'You haven't heard of anything, have you?'

George's tone had changed upon asking the question. He wanted to maintain his aggressive attitude toward this annoyance of a man, but he was so desperate for work he was willing to ask anyone even if it was his worst enemy and animosity wouldn't help.

'No, can't help I'm afraid, but hang in there, something will come up,' Bill said patting George on the back.

Bill leaned forward onto the bar to attract the landlord's attention with his cheeky grin.

'The usual please, John,' Bill called out.

The landlord took a pint glass from a rack and started filling it with ale from a filthy tap.

'How's the wife, George? Still on the game?' Bill said with a smirk.

'Shut up!' George said through gritted teeth trying to focus on his newspaper.

'What's this?' asked a second voice the other side of Bill.

George glanced up to see a short dumpy man with rosy cheeks standing next to Bill leaning on the bar. He didn't recognise the man, but assumed he was one of Bill's new lackeys. He collected them like stamps. Bullies rarely operate alone, always travelling with a sycophantic sidekick to cheer on their behaviour.

'Oh, of course, you don't know,' Bill grinned. 'On account of George here struggling to find work, his wife has turned to prostitution to pay the bills.'

'Jesus! And you're okay with that?' the dumpy man said incredulously to George.

'Doesn't have much choice does he?' Bill continued, much to George's embarrassment. 'It's either that or he's out on the street. She's doing alright though, keeping the customers flocking. We've all had her, haven't we George? Not bad if I say so myself. You've picked a winner there.'

George's fists clenched the newspaper, rustling as it creased between his fingers.

'That's enough, Bill,' the landlord said placing the pint of ale down in front of the despicable man.

'What? I'm only messing,' Bill protested. 'He doesn't mind, do you?'

Bill patted George on the back, this time much harder. George slapped his hand away with a swipe of his arm. Bill raised his hands up in defence trying not to laugh at this rare show of aggression.

'Alright, calm down, George. It's not my fault your wife's a whore,' Bill said with a hint of laughter as he lifted his pint to his lips.

That was the last straw. George could take everything people said, but the moment they referred to his wife as a whore, that was too much. He jumped up from his stool pushing it back so it toppled onto the floor. His fists had now released the newspaper. The right found itself flying through the air toward Bill's face. It made contact crushing Bill's bulbous nose and caused him to stumble, bumping into the dumpy man behind. The pint glass dropped to the floor and smashed, the foamy beverage seeping into the cracks of the wood.

A few seconds after, Bill had overcome the shock of George's act and he was ready to retaliate. Before he could, though, he felt two arms wrap around him, holding him back. The dumpy man was aware an all-out brawl could erupt and was keen to stifle it fast. The landlord flipped up the hinged bar top bashing it against the wall and cut in between the warring men.

'Alright, that's enough,' the landlord ordered.

Bill realised he wasn't going to be able to throw a much craved punch, so he turned to the landlord for justice.

'Oi! Aren't you going to bar him for that?' he said in an almost childlike manner.

'You were asking for it, Bill. I'd have done the same,' the landlord replied, well aware of who instigated the incident.

George, not willing to stay in this toxic environment any longer, grabbed his coat and rushed out of the pub.

George walked the streets of the East End for an hour unsure where to take himself. All this time, his mind kept thinking about what Mary was doing. Who she was with. How they were treating her. He couldn't take it anymore. He was becoming a laughing stock and he wondered whether he could ever get back the respect he'd spent most of his life earning. People like Bill would continue to mock him unless he finally put an end to this. He had to find work. *Well*, he thought to himself, *I will find work*. God as his witness he would get a job no matter what it was and he would put food on the table for his wife so she didn't have to. And until then, his wife would no longer sell herself to the underbelly of this decrepit city. He would march home right now and tell Mary that she's done enough. He would no longer stand by while she degraded herself. And one day he'd be able to enjoy a pint in the Dog and Bone without overhearing words that sent shivers down his spine. George then quickened his pace as he headed down the back alleys toward his home.

When he arrived outside the building, he noticed the curtains upstairs were drawn, a clear sign Mary was not alone. Many times he'd returned home early and had to wait outside until her current customer had finished. Well, not any more. He wasn't waiting around for whoever it was to finish. He wanted to put an end to this now. George climbed the wooden staircase at the side of the building and pushed his ear up against the door listening for voices. He heard the faint mumble of talking. Putting the brass key in the hole, he unlocked the door and burst into the room to find Mary lying on their bed. A tall, slim man was straddled on top, kissing her neck. Despite the intimacy between them, Mary was showing very little interest. It was just business for her after all. The sound of another presence in the room startled the man and he looked up at George with confusion. He had sinister eyes and a small scar above his top lip, the result of a harelip.

Mary sat up to see why the man had stopped and was shocked to find George staring at them. It was a surprise she got any business at all due to her frumpy figure and haggard looks, but her prices were rather competitive. It's easy to overlook missing teeth, unkempt hair and pocked skin at such a bargain.

'George? What are you doing? I'm working,' she said in a screeching tone.

'Not anymore,' George replied confidently.

He stomped over to the bed and grabbed the man by the arm yanking him off the bed and onto the floor.

'What the bloody hell do you think you're doing?' the man shouted.

'Time's up, mate,' George said dragging the man toward the door.

Mary was fuming at George's manner, especially as the man hadn't even paid yet, but at the same time, she was also impressed by her husband's prowess. Something George hadn't demonstrated to her in many years.

'Unhand me, you fiend,' the man insisted and a scuffle broke out between them.

The man pushed George across the room causing him to crash into a small dining table and chairs. As his rear hit the cold hardwood floor, he found himself wedged between the furniture. He could feel his blood boiling. He scowled at the man, watching him turn back to Mary and approach her as if to continue where they left off.

George reached out, wrapping his fingers around a brass candlestick in the middle of the dining table. He rose to his feet and lifted the heavy metal above his head like an axe, bringing it down in a wide arc, the man's head interrupting its journey. The connection sent a vibration down George's arm, he then felt a similar vibration in his feet as the man's body collapsed to the floor.

'Oh my God, George. What have you done?' Mary cried out.

She slipped off the bed to her knees beside the unconscious man. The blood was oozing from the back of his head, binding his hair around the open wound. She nudged him gently in the hope he would stir, but his body remained worryingly still. She reached up to a nearby bedside unit where a hand mirror lay. She placed the mirror in front of the man's mouth and nose and prayed that the familiar patch of steam appeared, but it didn't. She looked up at George with eyes wide like a stunned animal.

'George, I think he's dead,' she said.

The candlestick slipped from George's fingers and hit the floor with a thud making Mary jump. He fell to his knees and crawled over to the supposed corpse hoping Mary was mistaken. Unfortunately, his inspection garnered the same results.

'What do we do?' she asked.

'We can't tell the police, there'll be a noose around my neck before the judge can say guilty.'

'Well, we can't exactly leave him here.'

'We'll toss him in the river. No one'll find him there,' George proposed after a brief moment of thought.

'And how do you suppose you get his body to the river without anyone seeing?' Mary said placing her hands on her hips.

'We'll wait until it's dark and then carry him out wrapped in the rug,' he answered gesturing toward the rug the man currently lay on staining it with his blood.

'My mother gave me this rug before she died, I'm not having it sullied by a corpse.'

George was irritated Mary wasn't willing to sacrifice a useless possession to help save her husband from the gallows. He looked around the room for another option and spotted a large travelling trunk in the corner.

'Alright, we'll put him inside the trunk,' he said, thinking that was maybe a better idea anyway.

'You'll never fit him in there,' she replied with a snigger.

George was becoming incredibly impatient. Disposing of a body was a time sensitive thing and she was costing them valuable minutes arguing over the method.

'Jesus, Mary. Help me out here. We've got to do something,' he cried.

'Fine. Put him in the trunk,' she replied with a dismissive wave.

George pulled the trunk into the middle of the room and looked it over. He ran his fingers across the leather covered cuboid as if analysing its properties with his deft touch.

'Yeah, this'll do nicely. I'll punch some holes in it, add a bit more weight. It'll sink like a stone.'

Squeezing the corpse into the trunk took a lot longer than George was anticipating, especially as Mary refused to help. He had to twist the body in unnatural ways and he was certain he snapped a few bones along the way. If the man wasn't dead before, he certainly would be now. He filled out the rest of the space with some old broken bricks and drilled a few holes around the base and in the top to allow the air to flow out when it hit the water. He felt proud he'd thought of every conceivable detail. Science was always an interest to him and now it was paying off.

Once the sun had set, they lugged the trunk out the front door and it immediately slid down the stairs with a rattle before hitting the cobbled street below. George chased after it praying no neighbours appeared to see what all the noise was about. Satisfied no fellow residents were going to entertain their curiosity, they picked up the trunk and began the journey down to the Thames through the lamplit night.

The trunk was heavy, but it became much heavier when Mary dropped her end and it was dragging along the street with a horrific scraping sound. George stopped and looked over to find her shaking her hand to retain some feeling in her fingers.

'Mary, pick up the trunk,' he whispered.

'I can't, it's too heavy,' she replied through gritted teeth.

'Mary, pick it up!'

He stared daggers at her, hoping his penetrative vision would force her to buck up her ideas and inspire some haste in her.

'Just give me a second to catch my breath,' she pleaded.

George was ready to let loose with the insults, but the sight of a police officer walking toward them caught his breath. He looked at her nervously.

'Stay calm.'

'What?' Mary asked confused, then realised what George was referring to when she looked over her shoulder to see the bobby on the beat approaching.

'Oh my God,' she said under her breath.

The police officer stepped toward them, hands behind his back, a thick handlebar moustache beneath his nose. Mary's breathing quickened to a panting as he sidled up beside her.

'Evening, what are you two doing out so late? Are you oblivious to the fact there's a crazed killer on the loose?' the officer asked with an authoritative voice.

'No, officer. We just need to get this trunk to a friend of ours. He lives by the river,' George said with a smile, trying desperately not to panic.

'Do you need a hand?' the officer proffered gesturing toward the trunk.

'No, it's okay?' George snapped back. 'My wife can help.'

'Nonsense, you shouldn't be asking a lady to carry such an item. Allow me.'

Before George could protest, the officer had already gripped the trunk handle and lifted the heavy box. George grinned hoping his nerves would hold out. Better yet, he hoped Mary wouldn't crack. He could already see her hands shaking.

It was a rather long walk to the riverside and as nervous as George was about this police officer being so close to the body of a man he had just murdered, he did appreciate the physical strength the lawman contributed to make the transportation easier. When he heard the lapping of the water, George dropped his side of the trunk. One of the latches released itself and he had to quickly lock it back down. Of course there was no chance of the lid flipping open, but he was so on edge he didn't have time to think reasonably.

'This will do. My friend just lives in that house,' he said pointing to a random nearby building. 'I'll get him to help carry it the rest of the way.'

'Very well,' the officer accepted placing his side of the trunk down. 'Have a good evening, and stay vigilant.'

'We will. Thank you, officer.'

The officer gave a tip of his hat and walked off into the fog filled night. Both George and Mary let out a sigh of relief. Mary's legs almost buckled and she had to use the trunk to keep herself on her feet.

'That was close,' she said.

'Help me get it in the water. We're nearly done.'

Mary helped George lift the trunk onto the barrier wall. They then pushed it over and it toppled down into the water below with a mighty splash. They leaned over watching it bob up and down with the current.

'I thought you said it would sink,' Mary said concerned by its floatation.

'Give it a few seconds,' George replied confidently.

Eventually, the trunk slowly lowered into the water as it filled, until it disappeared completely. George smiled with relief.

They arrived back home exhausted. Mary stumbled over to the bed and sat down. George closed the front door and peered out the window to ensure nobody was watching them.

'What was that all about anyway? Coming home in the middle of the day when you know I'm working,' she asked.

George pulled over a chair and sat down. He was shaking from the adrenaline rush. He took a few deep breaths before answering her.

'I don't want you doing this anymore, Mary. I can't take it. The thought of you in bed with other men, people sniggering behind my back. It's over. Done.'

'And how do you expect us to pay the bills?'

'I'll find a job. I promise. Whatever it takes. Just not this.'

Mary stood and tiptoed over to him. She knelt down in front of his shivering frame and took his hands in hers. She kissed them softly and then looked up at him with a sweet smile.

'Okay, George. I'll stop. I wouldn't get much business anyway if you keep killing my customers, but you better find something quick. We've only got enough money for one more week's rent.'

'I'll find something,' he replied staring intently into her eyes.

Mary stood up straight and kissed George on the forehead. He truly did love her. After everything they'd been through he couldn't bear for them to be apart.

She made her way back over to the bed and collected a tatty old dressing gown, putting it on. As she tied the belt, she caught sight of a brown leather case by the bed.

'Oh, that man had a bag with him,' she said.

'Well, have a look what's in it. Maybe there's something we could sell.'

Mary picked up the case placing it down on the crumpled duvet of the bed. She unclipped the latch and yanked it open. She rummaged through it with curious fingers.

'It's all surgery tools,' she said taking out a scalpel.

She then pulled out several torn pieces of blood stained clothing. Each looked like offcuts of a different dress with various patterns and colours.

'Uh, George,' she said holding up the material for him to see.

George's eyes widened. The surgery tools. The blood stained clothing. Could it be? The man he just murdered and dumped in the river. Was he, the ripper? If that was the case, obviously the thought of his wife being the man's sixth victim was horrifying, but he was more disappointed about the five-hundred pound reward he missed out on.

A Seed of Misfortune

The old warehouse was draughty. An ice cold chill shot up
Frank's spine despite a three piece suit and dark raincoat shielding
him from the elements. He was towering over a bloody and beaten
man tied to a wooden chair, his head drooped almost unconscious.
Behind him stood two large heavy-set men in sharp suits, hands
clasped together, waiting patiently. Frank glanced at his gloved
hands, the blood residue a darker tone against the black leather.

'This can all end right now. Just tell me the truth,' Frank said
with exhaustion.

The seated man remained silent, his head lulling from side to
side. He felt Frank's hand against his forehead before being pushed
back. He could see a blurry face through swollen eyes and then
Frank's other hand forming a fist and pulling back ready to fly
toward him.

'Alright, it was me. I took it,' the concussed man blurted out.
Frank lowered his fist with relief.

'Where is it?' he asked.

'A locker at the train station. Number 126. The key is in my
pocket.'

Frank slipped off one of the gloves and, with a clean hand,
reached into the trouser pocket of the confessor. He pulled out a
small key with a numbered keyring attached. Frank wrapped his
hand around the man's chin and squeezed tight as he leaned in close.

'If you ever steal from me again, I won't be so kind next time,'
Frank threatened through gritted teeth. He released his grip and the
man's head dropped back down. Frank turned to the two men behind
him and held the key up for them to see.

'Go get the money, check it's all there, then take care of him,' he ordered them with authority. They both nodded as one of them took the key from Frank. He then turned and stepped out of the single beam of light coming through from the broken ceiling and into the darkness.

Frank pushed open the creaky metal door of the warehouse causing it to slam against its adjacent wall. He stepped out into the bright daylight squinting his eyes until they adjusted and breathed in the cool refreshing air. He pulled a squashed packet of cigarettes from his coat pocket and a gold zippo lighter. He lit a cigarette and closed his eyes as he drew in the delicious nicotine. Blowing out the smoke, he made his way over to his black BMW 5 Series and pulled open the driver's side door. Reluctant to stain his car with tobacco smoke, he tossed the cigarette to one side and climbed in. The engine started with a purr and he sped off kicking up dust in his wake.

The Lavender Club was a sophisticated bar with a very particular clientele. For those with power, money and influence who enjoy quiet places to listen to soft jazz music and socialise with friends and colleagues. As well as bankers, stock brokers and celebrities, it had become the chosen haunt of a few worldly criminals.

It was a quiet midday with only a few patrons dotted about and music playing through the sound system due to the live band only performing during evenings. The barman, a young, handsome Paulo was leaning up against the bar browsing social media on his smartphone. Frank entered as though he owned the place which nobody minded because he did own the place. He immediately caught Paulo's lax attitude at work and approached him with menace.

'Oi!' Frank called out to him. Paulo now alert to Frank's presence stood up straight and lowered his phone down and hid it behind him.

'Alright, Frank?' he replied with a friendly tone.

'Are you planning on doing some work today?' Frank asked rhetorically.

'Yeah, course,' Paulo answered not recognising the question didn't need answering.

Frank's eyebrows furrowed further than naturally possible.

'Then get on with it,' he screamed. 'I'm not paying you to stare at your phone all day!'

Frank carried on through the bar toward the back of the building. Paulo watched him leave and pulled a snarky face. He lifted his phone back up and continued from where he left off.

Frank's office was a tribute to himself and his achievements. On the walls were framed newspaper articles, the headlines reporting on his successes in business. Other pictures were of him with various celebrities from film, television and music. A glass cabinet in the corner of the room contained a menagerie of awards and trophies. In part it was to impress those who came into the room, but also to remind him of how far he had come from simple beginnings and a poor childhood. He was proud of what he had made of his life.

He sat down behind a large hardwood desk making himself comfortable. The bar manager, Graham, gently knocked on the open door yet didn't wait to be called in. He was a rotund man with thick glasses and a balding head. He was carrying a ledger.

'Morning, Frank. Here's the latest numbers for the month,' Graham wheezed, almost out of breath from the walk. Graham placed the ledger down on the desk. Frank snatched it toward him and flipped open the pages. 'I will warn you, it doesn't look good.'

'I don't like that new barman you hired,' Frank said as he browsed the columns and rows of numbers.

'Paulo? He's alright.'

'Maybe we should get rid.'

'You can't fire him just because you don't like him. We could end up facing legal action. That's the last thing we need right now,' Graham protested. Frank looked up at him with piercing eyes.

'He's lazy. That's why we should fire him. Every time I look over, he's not working.'

'I admit he can lack focus during the day, but in the evenings, the punters love him and he keeps them drinking. Just give it time. He'll grow on you.'

Graham chose to exit the office before Frank could reply to avoid a difficult conversation. Frank was distracted by the answer machine on his desk. The red light indicating new messages was flashing at him. He pressed the play button and listened to the automated voice tell him he had a new message and then leaned forward with interest as he heard the woman's voice start.

"Hi, Frank. It's Daphne. I need to see you. If you're free for a coffee later call me back," she said almost with desperation.

Frank wasted no time snatching up the phone receiver and dialling.

The cafe was busy, a cacophony of noise emanating around the room. Cutlery and porcelain tinkering and clattering, the low hum of conversation. Frank entered and scanned the room, spotting the young attractive Daphne sat at a table by the window. The warm sunlight glowing her like an angel. She caught sight of him and smiled sweetly. He grinned back at her as he made his way over. She stood up to greet him and the pregnant belly between them caused Frank to pause.

'You're pregnant?' he asked in disbelief.

'That's why I wanted to see you,' she replied.

Frank kissed her on the cheek. As they both sat down, he found it difficult to pull his focus away from the child growing inside her.

'I took the liberty of ordering for you. I hope that's okay,' she said softly.

Frank didn't even notice the steaming cup of coffee sat in front of him. He was transfixed on her stomach.

'You want to know if the baby is yours?' Daphne asked.

'Is it?' he snapped back after breaking free from his staring.

Daphne nodded with a cautious smile. She wasn't sure how he would react to this news, but was relieved to see the faint hint of a smirk on his face.

'How far…' Frank was about to ask before she pre-empted his question and interrupted.

'Nine months.'

'Nine months? Why didn't you tell me sooner?' he enquired with a frown.

'Because I'd left you. I'd spent three years suffering your attitude and abuse. I didn't want you to know. I didn't want you hounding me to get back together,' she explained.

'I get that.' Frank gave an understanding nod.

'The thing is, I thought I could do it by myself, but I'm only a few days away from my due date and I'm starting to have doubts about whether I'll cope. I'm willing to let you be involved, but I need your word you'll change,' Daphne maintained a stern eye contact as she posed this ultimatum.

Frank was surprised. She had certainly changed since he last saw her. She had become firm and confident. She'd never spoken to him like this before. He reached out a hand and placed it on top of hers.

'I already have changed. I'm a different man since you left. I understand how I treated you and I won't make that mistake again. I want to be there for you and our baby. I'll help any way I can,' he promised sincerely.

A large grin appeared on Daphne's face as tears welled up in her eyes.

'That's what I was hoping to hear.'

Frank stepped out into the street with a spring in his step and a smile on his face. All of a sudden, the problems in his life paled with the revelation of this news. Finally something good, life was looking up. As he started walking down the path, a middle-aged woman dressed in almost gypsy-like clothing appeared from around a corner and bumped into him spilling a cup of coffee all over his clean white shirt. At first he gasped in shock at the potential scolding he may suffer from the boiling hot liquid, but upon realising it was merely tepid, his shock turned to anger.

'Oh my, I'm so sorry,' she said with desperation. She pulled a tissue from her handbag and tried to mop at it. 'I'm so clumsy. I should look where I'm going.'

Frank was about ready to vent his anger and scream in her face, berating her for her lack of focus, but then he remembered the news he had just been given and this incident became a trivial thing.

'Don't worry about it. It's fine,' he assured her.

'I'd like to pay for the dry cleaning,' she offered.

'Not necessary,' he replied keen to keep on walking and take care of the mess himself.

'I insist,' she demanded blocking his path so he couldn't walk on. She rummaged through her handbag, but couldn't find what she was looking for.

'Oh, I don't seem to have my money on me. My flat is not far from here, I can get it for you,' she suggested with a hint of force.

Frank was about to tell her it's not a problem, but before he could finish his sentence, she cut in again, 'Please, I insist. I must balance this,' she said taking his hand and pulling him down the street.

The moment they entered the woman's flat, she zipped across the room to a back bedroom.

'I won't be long,' she called out.

Frank paced around the small one bedroom apartment analysing the various trinkets and memorabilia cluttering the many shelves lined along each wall of the living room. Animal bones and jars of pickled creatures immediately stood out to him. There were mystical pictures of star patterns and star signs hanging on the walls, but a crystal ball perched in the centre of a small round table caught his attention. The woman returned from the bedroom counting a wad of bank notes. She held them out to Frank.

'Here, that should cover it,' she said with relief.

Frank took the money with a thankful smile, but his mind was still on the crystal ball.

'What is this?' he asked.

'It's a crystal ball. I'm a fortune teller,' she replied with an air of arrogance.

'Oh, I see.' Frank was not impressed. He never bought into all that spiritual crap. He just took life as it came and never questioned why or how.

'Would you like me to read your fortune?' she offered.

'No, thanks.'

'It'll be on the house, as an apology for spoiling your day.'

Frank gave it some thought. He was never one to turn down something free. Very few things in life were free. After all, what was the harm. Either she'd be correct in her predictions and he can be prepared, or she'd be wrong and it won't matter.

'What do I have to do?' he asked curiously.

'Take a seat at the table,' she answered pulling out one of the chairs.

Frank sat down and she sat opposite him.

'Now, place your hands on the crystal ball either side. Close your eyes, take slow deep breaths and relax,' she continued.

Frank did as he was told. With both hands either side of the crystal ball, he was surprised by how warm it was. He closed his eyes and began to breathe deeply. She then placed her hands over the top of his and stared into the spherical glass.

'I'm getting a vision!' she said excitedly. 'I can see there is new life on the way.'

Frank's eyes whipped open in surprise. How did she know about his child? He only found out this morning.

'My girlfriend is pregnant. How did you…'

'Shh, I need to concentrate,' she snapped back. 'Close your eyes.'

Frank cautiously closed them again starting to believe in her abilities. He was a little nervous about what else she would tell him.

'You are suffering from financial difficulties. I see them ending soon,' she said with assurance.

Frank smirked. He was now convinced she was the real deal and she was telling him exactly what he wanted to hear. Finally, he could stop worrying about the fate of the club.

'Tell me more,' he pleaded.

Suddenly, her eyes opened wide in fear and she pulled her hands away from his. Frank opened his and looked at her in confusion. He could see she was startled and reluctant to continue.

'What's the problem?' he asked, not sure he wanted to know the answer.

'Maybe this was a bad idea,' she replied nervously. She tried to stand, but Frank reached out and grabbed her wrist preventing her from getting away from the table.

'What did you see?' Frank implored.

'I don't want to say,' she answered trying not to make eye contact with him.

'Tell me!' he demanded.

His tone frightened her and she was worried what he would do if she did not speak.

'I saw a death, your death.'

Frank was taken aback. He would be lying if he said this wasn't what he was worried about when he agreed to this charade, but at least if he had all the information he could be prepared, maybe even prevent it.

'I want to know more,' he insisted.

'I really don't think…'

'Tell me!'

She was shaking with fear. She slowly sat back down and took a deep breath.

'If you're sure.'

Frank nodded. She reluctantly placed her hands over his and stared into the ball. Frank watched as her eyes flickered slightly.

'I see a murder. A brutal murder,' she said with fear. Frank could see tears welling up in her eyes.

'Who kills me?'

She shook her head and frowned.

'I cannot see a face, but he is a young man with blond hair. He has a strange birthmark and I sense he was born during the first snow of winter for his heart is cold and vengeful.'

Frank stared at her with concern. How could she not see who it was? He tried pushing her for more, but her fragile state caused her to crumble into a blubbering wreck. She jumped up from the table and rushed into the back bedroom. He would have to take the signs she'd given and be cautious of them. It would have to be someone he knew, but who?

It was a long and cold walk back to the club. Frank ran through his mind the various people he knew who may hold a grudge and potentially murder him out of revenge. The list was long.

When he finally reached the club, it was getting dark and he found the place growing busy as usual. Passing through on the way to his office he scanned the bar, but found Paulo was nowhere to be seen. He frowned with frustration and rerouted himself making a beeline for it.

Stepping behind, he entered a small storage room filled with crates of bottles. Paulo was leaning against the wall downing a sneaky glass of vodka. Frank stared at him fuming.

'What the bloody hell do you think you're doing?' he screamed with fury.

Paulo almost jumped from his skin dropping the shot glass on the floor smashing it to pieces. He stood up straight trying to compose himself.

'Oh shit, sorry Frank. It was just a small one to perk me up ready for tonight's rush,' Paulo replied with a stutter.

'Well, you don't need to worry about that anymore. Get out!' Frank roared trying desperately not to wrap his hands around Paulo's throat.

'What?' Paulo answered, not quite believing the response he was getting to this minor infraction.

'Get out! You're fired!' Frank reiterated.

'Are you serious?'

'What do you think? Now, get out before I throw you out.' Frank could feel his blood boiling and if Paulo didn't leave immediately, he may have done something he later regretted.

'You know what? Stick your job!' Paulo snapped back pulling off the embroidered employee polo shirt and tossing it at Frank. Frank watched as Paulo stormed out of the back room and caught a glimpse of a strangely shaped birthmark on his back. Frank chased him out into the main room to find some of the patrons watching the drama play out having heard the commotion. Paulo was nearing the front door when Frank called out his name to stop him. Paulo paused before reaching out to the door handle and turned to him half expecting an apology.

'When were you born?' Frank bizarrely asked.

Paulo wasn't sure what he meant by that, but since it wasn't an apology he gave a simple two word answer back.

'Fuck you!'

Paulo opened the door and disappeared into the night. A worried look formed on Frank's face as he held the polo shirt in his fist. He noticed the patrons staring at him and hastily made his way through the room to his office.

Frank sat in his office for a couple of hours working his way through a bottle of whiskey he stored in his desk. He stared at the wall deep in thought. Could it really be Paulo who murders him? He has blond hair and the birthmark and he now has a motive. It must be. If it was anybody else, surely they would have acted by now if they had intentions to kill him. He had to do something. He slammed the glass down on the desk spilling its contents and jumped up from his seat. He grabbed his overcoat and rushed out of the room.

Paulo was sat on the sofa in his crummy one bedroom flat watching television with a bottle of beer. He was taking large swigs flicking through the channels with the remote. Several other empty beer bottles were scattered around the room and a half empty pizza box sat on the seat next to him. A knock on the door startled him. At first he wasn't going to answer it, comfortable in his wallowing, but the knocking didn't subside and there was only one way to make that

67

happen. He dragged himself to his feet and stumbled over to the door yanking it open to find Frank standing before him looking forlorn.

'What do you want?' he spat at Frank with a furrowed brow.

'Can I come in?'

Paulo reluctantly stepped aside allowing Frank to enter. He pushed the door closed behind him and watched as Frank stepped deeper into the room observing the detritus.

'Well?' Paulo asked impatiently.

'I want to apologise for what happened earlier,' Frank said softly.

'If you're here to beg me to come back, you can forget it. I'm done with that place and I'm done with you.' Paulo was pointing, still with the bottle in his hand, the beer swilling around inside.

'Let's just talk,' Frank gestured toward the bottle in Paulo's hand. 'How about a beer?'

'Fine!' Paulo said placing his bottle down on a side unit of the kitchenette. He pulled open the door of the small fridge and bent down to search for more bottles. As he was about to extend his arm to collect one, a thin wire wrapped around his neck from behind and was pulled taught. Paulo leaned back clutching at the wire cutting into his throat gasping for breath. Frank gritted his teeth as he pulled it tighter and tighter with all his might. A pair of leather gloves preventing the wire from cutting into his hands. Paulo's face was turning red and his legs became weak dropping to his knees. After a while, his hands fell from his neck and hung limp down by his side. Satisfied Paulo was dead, Frank released his grip allowing Paulo's body to collapsed to the floor with a thud. Frank took a deep breath. A slight smirk to himself. He had changed his fate. No more murder. His mobile phone started to buzz inside his coat pocket. He almost didn't notice it over the beating of his heart. It was a number he didn't recognise. He cautiously answered.

'Hello?'

The voice on the other end had his heart rate racing again.

'I'll be right there,' he shouted as he rushed to the front door of the flat.

Frank burst into the hospital room to find Daphne sat up in bed cradling a small bundle in her arms. She looked exhausted, but ecstatic. Upon hearing the sound of the doors swinging open, she turned to see who was interrupting the peace. Frank was approaching her slowly with a grin on his face. She smiled back through tear filled eyes.

'Say hello to your son,' she whispered.

Frank kissed her on the forehead and looked down at the tiny baby nestled in a hospital blanket. The child was fast asleep breathing quietly.

'I can't believe it,' Frank said still trying to comprehend what was lying before him. He always dreamed of becoming a father, but somewhere along the way he'd given up on that idea.

'Would you like to hold him?' she asked.

Frank didn't reply. He simply reached out and slid his arms under his son's makeshift cocoon and lifted him up to take a closer look. He began to rock him gently, a tear in his eye. *This is it,* he thought. *A turning point in my life, a new me.* He would do whatever it took to make sure Daphne and his son were happy.

A midwife entered the room to collect some spare unused blankets sitting upon a chair in the corner of the room. She glanced over at Frank and smiled.

'Is everything okay?' the midwife asked.

'Yes, everything's fine,' Daphne replied looking up at Frank with affection.

'Good. Let me know if you need anything,' the midwife offered before turning to leave the room. As she did so she caught a glimpse out the window and paused.

'Oh, it's started snowing,' she commented with surprise.

At first, the words didn't register in Frank's mind, too focused on who he was holding, but as they sank in, he began to think. He looked up at the window and sure enough a heavy snow was falling. His brain now kicked into over-gear and a darkness fell over him. He pulled back the blankets wrapped around his son to find a strangely shaped birthmark on his chest. Frank froze with worry as his eyes widened in shock.

Past Crimes

She placed her hands on her head, running slim fingers through her dark hair. Detective Inspector Abigail Pell could feel a headache developing as her tired eyes strained to read the files on the desk before her. She'd had difficult cases before, but this one was seriously testing her patience.

So far Abigail had had a one hundred percent solve rate. To say she was tenacious would be an understatement. Her colleagues always described her as a dog with a bone when she was working. She just couldn't let it go, no matter how futile it may seem. And so she persisted with this case. She needed to know who killed this victim, she needed an answer for her brain to rest.

It seemed so simple on the outset; a man in his mid-30s found dead in an alleyway, a laceration across his forehead caused by a heavy jagged object which was discovered to be a piece of stone found at the scene coated in the victim's blood. Except, there were no fingerprints, no DNA samples and no witnesses. If Abigail were more of a spiritual person, she would surmise the perpetrator was a ghost.

She'd poured over the crime scene photos multiple times, spoke to friends and family of the victim, interviewed locals who live near the alleyway, but there was nothing that could help crack the case. It had been three months of rinse and repeat, but no light at the end of the tunnel.

Twice the Chief Inspector suggested she pass the case over to another team so as they could throw a fresh pair of eyes over the details, but she refused. The Chief was not surprised, he was well aware of Abigail's persistence, it was something he'd encouraged in her early years of a detective and now it was consuming her.

He called her into his office for a review and immediately upon entering he could see she was tired and stressed. The bags under her eyes were dark and her hair straggled and unkempt. He was sure there was some kind of food stain on her shirt, but he thought it wise not to bring attention to it.

The moment she sat down she was prepared to defend herself and ensure she kept hold of the case, but the Chief raised a hand to silence her.

'I'm not taking the case from you,' he said assuring her.

'Good, because—' she snapped back before he cut her off again.

'Abigail, relax. Like I said, the case is still yours, but it's obvious you've hit a brick wall. You've exhausted all avenues of investigation and I can see you're all out of ideas. I think you could use some help.'

The Chief wrote down an address on a slip of paper and passed it over to Abigail. She took it and read the first line, it said 'The Institute'. Her eyes darted back up to the Chief and she scowled.

'I don't need therapy,' she said through gritted teeth.

'It's not therapy,' the Chief replied. 'It's a place I think could help solve the case. Just pay them a visit, see what they have to say.'

Abigail reluctantly pocketed the slip of paper and stood up.

'And try and get some sleep,' the Chief added.

'I'll sleep when I'm done with this case,' Abigail said as she exited the room.

The building was a large square shape of white walls and reflective windows. A well maintained garden of bright coloured flowers and a water feature welcomed you as you made your way toward the entrance. A large sign reading 'The Institute' hung above as Abigail entered via the double doors.

When she approached the front reception desk and gave her name, it seemed they had been expecting her. She was directed to an elevator and told to go down to the basement level where she would be greeted by a Dr. Thewlis. Abigail was overly cautious. She didn't want to be here in the first place and now she was being sent into the basement.

As she stood in the elevator feeling it descend, she was surprised by how long it took. Judging by the buttons, there was only one basement level, but it felt like it was a hundred feet below ground level. When the doors pinged opened, she found a grinning man with thick glasses and a laboratory overcoat waiting for her with his hands clasped behind his back. He extended a hand to shake as she stepped out of the elevator.

'Good morning, you must be Detective Inspector Pell,' he said. 'I'm Dr. Thewlis.'

Abigail nodded and shook his hand.

'Please, come through to my office where we can talk,' he said before heading off down a sparse corridor.

The facility, the doctor. Abigail was starting to feel like she'd been hoodwinked and this indeed was some kind of therapy. She wanted to turn and head back up to ground level, but at the same time was curious as to where this would go. At least if she suffered through whatever was planned she could tell her superior she tried and he would let her get back to the case.

Dr. Thewlis' office was rather small, but decorated with many accomplishments, such as PhDs and awards. She wasn't entirely sure, but there was something on the wall behind his desk that looked like a Nobel prize.

Thewlis gestured for her to have a seat as he sat behind his desk. Abigail perched herself opposite him, but didn't relax. She was ready to jump up and leave the moment therapy was mentioned.

Thewlis opened a drawer of his desk and took out a document placing it in front of her.

'Before we begin, I need you to sign this non-disclosure agreement,' he said passing her a pen.

'Why?'

'I just need to be sure you won't speak of what you see or hear in this facility. We have some very sensitive discoveries we are keen to keep secret from the world at present.'

Abigail scribbled her name on the dotted line and passed it back along with the pen. Thewlis acknowledged the signature and stored the document back in the drawer. He then leaned forward resting his hands on the desk and smiled.

'Excellent. So I assume you don't fully know why you are here,' he said.

'Not exactly.'

'Well, I assure you it is nothing sinister. But what I am about to tell you may be difficult to believe, so I will ask you to keep an open mind while I explain and do not interrupt.'

Abigail's curiosity was at an all-time high. The mystery and the NDA were certainly not something therapists use. Where had her Chief sent her?

'About ten years ago, a form of temporal traversal was invented. Time travel in layman's terms.'

'Excuse me?' Abigail blurted out.

'Please, do not interrupt,' Thewlis said. 'We have been doing regular tests ever since, but feel it necessary to keep it a secret from the world until we have complete knowledge of its parameters. We also want to make sure it doesn't fall into the wrong hands and prevent misuse. As a part of these tests, we have been offering our services to law enforcement to help in the investigation of crimes, but strictly only if all other options have been used and exhausted. As you can imagine, time travel is very sensitive and we cannot afford overuse. Your case file has been green lit for temporal traversal and we'd be more than happy to assist...' there was a long pause before Thewlis finished with, 'I'm sure you have questions.'

'You're genuinely telling me you've invented time travel?' Abigail asked.

Thewlis nodded with a grin.

'So you can travel into the future and see what life will be like?'

'Actually, it's not quite that simple. We can only travel to periods of time where we know the device exists in order to receive us. So we can go as far back as ten years, but in the future? Well, we have no idea how far forward the device will continue to exist. Perhaps months from now we make a disconcerting discovery and decide to destroy it.'

'And this has helped other criminal cases?'

'How can it not? We send you to say half hour before the event is thought to take place. You make your way there and witness it in real time. You then return and you have your suspect.'

'Why don't I just go back and stop it?'

'Out of the question, you cannot do anything to disrupt the space-time continuum. The slightest change back then could have dire consequences for the future. It's known as the butterfly effect. You can only observe. I understand for someone in your position that may be hard, but it's essential you do not change anything.'

'Will it hurt?'

'You'll feel a slight tingle, but there is no pain.'

'When can I do this?'

'There's no time like the present, or should I say the past,' Thewlis smirked.

Thewlis led Abigail into a large warehouse-like room. Set within its centre was a metallic box structure with a single vault door at the front. Hundreds of cables emanated from the walls connecting to large generators at the edge of the room. Around the box were dozens of scientists dressed in white overalls operating computer panels and checking clipboards.

'This is the device,' Thewlis said gesturing to the box. 'We call it the volume. When temporal traversal is activated, everything within will stay the same, everything outside will change.'

Thewlis beckoned a couple of scientists over and they jogged up to them prepared to take his orders.

'Get Detective Inspector Pell ready,' Thewlis said with authority.

The two scientists nodded before one of them took Abigail by the arm and led her over to a platform where they dressed her in white overalls.

'Is this necessary?' Abigail asked with a frown.

'It's anti-static. Once inside the volume, there is the possibility for electrocution,' one scientist replied.

'Are you sure this is safe?' she asked.

'This will protect you. Don't worry,' the other scientist remarked as he pulled a hood over her head, tucking her hair inside.

Abigail was then led over to the vault door. She glanced over her shoulder to see Dr. Thewlis standing by a control panel speaking to a scientist sat beside him pushing buttons. Thewlis caught her looking and gave a comforting thumbs up.

The vault door opened before her with a murmur and she got her first sight of the inside of the box. As the two scientists led her in, she rolled her head around to take in her surroundings. The space inside was huge and intimidating. The walls were lined with large, sealed beam lamps in a grid pattern. In the centre of the space a solitary wooden chair.

The two scientists sat her down on the chair.

'What do I do?' Abigail asked nervously.

'Do? You don't do anything. In about thirty seconds, these lights will start flashing. When they stop, the door will open and you'll be three months in the past,' the scientist said confidently.

The two scientists exited the volume leaving Abigail sat anxiously on the chair still looking around at the lights pointing at her. Her breathing was faster and her heart rate increased. She clutched onto the seat of the chair with both hands and squeezed tight as she waited. The vault door slammed shut making her jump.

She took a deep breath to calm herself, then suddenly the lights began to flash in various patterns. They were so bright she had to close her eyes. Then everything went dark. Abigail opened one eye, but all she could see was darkness. She opened the other eye, all was peaceful.

'Hello?' she called out.

The lights shone brightly one last time before dimming back to their original state. The vault door opened with a murmur.

Abigail cautiously stood up and approached the door. She stuck her head out of the volume to find the warehouse room silent. No scientists rushing around or manning controls. No Dr. Thewlis. She stepped out looking around.

'Hi there,' a voice said beside her.

Abigail nearly jumped out of her skin as she turned to see a scientist smiling at her.

'How are you feeling?' he asked.

'Fine,' she replied. 'Where is everyone?'

'It's just me during the night shift,' he said.

'Night shift? It's night?' Abigail questioned in disbelief. 'You mean it actually worked?'

'Yes, it worked,' the scientist said with a grin. 'Take a look.'

The scientist pointed up to a giant digital clock and calendar on the wall. Abigail took note of the date and time. Sure enough it was the date of the murder, half hour before they believed it took place.

'Here, you can take this off now,' the scientist said pulling the hood of the overalls from off her head. Abigail was still trying to take it all in as she unzipped the white outfit and pulled her feet from it.

'I really went back in time?' she said still catching her breath.

'Yes. Why did you come back out of interest?'

'I'm trying to solve a murder.'

'Oh, another one. Well then, I suggest you get to it.'

'You're right!' Abigail said as she headed for the exit with haste. Before she left, however, she suddenly had a horrifying thought. She turned to the scientist with concern.

'Hold on. How do I get back to the future?' she asked.

'When you're done come back here and I'll send you forward,' the scientist said with a comforting smile.

Abigail nodded with relief and then turned to leave, but was stopped by the scientist's call.

'Wait!'

She looked over to see a coat in his extended hand.

'It's awful cold out there tonight, take this. There are gloves and a hat in the pockets,' he said.

Abigail gave a grateful smile before heading out the large room.

Of all the taxi drivers in the city, Abigail had to get the slowest one. He was taking his time pottering along the road and Abigail was worried she would miss the murder occurring. Then again, she could always go back in time if she missed it. The thought caused a snigger to blurt out from her mouth and the driver glanced in his rear view mirror to see what she was laughing about. She caught sight of the alleyway coming up on her left side and checked her watch which she'd had the foresight to change as she left the Institute. She still had five minutes before the estimated time of death. Plenty of time.

The taxi pulled over and Abigail paid the driver hoping she would have enough for a taxi back. She climbed out of the car and approached the entrance of the alleyway. A cold chill blew through the air so she pulled up the collar of her coat, slipped on a pair of gloves from the pockets and tucked her hair under a woolly hat. As she ventured deeper inside, she could hear a woman crying for help and sounds of a struggle. She crept further down the wet narrow corridor and sure enough a young woman was pinned up against a wall by a man in a hooded jumper. She was squirming to break free, but was unable to under his immense strength.

Abigail's police officer instincts kicked in and she rushed the attacker tackling him to the ground. The young woman took the opportunity to escape, her high heels splashing in the puddles as she ran from the alleyway.

Abigail and the attacker struggled on the ground for several seconds before the attacker threw back an elbow cracking her in the face. She held up her hands to her nose to check it wasn't broken and the attacker took advantage of her vulnerability to climb on top of her and wrap his thick fingers around her neck. He began to squeeze the life from her. Abigail tried to pull his hands from her throat, but he was too strong. She could feel her breath shortening and her head lighten. She looked up at his face, but it was shadowed in darkness from the hood.

Her hands flailed around about her looking for a weapon. She stumbled upon a heavy piece of stone and grasped it with desperation. She lifted the weight as high as she could and it crashed into the attacker's head.

She felt his grip release and she gasped for oxygen as he toppled off of her hitting the concrete ground with a thud. Abigail sat up, still catching her breath. She looked over at the man lying next to her dead, a gash across his forehead. A chill rushed up her spine. She glanced down at the stone in her hand, the blood covering one side. It looked exactly like the murder weapon they found. She then got to her knees and leaned over the body of the attacker. It was him. The murder victim. The man who's death she was sent back to solve and now he was lying in the exact same position as the crime scene. She dropped the stone on the floor and got to her feet.

She analysed the area and couldn't believe how alike it was to the crime scene. It was all making sense to her now. How she couldn't gather any evidence connected to the perpetrator, how it had all seemed like a ghost killed him. She was the ghost.

'Shit,' was all she could muster.

She stepped back from the body looking around to ensure there was no witnesses. She then turned and sprinted out of the alleyway.

She arrived back at the Institute half hour later having found just enough money for a taxi back. The journey was not a pleasant one. She remained deep in thought about how she was going to deal with this. Should she say something? She was told not to intervene. Could she go back again and not stop him? But then she would have to witness a young woman suffering. Besides, he was clearly a bad man, suddenly his death no longer seemed a concern to her. But her Chief would be expecting a result.

She found the scientist asleep at the control panel and gently touched him on the shoulder. He woke from his dream and looked up at her with tired eyes.

'Oh, hey. How did it go?' he asked.

'Fine, just send me back,' she replied pulling on the white overalls.

'Sure thing,' the scientist said as he punched some buttons. The vault door opened and Abigail entered with trepidation. A part of her was worried she wouldn't be able to get back and she may be stuck in the past. What would happen if she bumped into herself?

She sat down on the chair and waited for the lights to begin flashing. She closed her eyes and clutched onto the chair. The darkness came and then the final flash before everything returned to normal and the vault door opened.

Abigail took a deep breath and stood up. She anxiously stepped toward the vault door and immediately heard the hustle and bustle of the scientists outside. She peered out and sure enough there was Dr. Thewlis waiting for her with a smile. She was back to the exact moment she left.

'Welcome back, or should I say welcome forward,' he said. Abigail was beginning to find his time-based jokes irritating.

She exited the volume and tore the white overalls from her body. She knew the question was coming and so wasn't surprised when Thewlis asked.

'How did it go?'

'Not good, I'm afraid. I couldn't get a clear view of the perpetrator's face. I guess we're still at square one with this investigation,' she replied.

'Well, we could send you back and you could try again,' he offered.

'No. It's okay. I think I'll just stick to good old fashioned police work. Thanks anyway.'

Abigail pushed past a confused Thewlis and headed for the exit. As she made her way through the serene garden out the front of the Institute, she decided she would pass the case over to someone else and learn in future to let things go if they seemed impossible.

A Deadly Suspicion

They stood opposite each other staring down at the corpse between them. It never ceased to amaze Cooper how one minute someone could be so full of life and the next they were just a lifeless piece of meat. Gabe seemed to be in his own little world, silent and motionless, oblivious to Cooper's words as he spoke.

'So the necklace he bought for his mistress he sent to his wife by mistake. Had her name engraved on it and everything,' Cooper said smirking from within his well-groomed goatee.

Cooper waited for a response, but Gabe was focused on the cadaver as though he were hypnotised by its presence.

'Can you believe that?' Cooper said slightly increasing his volume to get Gabe's attention.

Gabe broke from his daydream, looking up to meet Cooper's gaze despite his taller frame. He suddenly remembered where he was and needed to get his mind back in the zone.

'What?' Gabe said with a frown, scratching at his prickly stubble.

'Are you even listening to me?'

'Yeah, course. Something about Mr Green's wife cheating on him.'

'No, Mr Green was cheating on his wife. Jesus, where is your head at? Get the body bag,' Cooper said gesturing toward a duffel bag on the floor.

Gabe searched through the bag, his hands wearing blue surgical gloves. Cooper leaned up against a large hardwood desk in the ornately decorated office. He lit a cigarette taking a long drag. He too was wearing similar surgical gloves. Both men had multiple run ins with the law in the past and fingerprints would be their downfall if found.

'Did Mr Green say how he wants this done?' Gabe asked still rummaging through the bag.

'No, just that he wants it done, so I vote a quick disposal,' Cooper replied, exhaling smoke.

'You got somewhere better to be tonight?'

'As a matter of fact, I've got a hot date, so I don't want to be dealing with this shit all night.'

Gabe stopped his search and looked at Cooper with a piercing stare, the bags under his eyes giving away his tiredness.

'And I don't want to end up behind bars because you couldn't wait to blow your load.'

'Just get the body bag out and quit your moaning.'

Gabe yanked a black sack from the duffel bag and unfolded it.

'Where did you even hear that about Mr Green's wife?' Gabe asked with an air of scepticism.

'Sobieski.'

'I wouldn't listen to Sobieski, he's full of shit.'

Gabe laid out the body bag next to the corpse and unzipped it ready to be filled.

'No, this is straight up. Apparently, she came into the club and tore the place up wanting answers. Took 'em three hours to calm her down. She is one feisty bitch.'

Cooper stubbed out his cigarette in an ashtray on the desk and then pocketed the extinguished butt. DNA was another piece of evidence they didn't care to leave for the police. He approached Gabe who was suddenly deep in thought again.

'Alright, let's do this,' Cooper said.

As Cooper bent down to take hold of the dead man's shoulders, Gabe jumped up from his crouched position and headed for the door.

'I've got to make a phone call,' he said, his voice fading as he stepped out the room.

'I gotta do this by myself?' Cooper shouted as he watched Gabe disappear. 'Gabe?'

Stephanie was rushing around her apartment flustered, searching for something. She was wearing a dressing gown that billowed in the passing wind and her hair was tied up in a towel. Her cell phone rang and she snatched it up from the coffee table. Gabe's name appeared on the screen and she answered it speaking without hesitation.

'Hey, have you seen my earring?' she asked.

Gabe was stood in a dark hallway lit only by the moonlight. He was hunched over and had the cell phone pushed tight against his ear trying to shield his voice from Cooper's potential eavesdropping.

'What?' he replied.

Stephanie continued to pace around the room looking in drawers, under the sofa, still with the phone held to her ear.

'One of my earrings is missing. I can't find it. I wondered if you'd seen it anywhere,' she said, the impatience in her voice increasing.

'I don't know. What does it look like?' Gabe's voice crackled through the phone.

'It's a gold butterfly with two small red gems on the wings.'

'No, I don't think so. Listen, I'm probably going to be done early tonight. I was wondering if you wanted to go to dinner. I could book a table at your favourite restaurant.'

'Oh, I'd love to, but I already have plans.'

'What plans?'

Stephanie gave up the hunt and took a seat on the sofa slightly exhausted. She took a deep breath and relaxed her slim figure against the cushion behind her.

'I'm going to Charlie's Pub with Susan,' she said.

'Oh, okay. Well, how about tomorrow night?'

'Uh, sure, we'll see. I have to go.'

Stephanie hung up and Gabe was left listening to the ear-piercing line tone. This was not like her, she was definitely acting different. He was certain there was something going on. He put his cell phone back in his pocket and took out a small snuff box. He snorted a couple of shots of white powder up each nostril. Suddenly, he felt much better and so headed back to help Cooper.

Gabe found Cooper struggling to lift the body onto the waiting open body bag. He glanced up at Gabe with irritation.

'Will you give me a hand?' he asked through gasping breath.

Gabe took the other end and together they lifted the stiff weight onto the body bag.

'Who is she?' Gabe asked.

'Who?' Cooper replied wondering who his partner was referring to. Gabe was notorious for throwing up random questions out of context.

'This date of yours.'

'Oh, just some girl I met in a bar.'

'You make her sound so special,' Gabe said raising an eyebrow. 'Another notch on the bedpost, huh?'

'No, it's not like that this time. She's different. I feel a connection, you know?'

'Well, I'll be damned. Cooper has a heart. What's her name?'

'Uh, Jennifer.'

Gabe smiled with sincerity. He was genuinely happy for his friend's discovery of love, but at the same time it only made him remember his own situation. Why was Stephanie acting so strange around him?

'That's a nice name,' Gabe said zipping up the body bag.

The body was surprisingly light as they lifted it into the trunk of the car. Cooper wasn't sure how much his back could take these days and appreciated the ease with which they carried the corpse. Gabe slammed the trunk shut and without hesitation turned to Cooper and blurted out, 'I think my girl is cheating on me.'

Cooper froze. He wasn't quite sure how to react to this statement. He stayed silent and waited for more information.

'She's been acting real strange lately,' Gabe continued. 'I think she's screwing around with someone else.'

Cooper was happy to entertain this concern, but he was also keen to get the job done. He suggested they continue the conversation in the car.

They were driving down a quiet lane in the blackness of the night. The beam of the headlights reflecting back off the wet tarmac and onto them. Cooper was relaxed in the passenger seat and asked the question that was most curious to him.

'What do you mean acting strange?'

'She rarely has time for me and when we are together she's always hiding her phone. There's definitely something going on,' Gabe replied clutching the steering wheel tight as he guided the car along the almost non-existent road.

'I think you're just being paranoid.'

'How do you explain the way she's been acting then?'

'I don't know. She's busy and she likes her privacy,' Cooper offered with a shrug of his shoulders.

'She was never like this when we first got together. Something has changed.'

'People change, it doesn't necessarily mean there's something sinister behind it.'

The conversation dragged out much to Cooper's irritation even as they were stood in the middle of the woods digging a hole.

'It's not exactly good though, is it?' Gabe asked.

'Maybe you should talk to her. She may have a perfectly reasonable explanation.'

'Nah, I know what I see. And it ain't good.

Gabe paused his digging and looked around the grave-size pit they had cut from the earth.

'That's deep enough,' Gabe said tossing his shovel to the side. Cooper climbed out and extended a hand to help Gabe exit the hole. They pushed the body bag into the grave and admired their handy-work. It was a perfect fit. Something they had come to perfect over the years.

'I'll call Mr Green. Tell him it's done,' Cooper said walking over to the car.

An hour later, the body safely hidden from the world, the car pulled up outside Cooper's apartment block. Cooper was relieved that they had not taken longer than necessary and he still had plenty of time to get ready for his date. Cooper was about to climb out of the car, but paused turning to Gabe, 'Talk to her, Gabe,' he said. 'You'll find it's nothing.'

'I will, if I ever get a chance to.'

Gabe took out his snuff box and took a couple of hits. Cooper watched him with a face of disgust.

'Taking that shit ain't gonna help,' Cooper warned.

'I beg to differ. Where are you taking this girl of yours tonight anyway?'

'Charlie's Pub. Why, you want to chaperone?' Cooper asked with a grin.

Gabe held back a laugh and shook his head.

'I think I might drown my sorrows. I wouldn't want to run into you and cramp your style.'

Cooper opened the door and stepped one foot out of the vehicle.

'Wait, did you say Charlie's Pub?' Gabe asked.

'Yeah, why?'

'No reason,' Gabe answered, staring suspiciously at his friend.

'Take it easy, Gabe.'

Cooper climbed out of the car slamming the door shut behind him. Gabe watched him head inside his apartment building. Gabe knew that both Stephanie and Cooper going to the same joint could easily be a coincidence, but his paranoid mind wasn't willing to dismiss any possibility. He knew Stephanie was cheating on him, but could Cooper also be betraying him? If that was the case, he wasn't quite sure how he would react. He needed to dispel this idea before it consumed him, it could cost him if he got this wrong.

Gabe was sat in his favourite armchair in his small one bedroom apartment. He was sat in darkness with only the light of the television screen glowing on his face. He collected a small mirror from a coffee table, white lines of pure cocaine waiting upon its surface. He used a rolled bill to snort one of the lines and felt the burning in his nostril. He felt confident again.

He placed the mirror down and took out his cell phone. He found Stephanie's number in the contacts and dialled. He waited impatiently listening to the dialling tone, but it switched almost instantly to the voice-mail. This made him nervous. Now she wasn't even answering her phone to him.

He hung up and considered his options. It could be too hasty to go to the pub, it could all blow up in his face if he misjudged his approach. He then thought about calling Stephanie's friend, Susan. She was supposedly with Stephanie and could confirm if she was telling the truth.

He didn't have to wait long for Susan to pick up her phone. He could barely hear her voice with loud music playing in the background.

'Hey, Susan. It's Gabe. Can I speak to Stephanie? She's not answering her phone.'

Susan had to raise her voice to cut through the noise. She couldn't hear who it was and asked Gabe to repeat himself. He spoke louder and it became slightly clearer.

'I want to speak to Stephanie,' he almost shouted.

'Stephanie? She told me she was out of town this week,' Susan shouted back.

'What? Where?'

'Sorry, I can't hear you. I'll call you back later.'

The line went dead. Did she say Stephanie was out of town? So she wasn't going to Charlie's Pub with Susan, she wasn't even with Susan. Then who was she with? Gabe picked up the mirror and snorted another line. He couldn't relax until he'd figured this out, until the truth had come to light. He decided to pay Cooper a visit.

To say Cooper was vain would be an understatement, he was a man who regularly checked his appearance in every mirror he came across. He was adjusting his hair in front of a standing mirror in his bedroom making sure every hair was perfectly in place when he heard a banging at the front door. He wasn't expecting anyone so this concerned him. He played with the collar of his shirt as he made his way over to the door to answer it. Before he could get the door fully open, Gabe pushed his way in.

'Gabe? What the fuck are you doing here?' Cooper asked.

'Something's definitely going on.'

Gabe paced around the stylishly decorated room, his eyes darting as if his paranoid mind was causing a physical strain on them.

'What are you talking about?' Cooper asked, trying to catch a glimpse of Gabe's face to make a visual judgement on his mental state.

'I tried to call Stephanie. She didn't answer her phone. So, I called her friend Susan. Susan says she's not with her.'

'So?'

'Stephanie told me she was going out with Susan tonight. She fucking lied. Why?'

'Gabe, relax,' Cooper said softly placing his hands on Gabe's shoulders. 'Take a seat.'

Gabe felt a slight force of pressure from Cooper pushing him down into an armchair. He fought against it, eventually knocking Cooper's hands away and gaining some distance between them.

'No, I can't sit. I'm fucking fuming right now. I don't know what to do,' Gabe shouted continuing his pacing.

'Well, you need to calm down before you do something crazy.'

'Crazy sounds good right now.'

Cooper felt a chill down his spine as Gabe stared at him with sinister eyes. He knew what Gabe was capable of with a level head, God knows what he might do in this state. A phone rang in the other room and Cooper was glad for the distraction.

'I have to get that. Give me two minutes and then we can talk about this.'

Cooper rushed into the bedroom leaving Gabe still pacing up and down. Every so often he would glance over at the armchair. A part of him wanted to sit, his legs were aching and he wanted to relax, to collect himself. He eventually gave in to his wants and collapsed down onto the chair appreciating its comfort. He wasn't able to enjoy it for long, however, as something buried within the shag of the carpet glistened, grabbing his attention.

He leaned in for a closer look, reaching out with curious fingers to pick up the lost earring. It was a gold butterfly with red gems in the wings. He couldn't believe it, he didn't want to believe it. His worst fears were coming to fruition.

He looked over toward the bedroom door, the faint sound of Cooper's voice emanating from within.

Cooper was sat on the bed with the phone receiver held tightly to his ear, one hand cupping the mouthpiece.

'Yeah, I'll be there as soon as I can. I just have something to deal with first.'

Gabe appeared at the door almost making Cooper jump out of his skin. He turned away to prevent his voice from travelling and then hung up the phone.

'Okay, let's talk,' Cooper said.

'Later. I just spoke to Mr Green. He wants to see us.'

'He called you?' Cooper asked surprised. It wasn't like Mr Green to phone Gabe, he always spoke to Cooper.

'Said he tried to call you, the line was busy,' Gabe explained.

That made sense, after all, Cooper had just been on the phone, but still he would have imagined Mr Green could have waited until the line was free and tried again. Perhaps it was an emergency.

'Right now?' Cooper asked, wondering if this was going to spoil his date.

'Right now,' Gabe confirmed.

Cooper was about to reiterate he had plans, but knew it would fall on deaf ears. Gabe wasn't in the most sympathetic mood right now and when Mr Green calls, you drop everything, no matter what.

'I'll meet you at the car,' Gabe said before disappearing out the door.

Cooper exhaled with disappointment. He thought about calling his date, but hoped this wouldn't take long and he could still make it.

Gabe pulled up outside a small apartment block and left the engine running. Cooper looked around for any sign of Mr Green, but it was clear Mr Green wasn't there.

'Why have you stopped?' Cooper asked.

'This is Stephanie's place,' Gabe said guiding Cooper's attention to the building outside.

'And we're here because…'

Gabe extended his hand out the open window and pointed a finger toward a window. A light within was beaming through the closed curtains.

'She's still home. She told me she was going out.'

'Gabe, what are we doing here? What about Mr Green?'

'Mr Green doesn't want to see us. I just told you that so you'd come with me. I think Stephanie's meeting someone tonight and I want to see who.'

'So this is a stakeout?'

Gabe nodded.

'Jesus, Gabe. You are seriously losing your shit over this,' Cooper said aggressively.

'So why is she still at home?'

'Because she hasn't left yet?'

Gabe stared up at the window. The curtains twitched and Stephanie peered out as if looking for someone. Gabe pulled his phone from his pocket and dialled. He waited anxiously still watching Stephanie at the window. Stephanie glanced at the cell phone clutched in her hand and pressed a button. Gabe heard the voicemail message and the following beep. He hung up as she stepped away from the window.

'She declined my call. How do you explain that?' Gabe said turning to Cooper with fury.

'Let's just go, before she sees us.'

'She's cheating and sooner or later somebody is going to knock on her door and then I'll know for sure.'

'We could be here all night,' Cooper said, knowing full well his date was now off.

'If that's what it takes.'

Cooper's phone rang. He slipped it from his pocket hiding the screen from Gabe's sight line and declined the call. He shoved the phone back in his pocket.

'Who's calling? Your hot date?' Gabe said, an air of mockery in his voice.

'Gabe, listen to me. We need to leave, because if Stephanie sees you spying on her, it's only going to make things worse. Trust me.'

'Trust. Such a fragile idea. One lie, one deception and an entire faith in someone is fractured beyond repair. Some people think trust can be regained, but it can't. Once you know someone is willing to deceive, there's nothing to say they won't do it again. You can never believe a single word they say from then on. And so, if you can't trust someone, you may as well cut them from your life, that's the only way you can protect yourself. Do you agree?'

Cooper stared at Gabe with concern. He'd never heard him talk like this before, there was definitely something psychological deep within his mind affecting how he thinks. He was reluctant to provoke him any further and decided on a careful tact of humouring him.

'Yeah, I guess,' Cooper said with very little assuredness.

'You guess?' Gabe snapped back. 'You need more conviction in life, Cooper. It never pays to stay perched on the fence. You either shit or you get off the pot.'

Cooper's plan wasn't working. It seemed no matter what he said Gabe would continue down this path of insanity.

'Are you okay, Gabe?'

Gabe burst out laughing at this question like it was the punchline of a joke.

'I didn't know you cared,' Gabe said, still stifling laughter.

'Of course I care,' Cooper assured.

'Actions speak louder than words.'

'What's that supposed to mean?'

'You know what, you're right. This is crazy. What was I thinking?'

Cooper sighed with relief. Finally, Gabe was seeing this at it was, the ramblings of a fool. He began to relax as Gabe started the engine.

'Good. I'm glad you see it. Let's just go,' Cooper said, hoping he didn't provoke the unstable man further.

'I'll take you to Charlie's bar,' Gabe offered shifting the car into drive.

'Oh, there's no need. Just drop me at home,' Cooper replied, slight desperation in his voice.

'No, it's not a problem. Hopefully, you can still make your date.'

Before Cooper could protest any more, the car was moving and Gabe seemed to be intent on taking him to the bar. Cooper was glad for the quiet, the last hour had been stressful enough and now he was content with staring out the window. Until that is, he noticed Gabe taking the wrong route.

'You missed the turning,' Cooper said.

'Did I?' Gabe replied focusing on the road ahead. 'Well, we all make mistakes. You of all people should know that.'

Gabe glanced over at Cooper with deadly eyes. Cooper stared back nervously. There was no way Gabe could know about him and Stephanie, was there? He thought they had been so careful. How could he know? But if he did? Cooper pulled his focus away and stared out the window wondering if they would be heading back to the woods that night.

Short Term Stay

James sipped from his glass of beer and let out a satisfying exhale as the cool refreshing beverage slipped over his tongue and down his gullet. He always insisted on his beer being decanted into a glass. Allowing the liquid to breathe made it taste so much better. An argument he'd had with many barmen over the years. He scanned the other patrons of the Red Sun bar and sneered at those drinking beer from a bottle. They didn't have a clue. It was wasted on them.

James was a drifter, a nomad, making his way from town to town taking on odd jobs to fund his simple lifestyle of drinking beer, gambling and screwing. He had no friends, he had no family. No ties keeping him anywhere. He was truly a free man and he loved it.

The day had been a good one; the morning was spent working for a landscaping company as they made the finishing touches to the garden of a wealthy ex-politician, the afternoon he picked up some menial work on a construction site shifting rubble. A solid day's pay, he even had time after work to place a few bets on the horses of which he doubled his money.

He was now relaxing as he always did every evening, with money burning a hole in his pocket. All he needed was a young attractive woman to finish the day with. This served two purposes, the first was sex, obviously, but the second gave him a place to stay the night or if they chose a motel he would find a way to get her to pay saving him a pretty penny. James would always try to avoid paying for necessities whenever possible, it just meant more money for drinking and gambling.

His eye was caught by a seductively dressed blonde at the end of the bar. Her dress was strapless, the curvature of her soft shoulders unencumbered by restricting material. He shifted his focus down toward her heaving cleavage sitting upon a slim waist. The body was certainly to his liking. He raised his sightline to her small round face, big blue eyes staring back at him. Her plump red lips stretched into a smile. There was no doubt in his mind this woman was looking to be picked up, so he produced his most charming grin and winked back.

At this moment, a tall heavy-set man standing next to the woman talking to his friend glanced over at James and frowned at him.

'Oi! Are you winking at my girlfriend?' the heavy-set man shouted at him.

Of course she has a boyfriend, James thought. *How could someone like that not already be taken?* For most men, this knowledge would put to bed any further attempt at flirtation, but James didn't care. As far as he was concerned, nobody was off-limits.

'Fuck off!' James replied.

The heavy-set man slammed down his bottle of beer on the bar so hard it caused it to froth and charge up the neck until it exploded out like a volcano. He marched around the bar toward James, his boots stomping across the wooden floor with menace. James remained calm, staying sat on his stool, sipping at his drink. The heavy-set man pushed his face up into James' and he could smell the putrefying halitosis emanating from this neanderthal-like beast confronting him.

'If you look at my girl again, I'm going to put your face through the window,' the heavy-set man threatened through gritted teeth.

James took another sip of his beer and smiled. He couldn't believe what he was about to do next, after all, it was a delicious beer the barman had provided, but he refused to be threatened and so felt it needed an overreacted retort. He swung his hand around quickly, the beer swilling around in the glass until it crashed into the side of the heavy-set man's head shattering into pieces. The beer drenched him, mixing in with the blood that spilled from the many gashes caused by the slicing shards.

This, unfortunately, was not the end of the matter as James had hoped. The heavy-set man did not go down. Instead, he turned his moisten head back toward James and stared at him with such fury the bulbous veins in his head were no doubt pumping more blood toward his wounds.

He clenched his large hand into a fist and threw the mass of bone and flesh into James' face knocking him off his stool. James hit the floor hard, dazed and confused, but his attitude was one of humour. He always enjoyed a good bar fight and this time he had a worthy match.

He got back to his feet and charged at the heavy-set man like a bull, ramming into his stomach and winding him. The two men crashed into a table where a couple were enjoying a quiet romantic drink. The woman screamed in shock as the table and their drinks toppled over to be replaced by two animals growling at each other. The couple took each other's hands and scarpered from the scene before they got caught up in the scuffle.

James had the heavy-set man where he wanted him, on his back and he was now throwing a series of punches into his stomach. No matter how hard, he tried James never felt like he was doing any damage, the guy had rock hard abs. He hoped that if he kept hammering away, eventually, he would hit a sweet spot. Unfortunately, before that happened, the heavy-set man's friend had stepped up and was now lifting James up, his fists no longer able to reach the wall he was attempting to break through.

James threw up an elbow behind him catching the friend in the face breaking his glasses. The friend released his grip on James and stumbled back into another patron. A middle-aged man with thick beard and tired eyes. He was a regular of the bar and it was his sanctuary. He came to the bar as an escape from his annoying wife. He came to the bar for peace and now that peace was being interrupted. Not only that, but some idiot had bumped into him and spilt his long deserved beer. He stood up from his stool and punched the heavy-set man's friend in the face knocking him down. At this moment, the heavy-set man was now up on his feet. He reached into his pocket and pulled out a switchblade, his eyes targeting James.

Before long, the entire joint was at it. Chairs were flying across the room, bottles and glasses were smashing. The barman was cowering behind the bar on the phone to the police, hoping they would come quickly. This was only his second week working at the Red Sun and he didn't want it to be his last.

James was battling his way through the crowd, swinging fists and kicking legs at whoever tried to attack him. He was holding his own well, but knew it was only a matter of time before the police arrived to end the fun. With several priors, it could turn into a long night down at the police station for him. He needed to scarper and so headed for the back door.

Suddenly, he felt something cold and sharp in his abdomen. He looked down at the knife protruding from his gut and the large hand holding it. He followed the attached arm up to the grinning face connected to it. The heavy-set man winked at James before pulling the knife back out. James clutched his belly, his hands collecting the gushing blood. He was shocked at this turn of events, but the thought of retreat was still on his mind.

James burst through the back door of the bar into the dark of the alleyway. The door almost came off its hinges as it slammed against the adjacent wall. James stumbled across the wet concrete, blood running down his leg leaving a trail behind him. He needed to find somewhere to patch himself up. He knew of a rundown hotel around the corner that wouldn't cost too much. He set off into the night hoping he wouldn't collapse before he got there.

The hotel was modest, a simple building, nothing of note. Flat grey stone walls, like a tombstone with dirty windows. It felt cold and uninviting, but James couldn't care about that right now. He just needed a room, somewhere he could plug up the wound and ride out the pain. He climbed the steps to the front doors and slipped inside.

The interior was very similar to the external design. No fancy trimming, no pictures on the walls, no furniture. Just walls, floor and ceiling. James staggered through the lobby to a reception desk and fell up against it. His legs were weakening. He tapped a bell on the desk and waited impatiently for a tall, gaunt man to appear from a back room. He grinned at James.

'Ah, a guest,' he said hauntingly.

'I need a room for the night. Whatever you have available,' James requested gasping for breath.

'We always have rooms available,' the gaunt man said as he pushed over a signing in book to James. 'Please, sign your name.'

James picked up a pen and scribbled his name down, the handwriting almost illegible. He noticed a series of names in the check-in column, but none had checked out for several weeks.

'I'm surprised you have any rooms available. Doesn't anyone check out from this place?' James asked curiously.

'I guess we're the kind of establishment you just can't leave,' the gaunt man replied with a grin. He held up a key. 'Room twenty-six.'

James reached into his pocket to extract some money.

'No charge,' the gaunt man said.

James paused, slightly confused. He was about to question the remark, when he thought better of it. Any opportunity to avoid paying must be taken, so he took the key and made his way over to the elevator pushing the button to call it before the gaunt man could change his mind. The doors slid open with an ear-piercing screech and he stepped in. He reached out to press the number two button, but found no controls either side. Before he could call out to the gaunt man for help, the elevator sealed itself and began its ascent to the second level. James looked around the floor of the steel box and noticed burn marks along the base of the walls as if a fire had engulfed the tight space recently. He looked up and detected smoke staining across the ceiling. Perhaps the hotel was the victim of a pyromaniac. It seemed like the type of place that would attract criminals and nutcases who'd be capable of such a thing.

The elevator stopped with a juddering halt and the doors screeched open. James stepped out cautiously looking up and down the long corridor either side. It was eerily quiet. He made his way to the left and came upon door number twenty-six. He slid the key in, unlocking the door and pushed it open. The room was sparse, only a bed, a bedside table and a dresser with small television on top. It didn't matter to James. He just wanted to wrap something around his wound and collapse onto the bed with the television on. He shut the door behind him and tossed the key onto the dresser before making his way into the bathroom.

It was grimy and smelly. It had obviously been a while since anyone had cleaned it. The white bath was stained with something black and mould-like. The toilet clogged with tissue soaking in brown water. James almost threw up at the sight, but there was something more pressing he needed to attend to. He stepped up to the sink where a large mirror hung above it. He lifted up his blood stained shirt to assess the wound, but was stunned to find there wasn't one. His skin was clear of any penetration. It was a miracle or perhaps it was all in his head. Maybe the thought of being stabbed caused his brain to hallucinate the consequences. He felt pain, he saw blood. The heavy-set man must have punched him so hard it felt like a stab wound. That must be it. How else could he explain it?

He turned the tap on and, surprisingly, clean water ran from the faucet. He ran his hands under the cool water and closed his eyes, splashing his face to wash away the sweat and grit that he felt on his skin. Only it wasn't water. When he opened his eyes to look at his reflection his face was red. He looked down at his hands and they two were pure red, dripping into the sink. The taps were running furiously, spraying out what looked like blood. It was bouncing off the bowl and flicking up at his clothing. He hastily turned off the tap, but it wouldn't stop. The whole bathroom was being speckled by flecks of blood. He looked up at his reflection again to wipe the blood away from his eyes, but there was no blood. His face was clean. He looked down at his hands and they too were clean. The sink, although not as white as it should be, was not covered in blood. The tap was producing clean water like it had before. James was frozen with confusion. His mind was trying to comprehend what had just happened. Maybe this was a continuation of his delusion from before. He turned off the tap and took a few deep breaths.

As he looked up at his reflection again, his eye was drawn to the bath behind him. He was surprised to find it filled to the brim with red water. He sensed someone was in the bath, but couldn't be sure for a shower curtain had been pulled halfway across. He slowly turned around and discovered the overflowing red water was being channelled between the grooves of the tiled flooring. He wanted to know who was behind the curtain, he needed to know. He extended his hand and took hold of the edge of the plastic material. He took another deep breath and whipped the curtain across.

The dead eyes staring back at him were the first thing he noticed. The mouth agape, the face pale and bloated came next. The woman looked still and peaceful. Her sliced wrists oozing life into the warm bath water. She seemed familiar to him.

James stumbled back in horror. He tripped on a bath mat and fell to the cold wet floor. He scurried backwards on his rear until his back was pushed up against the opposite wall. His breathing intensified, his heart was beating so hard he felt it could burst through his rib cage. The shower curtain gently swung back into place covering the corpse. After a few seconds, his nerves calmed and he had regained his composure. He slowly got to his feet and reluctantly looked back at the bath. Once again, his senses were deceiving him. The bath was empty, no water, red or otherwise, and no body.

'I need a drink,' he said to himself.

He found a bottle of whiskey sat upon the dresser next to the television set. He was sure it wasn't there before, but he rarely took in his surroundings with any degree of accuracy. Perhaps it just blended in before. He poured himself a large glass and downed it in one. It was no beer, but it was something. He then refilled, taking the glass over to the bed where he lounged upon it and relaxed. As he sipped at the drink, he reached over to the bedside table and picked up the television remote. He flicked on the television, but was presented with only static and a loud fuzzing sound. Switching through the channels didn't help, each one the same black and white grain. He turned it off, tossing the remote onto the bed and continued sipping his whiskey.

The door to his room creaked open. He whipped his head around to see who was entering his room uninvited. He was pleasantly surprised to see a young attractive woman step inside. She was wearing a low cut dress and her hair was curled flowing down onto her shoulders. Her face half hidden in the darkness. She shut the door behind her and approached him.

'I think you have the wrong room,' he said.

She remained silent as she neared him. She bent over and kissed him on the lips passionately. He was stunned by this forward attitude, but at the same time, he wasn't going to complain. His hand went limp and he released the glass allowing it to fall helplessly to the floor. The woman pulled away from his lips and looked into his eyes. He furrowed his brow as he studied her face. He felt like he recognised her, but her features were hard to identify in the low light.

'Have we met before?' he asked.

She placed a finger on his lips to silence him.

'Take me now,' she whispered.

James didn't need telling twice. This is what he wanted, what he was hoping to find in the bar and now, as if a genie had granted his wish, a strange woman had entered his hotel room asking him to make love to her.

He took her, forcefully throwing her down onto the bed and began kissing down her neck and on her chest. She was moaning with ecstasy. She then took control rolling on top of him, straddling his waist like he was an animal to be tamed. He was a little stunned by the woman's strength, her slim figure did not suggest much muscle. Still, who was he to complain, she was an assertive woman, she clearly knew what she wanted and he was willing to give it to her.

She unbuttoned his shirt as she gyrated on his groin. He was finding it hard to moderate his excitement. Before the fun could start, however, the woman began to cough and convulse. It seemed like she was choking. James wanted to get out from under her, but he couldn't. He was pinned down to the bed unable to pull his way free and his hands were trapped beside him. The woman's mouth opened wide above him and he saw a large sticky sack bulge from between her lips. As she continued to gag, the sack grew like she was blowing bubble gum. It was a thin veiny membrane and the light bouncing off its green colour showed there was something squirming inside. Her bottom jaw widened so far her cheeks began to tear and eventually her jaw snapped causing it to hang loose. James was screaming in horror. The sack fell from her mouth and onto his bare chest. It was so close to his face he was trying to stretch his head away. The sack tore open and tentacles shot out whipping around as if searching for something. The woman collapsed off of him and his hands became free again. He pushed the tentacled blob from his chest and it rolled onto the floor leaving a slimy trail across the bed sheet. He did not hesitate to jump off the bed the other side and stood watching as the woman sat back up and looked over at him with drowsy eyes. Her face was battered and bruised.

'What's the matter? Don't you like me?' she said disappointed through a flapping jaw.

Suddenly, James felt something cold and slimy around his ankle. He looked down to find a tentacle had taken a fancy to him after sliding under the bed toward him. He tried to break away from the grip, but lost his footing and now found himself prostrate.

The tentacle dragged him along the carpeted flooring. He clutched at the deep shag hoping to win this tug of war, but his fingers couldn't get a grip. James spotted the broken whiskey glass and collected a shard before he was pulled under the bed to his doom. The jagged piece penetrated the fleshy tentacle with ease, a green ooze spewing from the opening followed by a screech from the tentacle's origin. It released its hold and James crawled away toward the door.

'Fuck this,' he said to himself.

He yanked open the door and stepped out into the dimly lit corridor. His feet ran faster than they ever had, passing room after room, each one zipping by with a blur. He ran and he ran, but the corridor never seemed to end. As he looked into the distance, it appeared as though the corridor just kept on going. Where was the elevator? Was he running in circles? He had to stop to catch his breath. He was not a regular runner, and so something as minor as this had a profound effect on his lungs. He thought about running again, but his mind was still confused by the never-ending stretch before him. Glancing up at the nearest door to him, he was amazed to find it was room number twenty-six. His room. How was that possible? Had he actually been running at all? He was curious to see if the woman and tentacled creature were still inside. Maybe this was all part of some fevered dream having fallen asleep on the bed. He would no doubt wake up soon.

He gently pushed open the door and peered inside. All was quiet and tidy as if nobody had ever been in the room prior. He tiptoed so as not to disturb any potential being within and closed the door behind him. James thought if he lay down on the bed and concentrated he could wake himself up.

Before he reached the comfort of the duvet however, the television turned itself on. He stopped in his tracks and turned to the glow coming from the screen. It depicted someone's point of view. They were looking at a scared woman. The woman who was in his room? The dead woman in the bath? He leaned in closer for a clearer look. It was definitely the same woman. She was begging and pleading for someone to stop. He then heard another voice tell her to shut up. A voice he recognised. It was his voice. James couldn't tell for sure from the pictures he was seeing, but he sensed this woman was being attacked and it was starting to make sense. A hand was placed over her mouth to keep her silent. James wanted to look away, but he couldn't. He felt compelled to watch.

The picture changed and he was now seeing the woman lying naked in a bath. She picked up a razor blade sitting innocently on the side of the tub and sliced open her wrists. James winced at the sight of the blood running down her arms and dripping into the water around her.

The picture changed once more and he was now looking at the woman's pale corpse lying on an autopsy table. Two men hidden in the shadows were talking. One of them commented on the woman's pregnancy. James threw up a hand over his mouth. Tears welled in his eyes.

The television cut to static and the door of the room slowly creaked open by itself. James looked over, but there was nobody there. He nervously approached the threshold and stuck his head out into the corridor. He looked down to the end where the elevator was. The doors opened as if beckoning him over. He made his way over to the elevator, his hands shaking, tears running down his cheeks. He knew where he was going. He stepped into the steel coffin and the doors closed.

At first, the elevator descended slowly, but it quickly picked up speed until it felt like it was free falling and would hit the bottom with a crash.

James looked up at the needle indicating which floor it was on to find it spinning erratically. Smoke seeped in from the crack between the floor and the walls. He coughed and spluttered as he breathed it in. The elevator then came to an abrupt halt. James waved away the smoke, waiting impatiently for the doors to open. As they parted, he was welcomed by a roar of fire charging toward him. He screamed in pain as he was engulfed in flames.

Several of the bar patrons were cuffed and loaded into the back of a police van. No doubt they would be released in the morning, but a night in the cells would be enough to punish their actions. The heavy-set man managed to get away before the cops burst into the establishment announcing their presence. He knew one night in the cell would not suffice for his crime. Twelve people were involved in the fight that night, but there was only one fatal victim. James lay on the booze soaked floor clutching his stab wound staring up at the ceiling with glassy eyes. A circle of blood surrounded him, staining the wood beneath. The coroner shook his head in disappointment as he pulled a white sheet over James' face hiding him from the world.

The Perfect Story

Sam Marlowe was a desperate man. An experienced journalist in his late 30s, he hadn't written a good story for the Daily Herald newspaper in months. He now found himself in the office of editor Rick Marshall, his head only inches away from the chopping block.

'Look, Sam, it's out of my hands. The paper's in deep shit right now. We can barely sell enough copies just to keep ourselves going. We need to trim the fat and you're the first to go,' the overweight editor said before taking a long drag on the cigar between his sausage-like fingers.

'Come on, Rick. I can't lose this job. I'm behind on rent, I have bills to pay. Just give me a chance to bring you something juicy. You know I'm good for it. I may not be a consistent writer, but when I get something good—' Sam pleaded before being cut off.

'Alright, because I like you so much here's what I'll do. You've got one day to get me an exclusive. Something that will sell millions of copies and hopefully get this paper back on its feet, or you're out.'

Sam scratched at his five o'clock shadow nervously. His tired eyes darted around the room as if searching for an answer. He hated to say it, but he longed for the days of the Second World War when every day there was something new to report and his fingers tapping away on the typewriter couldn't keep up with the ever-evolving news.

'Something exclusive in one day? It would be easier to get an interview with Donald Logan,' Sam said defeatedly.

Rick sat up in his chair and his eyes almost popped out of his head they were so wide with excitement.

'Hey, now you're talking. An interview with famous millionaire recluse, Donald Logan. We still don't know why he suddenly decided to shut himself away. You could be the man to tell the world. You get me the interview, you keep your job.'

Sam pulled down on his tie and unbuttoned his top shirt button so he could swallow freely. He really wished he hadn't suggested that. How was he going to get an interview with a recluse who nobody had seen in two years?

Sam was at his favourite cafe. The place he always came when a problem needed solving. Something about the smell of coffee and the low murmur of conversation helped him relax and allowed his mind to work. Laid out on the table were a series of documents; newspaper articles on Donald Logan's successes in the oil business, the death of his dearly departed wife and reports of his sudden disappearance from the public world. Sam took a sip of his black coffee and scowled at the papers before him. Maybe the simplest option would be the best. Just ask for an interview.

Sam made his way over to a payphone in the corner of the cafe and loaded it with coins.

'Hello, operator. Could you connect me to the residence of Mr Donald Logan? The address is Westlake Manor. Thank you.'

Sam waited nervously for the call to connect. He chewed at his finger nails impatiently. If there was one thing Sam hated, it was waiting. He began scanning the cafe, watching the other customers as a distraction. A watched pot never boils after all. Suddenly he heard the phone ring and he broke from his daydream. A well-mannered voice answered at the other end.

'Logan residence.'

'Hello, I'd like to speak to Mr Logan, please?' Sam said with a stutter.

'I'm afraid he can't come to the phone at this present time. Whom may I ask is calling?'

'My name is Sam Marlowe. I'm a reporter for the Daily Herald and I—'

Before Sam could finish his introduction the phone went dead on the other end. The monotonous dialling tone whining in his ear. Sam placed the receiver back on the hook and rooted around in his pocket for some more change. If there was one thing Sam was, it was persistent. He slid the coins into the slot and asked the operator to connect him again. The well-mannered voice answered, 'Logan residence.'

'Hello again. I believe we got cut off. My name is Sam Marlowe, I'd like to interview—'

The phone went dead again. Sam slammed the receiver down this time with such force it almost broke. He knew he shouldn't be so angry, it was always going to be a long shot. He scratched at his stubble then had a new idea before rushing out of the cafe.

Westlake Manor is a grand house in the Surrey countryside dating as far back as the 18th century. Its grounds cover fifty acres with landscaped gardens and a large reflecting pool. Sam stood outside the secure iron gates blocking his path up the driveway toward the front of the building. It was quiet and peaceful, nobody about. Nothing unusual for the middle of nowhere, but Sam's journalistic instincts were telling him there was something worth investigating and a steely determination was developing inside him. He pushed the nearby button for the intercom, but there was no answer. He pressed it again and while he was waiting for a reply, he caught sight of curtains in an upstairs window shifting back into their static position. He pushed his face between the gate railings to get a better look. Someone had definitely been peering out and clearly didn't want him to know they were in. He took a few steps back and looked up and down the tall hedge either side of the gate. He chose to head right and ventured round the side of the house.

Sam walked adjacent to a tall wall looking for a good place to climb over. Unfortunately for him, the wall had been well-maintained and there was no sign of any surreptitious entry. Climbing over was going to be an impossibility as well, its height well over seven feet. Out of nowhere, he began hearing voices. Very faint, but definitely voices coming from the other side of the wall. He pushed his ear up against the wall to try and decipher what was being said, but they were too mumbled.

Sam gave up on the wall and the voices and returned to the front gate to have another go at the intercom. He was surprised to find the gates closing by themselves. He quickened his pace to try and slip in before they met, but he was too slow sealing him out again. Out of the corner of his eye, he spotted a figure moving away from him. It was a young woman in a maids outfit casually making her way down the quiet single lane road. Finally some luck. Sam followed her ensuring he kept a safe distance. He didn't want to startle her, he needed to wait for the right time to approach.

Sam pursued the maid to the dry cleaners where she dropped off a suit bag, the butchers where she bought a large batch of freshly cut red meat and the market where she perused the various stalls and purchased fruits and vegetables. None felt like the right place or time to confront her until he saw her enter the very same cafe he liked to frequent. *Perfect*, he thought. Comfortable territory and she'll be sat long enough for him to work his magic.

The maid ordered herself a cup of coffee. Sam was in the queue behind her and requested the same. Two mugs of coffee were placed down on the counter. The maid retrieved her small coin purse ready to pay, but Sam threw a hand out in front of her holding a ten pound note.

'I'll get this,' he said with a charming smile stretched across his face.

The maid became very coy, reluctant to look him in the eye.

'Oh, that's very kind of you, but there's no need,' she said in a quiet voice.

'Please, I'd like to.'

'I'm not sure.'

'Come on. What has the world come to if a man can't buy a nice young lady a cup of coffee?'

'Okay, I guess. Thank you.'

Sam pushed the note forward closer to the cafe employee who took it without hesitation, tired of waiting for them to make their minds up. The maid collected her mug and scurried over to a small table in the centre of the room. She sat down surprised to see Sam approaching her.

'Mind if I join you?' he asked.

Before the maid could reply, Sam had already pulled the chair out and was sinking down onto it.

'You look like you could do with the company,' he said with a grin.

The maid reluctantly smiled back clearly not happy about this intrusion of her privacy, but she was too shy to say anything and potentially cause a scene.

'My name's Sam,' he said extending a hand to shake.

'Dorothy,' the maid replied keeping her head down, refusing to shake.

Sam pulled his hand back. Maybe he was being too forward, but at the same time he only had a day to bag this interview.

'You work for Donald Logan, don't you?'

Dorothy perked up and her eyes widened.

'How do you know that?'

Sam leaned in close.

'Listen, I'm a reporter for the Daily Herald. I would really like to get an interview with Mr Logan.'

'That's not possible.'

Sam pulled his chair round the table in order to be next to her. Intimacy was always a winner, if the charm didn't work then the pressure would.

'Come on, don't give me that. You must agree with me it's rather strange for him to suddenly seal himself away like he has. What's he hiding?'

'Nothing. Mr Logan is a very personal man.'

'All I want is two minutes just to ask a couple of questions. People are curious to know.'

'My mother always told me curiosity killed the cat.'

'Well, in this world, curiosity sells hundreds of newspapers. I really need this story and you'd be doing me a huge favour.'

Sam placed his hand on Dorothy's and stared deeply into her eyes. He'd always relied on his charisma to get him what he wanted and Dorothy seemed like an easy target. Unfortunately, Dorothy snatched her hand out from under his, placing it on her lap.

'There's nothing I can do. Mr Logan will not give you an interview.'

Sam had to try a different tactic. Clearly this woman wasn't going to fall for his sweet talking, maybe she needed something more tactile. He reached into his jacket pocket and took out a twenty pound note placing it down on the table. He slid it toward Dorothy.

'Will this help?' he said with a raised eyebrow.

'I'm sorry Mr…'

'Call me Sam.'

'I'm sorry, Sam, but Mr Logan cannot give you your interview and nothing you say or do will change that.'

Dorothy stood up and collected her shopping bags.

'Thank you for the coffee,' she said before making her way to the door. Sam watched her exit and then sighed as he placed the money back inside his pocket.

Sam stood outside the main gates of Westlake Manor pondering his options. Desperate times call for desperate measures. He knew if he could just get to Logan he could persuade him to give an interview. Perhaps there was a way onto the property. To the left of the grounds was a large wood. Sam made his way deep into the trees to find where it met with the gardens, in the hope of finding a gap he could slip through. As luck would have it a tall hedge ran along the border between the wood and the gardens and it had not been well kept for a while. There were several holes where Sam could easily slip his slim frame through. Once on the other side, he could see the house in the distance and slowly made his way over, cautiously looking around for anyone who may have seen him.

As he neared the house, he could hear voices talking. He ventured toward the noise and peering around the corner of the large building found three people lounging by a large swimming pool. He crept closer taking cover behind a bush and analysed the faces. There was a tall and thin man in a dress shirt and shorts, bald with evil eyes and a face like a vulture. He was sat at a small table under a parasol sipping at a glass of Pimms. Next to him sat a well-built man with a worn face and rough stubble. He wore a tatty green polo shirt. The third man was laid back on a sun lounger getting a tan from the warm sun. He was shirtless and slightly overweight, his rolls of fat disgusting Sam. His greasy rosy cheeked face and bald head made him look like a giant baby. Sam wondered who they were. Friends of Logan's? Business partners? There was no Donald Logan though to confirm.

Sam watched as Dorothy stepped through a set of patio doors from the house and approached the three men. She stood nervously, avoiding eye contact. As she spoke, Sam couldn't hear what she was saying.

'Mr Warwick?' Dorothy said with a nervous whisper.

The vulture like man turned to her and smiled.

'Yes, my dear?' he asked with a well-mannered voice.

'I need to tell you something.'

'Go on, my dear.'

'I was approached today, by a newspaper reporter.'

Suddenly, Mr Warwick was very interested in what Dorothy had to say as he turned his full body around to face her.

'Really? And what did this reporter want?' he asked curiously.

'He wanted an interview with Mr Logan.'

'I see. Probably the same gentleman who telephoned this morning. What did you tell him?'

'That it wasn't possible to speak to Mr Logan and there was nothing he could say or do to change that?' she said desperately, hoping she did the right thing.

'And how did he react to this?'

The other two men were less relaxed now, keen to know the result of this meeting.

'I don't know, I walked away. I was so nervous. I thought maybe he knew—'

Mr Warwick stood and placed his hands gently on Dorothy's shoulders to comfort her.

'Calm down, my dear. Nobody knows and nobody ever will. As long as we all keep quiet, there is nothing to worry about. You did the right thing, Dorothy.'

'Thank you, Mr Warwick.'

'Now, carry on with your duties.'

'Yes, Mr Warwick.'

Dorothy turned and headed back inside the house. Mr Warwick sat back down and was deep in thought. His thinking was interrupted by the worn faced man sat next to him. His west country accent was something he always found irritating.

'I think the girl may be a liability. We should deal with her.'

'What are you suggesting?' Mr Warwick asked as he glanced over at the man.

'If anyone is going to crack it's her. Maybe it would be best if she were no longer a part of this. We should get rid.'

'No, I don't think that's necessary. If she was going to tell, she would have done it by now. We'll just have to keep a close eye on her.'

Sam watched as a tall skinny woman stepped through the patio doors toward Mr Warwick. Her face lacked kindness with pinched lips and a low brow. She wore thin glasses attached to string around her neck. Again, Sam could only hear mumbles.

'Mr Warwick,' the tall woman called out.

Mr Warwick turned and smiled at her.

'Meredith, come join us. Take a seat and relax,' he said gesturing toward the table.

She stood before him rigid.

'No, thank you. I've transferred this month's sum to everyone's accounts. Mr Logan was rather generous on this occasion, he gave us all a bonus,' she said almost robotically.

'Wonderful. We must thank him when we get the chance,' Mr Warwick said with a smirk. 'And the charitable donations?'

'Twice as much,' Meredith smiled, although it was an odd smile, clearly not something she was used to.

'I must say Mr Logan has become rather munificent of late.'

Mr Warwick raised his glass as if to toast his employers endeavours before taking a sip. Meredith turned on a six-pence and headed back inside the house with no emotion at all.

'I'm not too sure about her either,' the west country accent cut in again.

Mr Warwick stared at the worn faced man with a squint.

'Your opinion of women is not a positive one, is it Jim?'

'I'm just saying, is all,' Jim snapped back.

'Well, don't just say. Meredith is a very astute woman, not to be underestimated. She was Logan's finest personal assistant and, without her, we have nothing. So I suggest you be nice. I have witnessed that woman's fire, and I for one would not wish to be on the receiving end.'

Jim turned away speechless as Mr Warwick took a sip of his Pimms.

Sam made his way along the side of the house and found a window slightly ajar. He quietly slid it fully open and peered in to ensure the coast was clear. He then lifted a leg and slipped into the house like a cat burglar. The living room was larger than he anticipated with an imposing ornate fireplace and grand piano dominating the area. He crept along the carpeted floor, his eyes drawn to various photographs on the walls of Logan with celebrities and politicians. He was certainly a popular man and everybody wanted to be his friend, why would he want to give that up?

Sam reached a door the other side of the room and pulled it open peering out into a hallway. It was clear. He made his way down the wide corridor reaching the front door of the house. He passed a coat stand with hat and coat hanging on it. On the floor were a pair of smart shoes. He then turned to look up the grand staircase winding to the first floor. He had a hunch Logan would be upstairs and so he began to ascend the steps being careful not to make any noise. If a step sounded like it was going to creak, he immediately removed his pressure and skipped it completely.

Sam entered a small study, incredibly tidy as if nobody had been in the room for a long time. At a small writing desk, he found a framed photograph of Logan with his deceased wife. She was an incredibly glamorous woman despite her age. She always managed to keep up to date with the latest fashions, but was always aware of her years. He flicked through some nearby documents and letters, but there was nothing of interest. A glass ashtray caught his eye and he picked it up for a closer inspection. It wasn't so much the ashtray he was intrigued by, but the small blob of dried blood hidden within its jagged surface. He frowned with suspicion. There was definitely something going on here and he was going to get to the bottom of it.

Sam didn't find Logan upstairs having tried every bedroom and bathroom. He returned to the ground floor, but upon hearing voices approach, scarpered into the obscenely large kitchen. Unfortunately, the voices continued to near and he needed to find somewhere to hide. He yanked open the heavy door of the walk-in freezer and slipped inside pulling the door closed behind him.

He stood shivering as he listened to the muffled voices talking outside. He hoped they wouldn't be too long otherwise he was going to freeze to death. He decided to pace up and down to keep himself warm, but as he turned, he was confronted by the frozen corpse of Donald Logan hanging from the ceiling. A gaping wound in his temple. Sam wanted to scream in horror, but he had to clasp a hand over his mouth so as not to alert anyone.

He heard the voices fade away and he hastily grabbed the door handle pushing it open and rushing out. He slammed the door shut and tried to catch his breath. Now it was all making sense. Logan had been murdered, most likely by the staff and now they were keeping his death hidden claiming he had become a recluse so they could continue living at the house. He had to get out of there. Before he could make it to the door, though, he saw a rolling pin come crashing down onto his head.

Sam opened his eyes to find himself in a dark and dingy cellar tied to a wooden chair. He tried to pull his hands free, but his wrists were tightly bound. He looked around at the many shelves housing hundreds if not thousands of bottles of wine. Mr Warwick stepped out of the darkness and into a thin beam of light emanating from a small light above Sam's head.

'You must be the reporter. You're a very persistent man. Did you find what you were looking for?' Mr Warwick said.

'You killed him, didn't you. You killed Logan,' Sam replied.

'I was really hoping nobody would find out. Murder is not something I enjoy and it could damage my reputation.'

'Why did you do it?'

'Because the man was insufferable. He was demanding, abusive and exploitative. If the world only knew, they'd see justification in our actions.'

'Murder seems a bit extreme, don't you think,' Sam said, still trying to break free from the rope holding him to the chair.

'Maybe, but it was a means to an end. We no longer have to tolerate his incessant gross behaviour and yet we maintain a certain quality of life. Things were going rather swimmingly, the world had accepted Logan had become a recluse and we lived in peace, until you started poking your nose around. You've put us in a very awkward position. I see only one option.'

'I suppose it wouldn't help if I promised to keep this quiet,' Sam said with a smirk.

Mr Warwick smiled back. 'I'd find the audacity amusing. You're a reporter, I'd be surprised if you did keep it quiet. Anyway, time is of the essence. We must quash this before it gets too complicated.'

Mr Warwick disappeared back into the darkness.

'You won't keep this quiet forever. Someone will eventually expose you. I could help you, I could tell your side of the story, get the public on your side,' Sam called out desperately.

'I wish I could trust you, but I don't,' Mr Warwick replied from the black void.

Sam then heard footsteps going up the staircase. He threw his arms around trying anything to loosen the rope, but it was too tight. The sound of the basement door opening and then closing again unnerved him before another set of heavier footsteps came down the stairs.

The large man-baby stepped into the light placing a key in his pocket. He was wearing dirty chef's whites. He pulled a kitchen knife from his belt and held it up so it glistened in the light. A devilish grin formed on his face.

'You must be the cook,' Sam quipped.

The man-baby slowly approached Sam, savouring the moment, waving the knife around. As he got closer, Sam had a bright idea. He was able to stand lifting the chair with him. He then spun on his heels swinging the chair around, the legs knocking the knife from the cook's hand. The metallic instrument tinkled as it slid across the stone floor. The cook pushed Sam and he stumbled landing on his side. The harsh movement had caused the rope around his right hand to come loose.

The cook made his way over to the knife and picked it up. As he turned back around, he was met with a wooden chair crashing down onto him. He dropped the knife and fell to the floor. Sam gave him an extra kick in the face for good measure and then ran up the stairs. He tried to open the door, but it was locked. He remembered the cook placing a key in his pocket and rushed back down to retrieve it. Unfortunately, Sam's kick wasn't enough to incapacitate the large man and he was standing at the bottom of the stairs holding the key and grinning. He placed the key back in his pocket and held up his fists enticing Sam to fight.

Sam carefully made his way down the stairs. As he reached the bottom, he raised both his fists ready to rumble. He managed to punch the cook twice in his baby face, but he didn't even flinch. A retaliatory punch came back at Sam in his stomach and he was winded, falling to the floor gasping for breath. He was lifted by his shirt so he was back on his feet and the cook threw him up against one of the shelves, the force knocking several bottles onto the floor. Sam then felt the cook's chubby little fingers around his neck choking him. He grabbed the man's wrists trying to pull his grip from his gullet, but he was too strong. Sam was struggling for air and could feel himself weakening. He used what little strength he had left to reach up and pull a bottle of wine from the shelf by its neck. He raised it high ready to bring down onto the cook's head, but the man-baby saw the intention and released one hand from Sam's neck and grabbed his raised wrist to stop the attack. Sam had one last option. He swung his knee up into the cook's groin. The cook's eyes widened in shock. He released his grip from both Sam's neck and his wrist so he could clutch his testicles to ensure they were still outside his body. Sam then brought the wine bottle down hard and it smashed onto the cook's cranium drenching him in a 1947 Châteauneuf-du-Pape. The cook collapsed to the floor unconscious. Sam took a few deep breaths and then extracted the key from the still man's pocket. He raced up the stairs and unlocked the door.

Sam needed to get out of the house quickly. He needed to get back to his office and write this story so the world could know the truth about Donald Logan and he could save his job.

Sam cut through the dining room and burst through the patio doors onto the veranda. Torrential rain was hammering down. He ran through the garden as fast as he could. He could barely see where he was going the rain was so thick. He reached the hedge by which he had gained entry and slipped back through the gap.

Mr Warwick passed by the basement door and was alarmed to see it wide open. He rushed in and down the stairs.

'Gunther, I told you to lock the door!' he shouted.

He found Gunther sat on the floor, holding his head as he looked around trying to get his bearings. Mr Warwick helped him to his feet.

'Gunther. Where is he?' Mr Warwick asked in a panicked voice.

'Gone.'

Mr Warwick, Dorothy and Gunther rushed out the open patio doors into the pouring rain. They scanned the horizon for any sign of Sam, but he was nowhere to be seen.

'What do we do now?' Dorothy asked, the worry shaking her voice.

'I think we better initiate our contingency plan. Gunther, get the body from the freezer. Dorothy, phone the police,' Mr Warwick answered confidently.

'What should I tell them?'

'That there's been a murder.'

While Gunther and Dorothy enacted their tasks, Mr Warwick made his way down to the basement and analysed the broken wine bottle on the floor.

Several hours later, Sam was sat at his desk in his small rundown apartment furiously typing away on his typewriter trying to get this story down on paper as quickly as possible. He was excited to submit it to Rick. He knew he had something good here and if this didn't save his job, then nothing would. Before he could finish however, a knock at the door interrupted him. He answered it to find two men in suits standing before him. They both held up police badges.

'Mr Marlowe?' one of them asked.

'Yes?' he replied.

He was confused to find the police at his door. He hadn't intended to call them until he'd sent the article to Rick, but now they were here he guessed he had to tell them.

'Look, I...'

'You're under arrest on the suspicion of murder,' the officer interrupted.

Sam couldn't believe it. There must have been some mistake, but before he could protest his innocence, they had already slapped a pair of handcuffs on him and were leading him down the corridor.

Sam was in a police interview room sat nervously. The two detectives entered and sat down opposite him placing a file on the table.

'Listen, this is ridiculous. I haven't murdered anybody,' Sam stressed.

One of the detectives flipped open the file and began reading from a statement.

'Mr Marlowe, we have witnesses who claim you visited Mr Logan's residence to conduct an interview for your newspaper. You and Mr Logan were in his wine cellar when you attacked him with a wine bottle. We have the murder weapon with your prints on it. How do you explain that?'

'I didn't murder him. He was already dead. He was in the freezer. They killed him, not me,' Sam replied.

'They?'

'The butler, the cook, his entire staff. It was a conspiracy,' Sam said waving his hands about hoping the additional action would get his point across clearer.

'Why would they murder Mr Logan?'

'Because they hated him. Why would I kill him?' Sam couldn't believe this was happening.

'That's what we're here to find out.'

'I don't believe this. I did not murder Donald Logan!' Sam screamed.

The two detectives stood up towering over him.

'You'd better get yourself a lawyer. It's not looking very good for you,' one of them said before they both left the room.

The following day, The Daily Herald published a story with the headline "Donald Logan Slain by Reporter." It included an exclusive interview with the "murderer". They sold every copy. Sam received a letter in prison from Rick thanking him for helping to save the newspaper. He also pointed out that had Sam not been convicted of murder the story no doubt would have saved his job. Sam did not take comfort in that fact.

As for Mr Warwick and his fellow staff, they had to leave the house now that Donald Logan was dead and his estate up for sale. They loaded their things into a moving van ready to find another employer to take them in. As Mr Warwick looked up at the house one last time, Meredith sidled up beside him.

'I guess it was good while it lasted. What now?' she asked.

Mr Warwick turned to Meredith and smiled.

'We've done it once. We can do it again,' he said.

Devil's Offer

He wondered why he still had that irritating alarm clock. It cut through his eardrum like a knife. Then again, it was the perfect incentive to wake up. Paul Sanders turned under the duvet and swung his arm out to hit the snooze button. The resulting silence was a relief. He opened his tired eyes and stared at the empty space in the bed beside him. His arm stretched out and stroked the mattress softly. Another night sleeping alone and he still hadn't got used to it. Granted he had control over the covers and enough space to spread out, but he missed that comforting presence slumbering beside him.

Breakfast alone was just as bad. The house was so quiet as he sat at the breakfast bar cutting into a plate of overcooked scrambled eggs and bacon. Paul adjusted the tie of his police deputy uniform feeling he had pulled it too tight to survive the day. As his finger brushed his chin, he realised he was still sporting stubble, but couldn't be bothered to shave. Everything seemed so trivial and unimportant.

He was clipping on a name badge when the sound of the phone made him jump. He felt he was constantly on edge these days and little noises like that weren't helping. Paul knew it would be Amy with news and this worried him. As far as he was concerned, no news was good news. His heart quickened its pace as he reluctantly answered it.

'Hello,' he said softly.

It was Amy calling to see how he was. He gave her a cursory reply before taking control of the conversation. He threw questions back at her asking if the doctors had said anything more yet, but Amy explained they were still waiting on test results. An operation was still looking likely and she was concerned with the financial issue. Paul promised her he would get the money, a promise he was determined not to break. He glanced at the clock and realised he was going to be late for work so cut the call short. They exchanged the expected I love yous before hanging up. It wasn't the bad news Paul was anticipating, but he no longer felt hungry, pushing the plate away from him.

The local police station of Harbinger Creek, Washington was a small modest building slap bang in the centre of the remote logging town. Paul entered the front reception finding his colleague, Deputy Ross Kovacic, on the pay phone. As Paul passed by, they gave each other a nod of acknowledgement and Paul noticed Kovacic appeared distressed as he clutched the phone receiver tight in his fist. He was a tall man, but stood with a hunch as he leaned against the wall. His furrowed brows were not unique to the situation, it was an expression he seemed to use permanently. Paul chose not to concern himself as he had his own problems to worry about and so he continued through a set of double doors.

Kovacic began pacing up and down with frustration, the phone cable limiting his area of roaming.

'Look, I'm trying my best. I'm just finding the cash a little hard to come by right now. I promise I will get you the money, you just need to give me a bit more time. Just another day or two, please.' Kovacic waited for a reply, but heard nothing but a dead line tone. He slammed the receiver down.

Paul entered the main bullpen of the station. Four desks lined up two by two in the centre of the room with doors leading off into offices, interview or storage rooms. Two jail cells were erected at the side of the room like lion cages. The slightly chubby Deputy Tim Mulligan was sat at one of the desks writing. Paul approached and sat down on the edge of Mulligan's desk blocking his light. Mulligan glanced up, at first annoyed, but upon seeing Paul, he smiled with his round face accentuating his red cheeks. There was an air of childlike innocence in his eyes.

'Hey, look who's back. How are you?' Mulligan said with delight in his voice.

'Not too bad, considering.'

'Still not good?' Mulligan asked putting his pen down and giving Paul his full attention.

Paul replied with a simple shake of his head.

'He'll be fine. He's a tough kid,' Mulligan tried to reassure.

Paul appreciated the effort, but it didn't feel like enough. He offered a subtle smile of gratitude.

'What about you? How are you getting on living with your in-laws?' Paul asked, desperate to change the subject.

'They're not my in-laws yet, and at this rate, they probably won't *ever* be.'

'That bad, huh?'

'People warned me, but I thought they were just yanking me. They were right though, the sooner me and Zoe can afford our own place, the better. Then we can start living our lives and thinking about a wedding,' Mulligan punched his finger down onto the desk.

'I'm sure that won't be too long though, right?'

'I don't know. Zoe was supposed to get a promotion and a pay rise, but that never happened. We could be looking at another three to four months at best, a year at worst.'

Paul sucked in air through his teeth.

'I feel for you. I couldn't live with Amy's parents. Still, at least you have somewhere to live. Others might not be so lucky.'

Paul was now returning the favour helping boost Mulligan's morale. Two men keeping each other going.

'I know. I try to appreciate it.'

A crash from the sheriff's office interrupted their conversation. Paul glanced over at the closed door then back at Mulligan, confusion on his face.

'Who's in the sheriff's office?' Paul asked.

'The sheriff.'

'I thought he was on vacation.'

'He will be, once he finds what he's looking for. He's been making enough noise,' Mulligan replied with a smirk.

Paul slid off the desk and gently knocked on the sheriff's office door. He didn't hear a reply, so risked entering anyway.

The large, rotund Sheriff Parker was knelt on the floor rummaging through a cardboard box full of clutter. Sweat was dripping from his forehead and he was breathing heavily. Paul leaned up against the door frame folding his arms as he watched. He always found it unusual seeing his superior in civilian clothes. He always assumed the sheriff slept in his uniform.

'I thought you'd be gone by now,' he said.

The sheriff paused turning his attention to the voice by the door.

'Oh, how are you doing, kiddo? Glad to see you back,' the sheriff said before continuing his search.

'Everything okay?'

'Oh, I'm trying to find my damn binoculars. Can't do much bird-watching without them. I'm sure I left them here somewhere.'

Suddenly, his eyes lit up with excitement and he snatched out a pair of binoculars.

'Ah!' he cheered holding them up in victory.

A keen twitcher nearing seventy, he refused to retire and was only taking this vacation on the insistence of his dear wife. If she was going to force him to spend time relaxing, he would at least observe some of his favourite species.

'Alright, I'll be out of here then,' the sheriff said with some relief as he stood up.

The sheriff grabbed his coat off the back of his leather desk chair and headed over to the door.

'Listen, I'm putting you in charge while I'm gone.'

'Me? Kovacic is the senior officer,' Paul said surprised.

'I know, but I trust you more than him. Don't worry, he knows the situation. If he causes you any problems, you give me a call.'

'Sure, no problem.'

123

'How's your boy doing anyway?' the sheriff asked with genuine concern.

'You know Charlie, he's a fighter.'

'He certainly is, just like his father. Anything you and Amy need, just ask. Pamela and I are more than happy to help.'

'I appreciate that.'

The sheriff patted Paul on the shoulder and gave a warm smile. Paul never took for granted how much the sheriff cared for his deputies. He acted like their father and treated them like they were family. No doubt due to his wife being unable to bear children of their own. Paul knew for sure the sheriff would not hesitate to give his life to save one of them.

'I'll see you when I get back,' the sheriff said stepping out of the office.

'Have a nice time,' Paul called out.

Paul watched the sheriff say his goodbyes to Mulligan and Kovacic before disappearing out through the double doors.

Paul wasted no time stamping his authority on the others. He knew what Kovacic could be like and if he didn't make it clear from the start, the man could make things difficult. He stepped into the bullpen where Mulligan was sat at his desk reading and Kovacic was playing a game on his cell phone.

'Alright, roles for tonight. Mulligan, you and I are on patrol. Kovacic, you're on dispatch,' Paul said clearly so there would be no question of mishearing.

Kovacic wasn't really paying attention until he heard his role. He put his phone down and looked over at Paul incredulously.

'Me? Dispatch? You're kidding?' he shouted.

Paul didn't give a verbal reply, but opted for a stern look in Kovacic's direction. There would be less chance of an argument this way and it turned out he was right.

'This is bullshit!' Kovacic said before storming out of the room.

Mulligan smiled. 'Thanks, Sanders. I hate dispatch.'

'I think so does Kovacic,' Paul grinned, slightly revelling in this opportunity to wind up the one man he had no real affection for. No doubt Kovacic would be straight on the phone to the sheriff, and on top of screaming at him for interrupting his vacation, he would reiterate his choice that Paul was in charge and that Kovacic was to do as he was told or find another job.

Later that night, Paul and Mulligan had been out on patrol for two hours working their way through the heavy rain. As usual, it was a quiet night. Harbinger Creek was such a small town it never attracted much crime. Most of the locals knew each other and it was a tight knit community. Sometimes they wondered why they even had a police department. Many of their call outs were petty disputes between locals and all was needed was someone to arbitrate. It always resulted in a handshake.

To pass the time, they would check in on Kovacic to see how he was doing. He wasn't enjoying their joshing replying with a simple "shut up" whenever they stopped to laugh. This mocking had to stop however as they were making their way down a residential street when Paul caught sight of something up ahead that required their attention.

Paul pulled the squad car up alongside a tall stranger in a long dark coat stood by a parked car trying to pick the door lock. A quick blast of the siren attracted their attention. The stranger turned around startled, the headlights blinding him. He had a thick moustache and was wearing spectacles that glimmered in the light as he moved.

Paul and Mulligan climbed out of the car, their hands resting on their Glock 22 sidearms. The stranger raised his hands in surrender as they approached him.

'Sir, would you mind explaining what it is you're doing?' Paul asked.

The stranger stayed silent, just glaring at them with bright blue beady eyes. Paul and Mulligan looked at each other both feeling slightly uneasy in this man's presence. It felt like he was staring into their very souls.

'Turn around and place your hands on the vehicle,' Paul requested firmly.

The stranger complied without hesitation. Paul cautiously approached taking a set of handcuffs from his belt. He cuffed the stranger as Mulligan watched, still prepared to draw his weapon if the situation escalated.

'Do you have any sharp objects in your pockets?' Paul asked the stranger.

He received a silent head shake from the man and so proceeded to pat him down and check his pockets. He found a wallet, a motel key and a locker key. He placed each item on the hood of the car. A Beretta M9 handgun was holstered in the back of the strangers trousers. Paul removed it and held it up for closer inspection.

'Look what we have here,' Paul said slightly thrilled by how this was developing.

He placed the firearm down on the hood with the other items, then collected the wallet and flipped it open discovering a driver's licence inside. Paul pulled his radio up closer to his mouth.

'Dispatch. I need a check on a Mr Aksel Madsen.'

'Copy that,' Kovacic replied.

He waited impatiently for Kovacic to get back to him. He wondered if the constant pranks would result in some revenge. Kovacic would either make him wait an uncomfortable period or may not even reply at all. That would make the situation awkward and could undermine his authority in front of this perpetrator. However, after only a few seconds, Kovacic's voice come back and in a very excited tone.

'Holy shit. There's a federal arrest warrant out for this guy. You should see his rap sheet; murder, theft, fraud. Multiple aliases,' Kovacic's voice crackled through the radio.

'Alright, we're bringing him in. Have a cell ready,' Paul replied.

Kovacic watched as Mulligan pushed the stranger inside the open cell and then slammed the door shut locking it with a large key on a key chain. He couldn't remember the last time he'd put a genuine criminal in one of the jail cells other than the odd drunkard sleeping off the intoxication. Incarceration was so rare one of the cages was being used as storage.

'He doesn't look very dangerous,' Kovacic said looking the stranger up and down.

'Looks can be deceiving,' Mulligan replied clipping the key chain to his belt.

Paul stepped out of the sheriff's office to see how they were dealing with the prisoner. He was relieved to see they had him safely locked away. The last thing he wanted was any trouble with this man. They didn't have much experience with dangerous criminals and he hoped to keep it that way.

'I just spoke to someone at the FBI, they can't get anyone down here until the morning. We need to babysit him until then,' Paul projected across the room.

'Easy enough,' Kovacic said walking away feeling it was more the others' responsibility than his.

A couple of hours had passed by without incident. It seemed their run in with the stranger would be as exciting as it got for the night. Paul was in the sheriff's office still completing paperwork. It was the one part of the job he hated and it took him forever to complete. Crossing T's and dotting I's was not why he joined the force and certainly not something he was expecting to be part of the job. So much red tape to wade through, the bureaucracy of the law was enough to make someone give up.

Mulligan had been sat at his desk knocking back coffee as it was the only thing keeping him awake during these long night shifts. Unfortunately, it was going straight through him like a waterfall and so he made his seventh visit to the bathroom.

Kovacic felt his stomach rumble and needed to eat. He stepped up to the vending machine adjacent to the jail cell and slotted a few coins in. The stranger watched as he pressed the buttons of his choice and waited for the chocolate treat to reach the access point. Kovacic tore off the wrapper and took a large bite.

'Could you get me something? I'm pretty hungry,' the stranger said, approaching the bars.

Kovacic turned to him munching and shook his head.

'No can do, my friend,' he said in between chews, spitting everywhere.

'You're going to let me starve?'

'I am under no obligation to feed you.'

Kovacic looked at his watch.

'You've got six hours until the Feds arrive to pick you up. I hear you can survive three weeks without food, so you'll be fine,' Kovacic said with a wink before walking away.

Kovacic barely made two steps before he was stopped by the stranger's call to him. Kovacic turned, becoming impatient with this prisoners audacity.

'You see those two keys you took off me?' the stranger said gesturing toward the motel key and locker key in an evidence tray on one of the desks. Kovacic glanced over at them before returning his attention to the imprisoned man.

'The first key is for my motel room. Under the bed, you'll find a sports bag. Inside, fifty grand. Consider that a down-payment.'

'A down-payment for what?' Kovacic asked curiously.

'The other key opens a locker. Contained within, two hundred grand in cash. You let me go and I tell you where to find it.'

'Why should I believe you?' Kovacic said, knowing full well prisoners will say anything to get free.

'You don't have to take my word for it. Check the bag in the motel room. You find the fifty grand, what's to say I'm not telling the truth about the rest?'

'Alright, say I do find fifty grand. I could just keep that and leave you inside this cell,' Kovacic smirked taking another bite of his candy bar.

'You don't seem like the type of guy to turn down two hundred grand, especially when you've got debts to pay,' the stranger smiled back.

Kovacic didn't know if that was a generic assumption or a specific reference to his situation, but he didn't care because either way it reminded him of the dire straits he was facing and desperate to escape from. If he did find fifty grand in the hotel, it would be difficult for him to pretend there wasn't more stashed away somewhere. It would eat away at him, especially if it could save his life. Still there was no point worrying about that until the motel money was proven to be true.

Kovacic poked his head into the sheriff's office and told Paul he'd received a call that Mr Womack was stalking the streets wasted again. This was a weekly occurrence so not exactly a lie that would arouse suspicion. Paul stood up ready to call for Mulligan, but Kovacic quickly stopped him suggesting he go. After all, Paul still had paperwork to finish and this would result in that job taking a lot longer. Paul wanted to get it finished as soon as so he agreed to let Kovacic take it. He was also feeling bad keeping him cooped up in the station all night. Kovacic assured him he wouldn't be long and would be back on dispatch before he knew it.

The Cherry Tree Motel was a small rundown establishment on the outskirts of town. It was not the type of place tourists stayed. It was more a haunt for prostitution, drug dealing and wanted criminals on the run. As Kovacic pulled up the squad car in the car park, he was a little concerned his presence would spark panic. People would either start running or start shooting. He needed to get in and out before anyone noticed he was there. He put on his raincoat, made his way through the torrential downpour over to room number 12 and slipped the key into the lock.

The room was dark and gloomy. He switched on the lights, but that didn't make the place look any nicer. Kovacic guessed the decor hadn't been updated for well over thirty years. He dropped to his knees and pulled back the hang of the duvet like a curtain. He peered under the bed shining his standard issue torch into the blackness. There it was. A sports bag. He reached in and dragged it out. He hastily unzipped it and looked inside, his eyes widening with surprise.

Paul and Mulligan were standing by the water cooler drinking from paper cups. Paul had finally finished the paperwork and was now relaxing until his shift finished and the daytime watch started.

Mulligan was trying to persuade him the Harbinger Rams football team were going all the way this year. Paul said he'd believe it when he sees it. Paul wasn't the ever optimistic fan like Mulligan. He was a realist, and took each week of games as they came. Much like life.

Kovacic burst through the doors exhausted and sweating. They both turned to him half expecting the doors to fly off their hinges.

'Hey, can you guys come outside a second,' Kovacic said glancing over at the stranger staring back at him with a cold stare.

They were a bit concerned by his manner, but knowing Kovacic, it was probably something that had been blown out of proportion.

'What is it?' Paul asked.

'I need to show you something.'

'If Mr Womack shit in the patrol car again, you're cleaning it up,' Mulligan threatened.

'Just come outside,' Kovacic said impatiently.

Paul was thankful the rain had subsided. He didn't fancy getting wet for whatever bullshit Kovacic was pulling. No doubt this was the revenge he was anticipating. Yet as Kovacic led the two deputies out to the squad car, they found it parked at a slight angle. Paul could tell Kovacic drove into the car park with haste and was becoming very concerned as to what had happened.

Kovacic popped the trunk open to reveal the sports bag sitting solitarily in the middle. Paul and Mulligan cautiously looked down at it as Kovacic unzipped it to reveal bundles of cash. They both moved in for a closer inspection, the notes were crisp and new..

'Where did you find this?' Paul asked.

'In a motel room,' Kovacic replied still breathing heavy.

'What motel room?'

'That guy we got locked away in there. He told me he had fifty grand in a bag in his motel room,' Kovacic explained.

'Why did he tell you that?'

'He wants us to let him go.'

Paul stepped away from the trunk. Suddenly, he didn't want to be so close to the money.

'You're kidding me,' Paul said, hoping this was just a prank.

'He says he has more. Two-hundred grand more. This is just upfront. If we let him go, we get the rest,' Kovacic was becoming excitable.

'You're really going to trust that man? He's a wanted criminal. He's playing you.'

'This looks pretty genuine to me,' Kovacic protested.

Paul knew Kovacic could be short-sighted in most situations, but this one really took the biscuit. What little respect he had for the man was slowly fading away to nothing.

'It could be counterfeit,' Paul suggested, hoping to sew a seed of doubt.

'I don't think so. I've seen enough counterfeit money to know this looks pretty real,' Mulligan interjected with a shake of his head.

Paul stared daggers at Mulligan. He always relied on him to support his side in these types of matters and now he was making things worse. The last thing he needed was a humoured Kovacic.

'Even so,' Paul said increasing his volume. 'He could be lying about the rest.'

'So you're saying you don't want this?' Kovacic said waving a bundle of the money in front of Paul's face.

Paul slapped his hand away and the money almost spilled from his fingers.

'Here's what you're going to do. You're going to log that into evidence and hand it over to the FBI when they arrive,' Paul instructed with a point of his finger before heading back toward the station.

Kovacic chased after him. He grabbed Paul's shoulder, stopping him and turning him around. He looked deep into Paul's eyes hoping that would help sell his case.

'Hey, this money could change our lives and all we've got to do is let him walk out the door. There's nothing to it.'

'We could lose our jobs, or worse.'

'Only if people find out, which they won't. I know you need this money, Sanders.'

'What are you talking about?' Paul said furrowing his brow.

'Your kid, he needs an operation, right?'

'How do you know about that?'

Kovacic glanced over at Mulligan, a silent method of throwing him under the bus. Paul couldn't believe it. Betrayed again by the one person he thought he could trust.

'You told him?' Paul shouted at Mulligan.

'It slipped out. I thought he already knew,' Mulligan confessed raising his hands in apology.

'Look, this could solve all our problems. He's offering two-hundred grand. That's over sixty grand each,' Kovacic continued his pitch with ferocity like a politician in the midst of a debate.

For a split second, Paul considered it. The idea ran through his mind, he could pay for his son's operation and then some. No more worry for Amy and him. Things could get back to normal, his son could live a long and happy life. But his conscience wouldn't let him go through with it.

'No, I'm not going to risk it,' Paul said shaking his head. 'Log the evidence and stay away from the prisoner.'

'You know what? Fuck you! You're not my boss!' Kovacic shouted, losing patience as he slammed the trunk shut.

'Until the sheriff gets back, I am. So do as you're told,' Paul commanded before heading back inside the station. Once he'd disappeared inside, Kovacic and Mulligan looked at each other.

'You know you need this too, Mulligan. What do you say? Two hundred grand divides a lot easier two ways.'

'Hey, I agree I could do with the money, but if we get caught—'

'We won't get caught. We disable the CCTV, claim he overpowered us and escaped.'

'But Sanders.'

'Sanders can't see the bigger picture, he had his chance. Just think, no more in-laws. No more stepping on each other's toes. You and your girl in your own place.'

Mulligan was always less resistant to Kovacic's persuasions. He always knew exactly what to say to get him on-board.

After switching off the CCTV cameras at the reception desk, Kovacic and Mulligan enacted their plan. Mulligan checked in on Paul still in the sheriff's office where he was looking through the job listings in the local paper. He was hoping to pick up some work on the side to help pay for his son's operation. If he could find something suitable, it would put to bed the niggling thought that had grown in his brain regarding the stranger's offer.

When he noticed Mulligan by the door he put the paper away, slightly embarrassed. He didn't want anyone to know his intentions, not that Mulligan would have criticised, but he was feeling a sense of shame he didn't want exposed.

'What's up, Mulligan?'

'I just wondered if you could read over my report on tonight's arrest,' Mulligan said holding up a document for Paul to see.

'Do you need me to?' Paul asked, confused.

'I worry about my grammar. In case it doesn't make sense. The sheriff usually does.'

Paul nodded reaching out to take the document. Mulligan hesitated a brief moment before passing it over so Paul could begin reading. Mulligan waited impatiently, picking at his nails with shaking fingers. He glanced over his shoulder out the door as if he were aware of something happening behind him. At this moment, Paul looked up about to speak, but paused as Mulligan snapped his head back.

'What's going on?' Paul asked frowning with suspicion.

'Nothing,' Mulligan replied, shaking his head.

Paul could see through Mulligan's lie like it were a piece of cellophane. He was never good at deception. He stood up tall and looked past Mulligan out the door to see Kovacic the other side of the bullpen by the jail cell fumbling with a set of keys. He couldn't believe it.

Paul pushed his way past Mulligan almost knocking the man over. He stepped out of the office and marched over to Kovacic at a quick pace.

'Kovacic, what are you doing?' he asked.

'You don't need to be involved in this, Sanders,' Kovacic said, turning to him still trying to pick out the correct key. 'You just go back to the office and we'll take care of it.'

'You can't do this, Kovacic. He's lying and you're going to get caught. What about the CCTV?'

'I disabled the cameras, so we're not going to get caught. I have it all figured out. You didn't see a thing. So go back to the office and pretend this ain't happening. I'll deal with the Feds.'

Kovacic turned back to the cell door and plucked out the winning key from the bunch. He was about to slide it into the lock when Paul drew his sidearm pointing it at Kovacic.

'Step away from the jail cell,' Paul ordered, surprised it had come to this.

Kovacic glanced at the gun and smiled.

'You're not going to shoot me, Paul,' he replied confidently.

Kovacic put the key in the lock ready to turn. Paul holstered his weapon and grabbed the disobedient deputy around the shoulders pulling him back. The key still in Kovacic's hand slipped back out of the lock. He stumbled and the two of them fell to the floor, the keys spilling from Kovacic's hand sliding across the floor. Mulligan and the stranger watched as the two men wrestled. Kovacic had his arms around Paul trying to get him into some kind of sleeper hold, but he was resisting. Paul threw a couple of punches and his oppressor released his grip allowing him to get to his feet and collect the keys.

'I'm keeping these until the Feds get here,' Paul said, catching his breath as he jangled the keys in the air. 'You try anything like that again and I'll put you in a cell myself. Stay away from the prisoner and get back on dispatch.'

Kovacic stood up and wiped a stream of blood from his nose with his sleeve. He analysed the blood then gave Paul a look that said this wasn't over. Paul was sure Kovacic would attack him again, but he didn't. He simply turned away and disappeared through the double doors.

'Paul,' Mulligan said, sorrow in his voice.

Paul glanced over at him with contempt before returning to the office.

It was coming up to 6AM. An hour before the Feds would arrive to collect the prisoner and two hours before shift end. Mulligan was sat alone at his desk reading a book. It was something he had only recently developed an interest in. Living with Zoe's parents meant very little access to the television and so he needed something else to entertain himself. He found the book at the bottom of a box. A Christmas present from his father to try and encourage him to read. How he appreciated it now.

The stranger was sat staring intently at Mulligan through the bars, his devilish eyes peering over the top of his glasses.

'How long have you been living with your fiancée's folks?' he asked.

Mulligan was pulled from his book and turned to the stranger startled by the question.

'How do you know that?' Mulligan asked with concern. He wasn't the type to believe in psychic abilities no matter how impressive, suspecting maybe Kovacic had said something. At least, he hoped that was the case, but a sense of doubt lingered in his neurotic mind.

'It sure can be tough,' the stranger continued. 'At first it seems easy; you work out your routines, you're happy seeing each other. Breakfast together, dinner together. You think the time will fly by. But then you start stepping on each other, hogging the bathroom, finishing the milk, the walls start closing in and you feel like their sucking up all the air. Just the sight of them is enough to drive you crazy, and you wonder how you ever put up with them those first few weeks.

'I can understand how desperate you must be to escape, I've been there myself. Once you get your own place, the sense of freedom is incredible. Trust me, the sooner the better. You could get a real nice place with two hundred grand,' the stranger grinned like a Cheshire Cat.

Mulligan put down his book. He was so deep in thought he couldn't comprehend reading right now. He was thinking about the three bedroom house he and Zoe saw on Pinewood Drive for sale, with the two-car garage, front yard and white picket fence. It was way out of their price range and was always considered a "dream" house, but now that dream could become a reality.

Paul jingled the jail cell keys in his fingers, pondering whether to mention this incident to the sheriff when he returned. It didn't seem right having an officer in the department so easily swayed by those running on the other side of the law. He wondered if this had happened before or if Kovacic was corrupt through and through. He decided he would raise the issue with the sheriff and let him decide how to act. Chances are, Kovacic would be out the door within the hour. The sheriff didn't stand for any kind of misconduct.

His train of thought was interrupted by a knock at the door. It was Mulligan standing sheepishly rubbing his arm, trying not to meet Paul's gaze. Paul put the keys in his pocket. Prior to today he would have trusted Mulligan, but now he wasn't so sure.

'Hey, I just wanted to apologise for earlier. I let Kovacic get to me,' Mulligan said softly.

'Don't worry about it. It's over. No harm done. I know what he's like.'

Mulligan paced over to a shelving unit behind Paul and admired the many awards that filled it.

'I forget how many awards the sheriff has received,' Mulligan said running his fingers over a large gold Officer of the Year award.

'He's a damn fine officer,' Paul replied.

Mulligan picked up the award for a closer look, he picked at the gold plating.

'I hope you forgive me,' Mulligan said.

'Forgive you for what?'

Paul was about to turn around, but before he could, he felt a sharp pain in the back of his head. He felt dizzy collapsing to the floor until everything went black. Mulligan put the blood stained award back on the shelf and rummaged through Paul's pockets for the cell keys. He found them with ease and rushed out of the office almost tripping over a chair.

Mulligan weaved between the desks of the bullpen reaching the cell door and unlocked it with haste. He pulled the heavy door open and the grinning stranger stepped out.

'So, where's the money?' Mulligan asked impatiently.

The stranger beckoned Mulligan with his finger to come closer. Mulligan leaned in expecting the stranger to whisper in his ear. However, much to his surprise, the stranger grabbed Mulligan around the neck and pulled him close into a sleeper hold. He then drew a knife hidden within his coat sleeve and held it up to Mulligan's neck.

'What the fuck?' Mulligan cried out.

Kovacic pushed through the double doors like a sulking child looking to get another sugar fix when he saw Mulligan being held hostage by the prisoner. He drew his sidearm like a gunslinger, aiming it at the stranger and stepped closer looking every bit the police officer again.

'Drop it, asshole. Let him go!' Kovacic shouted.

The stranger refused to comply offering up only a sinister grin that sent a chill down his spine.

'Look, you let him go and you walk out the door. Nobody needs to get hurt here,' Kovacic said trying desperately to control the situation.

'Don't you want the money?' the stranger asked with a raise of one eyebrow.

'That's still on the table?'

'I said it was yours if you released me.'

'Okay, you let him go first.'

Paul stepped out of the sheriff's office holding his bleeding head trying to get his bearings. He had a pounding headache and his vision was blurry. As soon as he saw the commotion in front of him, he had to overcome his fragile state and whipped out his gun pointing it at the stranger.

'Drop the knife!' Paul screamed.

'I'm sorry, Paul,' Mulligan strained to say with the stranger's arm around his throat.

'Let him go and get back inside the cell,' Paul shouted, hoping a louder tone would suffice. He wasn't really in the mood to kill anyone tonight. Especially with his senses incapacitated as they were, he was liable to shoot Mulligan by mistake.

'If I go back inside the cell, you don't get the money,' the stranger warned.

'We don't want the fucking money,' Paul insisted, cocking his gun.

The stranger looked over at Kovacic expecting a second opinion.

'Is that right?' he asked.

'Back off, Sanders. I've got this,' Kovacic called out to his side, maintaining his focus on the stranger.

'It doesn't look like that to me,' Paul replied. 'Let him go,' he shouted again.

The stranger released Mulligan pushing him down to the floor. Mulligan had to prevent his face from slamming against the parquet and sprained his wrist as he caught himself. He got to his feet as the stranger dropped the knife and raised his hands in surrender.

'I guess I'll go back inside my cell then,' the stranger said taking two steps back. 'Goodbye, money.'

'Stop!' Kovacic called out before turning his gun on Paul. 'Drop it, Sanders.'

Paul couldn't believe his eyes. He knew Kovacic could be unpredictable, but taking the side of a criminal over a fellow officer? This was a new one.

'What the hell are you doing, Ross?' Paul said switching his aim to Kovacic.

'I want that money and I won't let you get in my way. Drop your gun.'

'You don't want to do this, Ross.'

'Drop it, or I drop you,' Kovacic threatened.

'Tim, I want you to arrest Deputy Kovacic,' Paul demanded, slightly amazed at what he was saying.

Even Mulligan couldn't believe the order he was being given. He looked over at Paul expecting him to burst out laughing and reveal this was all some joke, but he didn't. He just reiterated his order.

'You want the money too, Mulligan. I know you do, otherwise you wouldn't have let this guy out of his cell,' Kovacic said trying to get Mulligan on side as he knew he could.

Mulligan panicked and drew his gun aiming it at Kovacic, but then something inside him made him turn his sights on Paul. It was now a Mexican standoff.

'I'm sorry, Paul, but I need that money,' Mulligan said, his voice shaking.

'You're making a big mistake, Tim,' Paul warned.

'It's only you making a mistake, Paul. Think of your son. You could pay for that operation and save his life,' Kovacic said.

'You leave my son out of this!' Paul snapped back.

'Put aside your morals and open your eyes. I'll give you one last chance to put down your gun and walk away,' Kovacic offered, though he knew Paul wouldn't comply.

'Can't you see this asshole is lying to you. There's no money,' Paul stressed.

'I'm willing to take that risk.'

'You may have nothing to lose, but Tim does,' Paul argued turning to Mulligan with sympathetic eyes. 'You've got a fiancée, Tim. What happens if you get caught?'

'We won't get caught!' Kovacic screamed, tiring of this argument.

'You can't be sure of that.'

'He's right,' Mulligan interjected, 'If there's no money and we get caught—'

'We're not going to get caught!'

Mulligan felt torn. He wanted it both ways but knew it couldn't be so. He decided to choose the path of least resistance.

'I don't know if I can do this. Sanders is right,' Mulligan reluctantly said as he turned his gun back toward Kovacic.

'Are you kidding me?' Kovacic said aggressively trying desperately not to pull his trigger. He was angry, but he too didn't want to kill anyone.

'It's too risky, Ross,' Mulligan tried to reason, but Kovacic wasn't having it.

'You son of a bitch!'

Kovacic turned his gun on Mulligan, his finger slipping down to the trigger. Mulligan panicked expecting a shot to be fired his way and so pre-emptively fired one at Kovacic. The bullet clipped his neck sending out a stream of blood. Kovacic threw a hand up to his neck to stem the flow, but it was spraying like a hose. Mulligan stared, his eyes wide, his bottom jaw hanging open.

'I'm sorry. I thought you were—'

Mulligan's sentence was cut off by another gunshot, this time from Kovacic's gun. Mulligan felt like he'd been punched in the chest. A burning sensation around his heart. He collapsed to the floor as Kovacic dropped to his knees joining him on the cold surface.

Paul holstered his gun and rushed over to Mulligan in a panicked state. He took Mulligan's hand and squeezed it tight as the dying man looked up at him with sorrowful eyes.

'I'm sorry, Paul. I was weak.'

'It's okay. Hold on, I'll get help.'

Kovacic himself was trying to hold on, but the amount of blood gushing from his neck was too much. The last sound Kovacic heard was Mulligan coughing up blood and releasing his last breath.

Kovacic's hand then dropped from his throat as he too gave up the ghost.

Paul looked down at Mulligan and then over at Kovacic. Both men now silent after all the screaming and shouting.

The stranger stepped out of the cell and tutted at the mess before him. Paul looked up at him, wondering what he would do. All he did, was wink and turn to walk away.

Paul grabbed his gun and pointed it at the departing man.

'Freeze!' Paul shouted.

The stranger stopped, closed his eyes and took a deep breath. He turned and walked back over to Paul collecting the locker key from the evidence tray on the desk. He crouched down in front of Paul staring straight down the gun barrel. There was no fear in his face, as though he'd had a thousand guns pointed at him in his life.

'You can shoot me, or you can save your son,' the stranger said holding up the locker key, 'Bus station, locker 24. It's all yours.'

The stranger placed the key down on the floor in front of Paul. He stood and turned to walk away. Paul looked down at the key for a moment and then he looked at Mulligan and Kovacic's bodies still oozing blood, turning pale as their souls drifted from their mortal shells. Paul's grip around the gun tightened. He aimed the weapon and fired a shot straight into the stranger's back. The stranger, hearing the bang echo around the room, paused and smiled. Paul waited for the man to drop to the floor, but he didn't. There was no reaction of pain, no screaming, it was as if the bullet had passed straight through him. He then casually strolled out of the station as though nothing had happened. Paul looked at his gun confused.

The Feds arrived precisely when they said they would and sure enough they had some questions that needed answering. Paul was sat in the sheriff's office with a thousand yard stare. A paramedic was patching up his head wound and a Federal Agent was sat on the desk with a notepad and pen. He leaned in to Paul trying to catch his gaze.

'Paul, tell me again what happened,' the agent asked.

Paul broke from his daydream and tried to gather his thoughts. He'd already been through this several times, but it seemed they weren't satisfied.

'I was in the office. I heard a commotion and two gun shots. I came in and found deputies Kovacic and Mulligan on the floor and the jail cell empty. I was then hit over the side of the head and knocked unconscious. I don't know what happened exactly.'

The agent gave a nod of acceptance, making a final note in his pad.

'When you brought in the suspect, did he have anything on his person?'

'Just a wallet, a motel room key and a Beretta,' Paul said quietly.

'Nothing else?'

'No,' Paul said reaching into his pocket and caressing the locker key.

Twisted

The basement was dark, at least he thought it was a basement. The only light was that of the moon beaming in through a high window. He could feel the damp floor beneath him soaking his trousers. As he moved, the chains rattled and then went taught as it restricted his movement. Both his wrists were bound, the metal links winding along the floor and looping through a metal bracket bolted to the stone wall behind him. The chain ended at a winch on the floor either side of him. A cold draft swept along the floor sending a chill up his spine.

He needed to get free and hope came in the form of a rusty nail wedged in between the cracks of the tiled floor. He pushed his fingers into the jagged whole and managed to find just enough purchase to extract the potential tool. He found the lock on the manacle around his wrist and slipped the nail into the hole wiggling it around.

The sound of a door opening and slamming shut made him jump. His captor was coming back. He hid the nail behind him and waited anxiously for the footsteps to get closer and the figure to step into the light.

The jailer stood before him tall and foreboding. His eyes scowling, teeth grinding as he looked his prisoner up and down. He was carrying a tray of food. If you can call bread and water food. He placed the tray down in front of the chained man, like some archaic waiter.

'Eat up. I don't want you dying on me. Not yet anyway,' the jailer said with a sinister tone.

'How long are you planning on keeping me here?' he replied desperately.

The jailer said nothing, standing up straight, but keeping his focus on the pleading man before him. He turned and disappeared into the darkness. His footsteps echoing around the small room.

The prisoner waited for the door to open and close again before collecting the rusty nail and working on picking the lock again. Several attempts later and he was still not free. The nail proved useless and so he tossed it across the room with frustration hearing a slight tinkle as it bounced off the opposite wall.

He looked down at the food and felt his stomach rumble. He couldn't remember how long it had been since he last ate. He snatched up the bread and rammed it into his mouth. It was dry and stale, but it would suffice, for now. He took a swig of the water to wash it down and tried to think how he ended up here and why this man had imprisoned him. He had patches of memory such as climbing into a car. He was heading somewhere, where, he was not sure. Before he could get in the car though, he felt pain in his head. He wasn't even sure who he was. He tried to conjure a name in his head, but nothing felt right. Was he suffering from amnesia? How could he know? He wondered what this man wanted from him. Who was he? Some kind of serial killer who liked to torture his victims before death? The thought of death had him suspecting it would come somewhere down the line and he needed to escape fast.

Suddenly, he could hear the sound of the door opening and closing again. The footsteps nearing and the jailer standing before him, this time holding an old pair of dirty pliers. The prisoner could sense something sinister was afoot and his fears were confirmed when the chains went taught and his hands slammed against the wall. The winch operated by the jailer had wound in the metallic links. His arms were out like he were about to be crucified. The jailer stepped closer and leaned in breathing heavily, excitement in his eyes. He shoved the pliers into the prisoner's mouth and he could taste the metal and grease. He tried to shout, but his tongue was pushed back against his throat. The pliers wrapped themselves around a tooth and clamped tightly. The prisoner winced and moaned, gurgling saliva from the corner of his mouth. He could feel each nerve ripping as the tooth lifted from its gummy crater. Blood mixed with the drool and ran down his chin dripping onto his shirt.

The jailer extracted the tooth and studied it with joy.

'An eye for an eye, a tooth for a tooth,' the jailer whispered.

The prisoner spat the excess blood and looked up at the jailer with tear filled eyes.

'Why are you doing this?' he cried.

'You know why,' the jailer snapped back, his face creasing like a Rottweiler barking.

The jailer tossed the tooth away and leaned in ready to take a second, but he was interrupted by the sound of a doorbell upstairs.

'Saved by the bell,' he said, wiping the traces of blood from his hands on a dirty rag.

The prisoner watched the amateur dentist disappear into the darkness and waited for the sound of the door slamming shut. He couldn't take anymore of this. He had to escape, but how? His hands were now more restricted than before. He could barely breathe. His heart was pumping so fast and his mouth was filling with blood again. He cried out for help in the hope that whoever was at the door would hear. He filled his lungs with as much air as possible and strained his voice to scream. The veins in his head bulged and his face turned red, but it just felt like his voice was echoing around the room and returning to him.

The jailer exited the basement and cautiously approached the front door of the house. Through the glass window, he could see a jaded man he recognised waiting for him to answer. He slipped the bloody pliers into his trouser pocket and pulled open the door.

'Detective,' the jailer said with a warm smile. 'What can I do for you?'

'Do you mind if I come in?' the detective asked.

'Of course not. Come through.'

The jailer stepped aside allowing the dishevelled police officer to enter. The two men made their way down a hallway into a quaint living room, neat and tidy with a feminine touch. The police officer declined the offer of a drink and took a seat on the sofa trying to make himself comfortable. The jailer sat opposite him nervously, the pliers digging into his thigh.

'We have a lead that looks very promising,' the detective said hopefully. 'We believe a man called William Bernstein may be responsible for your wife's kidnapping and death. Does the name sound familiar to you?'

'No, it doesn't,' the jailer replied calmly.

The two men stared at each other silently for a moment. The jailer's heartbeat increased as the detective tried to study him.

'Is everything okay?' the officer asked curious to his manner.

'Everything's fine, why?'

'I don't know. I guess I was expecting a different reaction to my news. A little more emotion perhaps.'

The jailer frowned. 'What are you saying, I don't care? Of course I care. The man kidnapped my wife. He tortured and raped her for three weeks. She suffered pain and torment until he murdered her and dumped her body in a junkyard. I'm sorry if I'm not skipping around the room singing! But until he's suffered as much as she did, this isn't over.'

The officer stood up and raised his hands in surrender.

'Look, I shouldn't have said that. I apologise. I can't imagine what you're going through. I didn't think. I'll keep you updated if and when we find him.'

'Thank you, Detective. I appreciate it.'

'I'll let myself out.'

The detective stood and walked out of the living room sheepishly. The jailer waited for the front door to close before retrieving the pliers from his pocket and heading back down into the basement.

The jailer stepped back into the light to find his prisoner still bound, unable to move. His mouth bloody and tears streaming from his eyes, exhausted from incessant screaming. There was nothing he could do.

'Well, William. Looks like the police have finally caught up to you, but I'm afraid it's too late. They can't save you now,' the jailer said before leaning in with the pliers again.

Fatal Infidelity

Russell was never keen on driving, he found it monotonous and slow. However, he was enjoying this particular journey. He was returning home from a meeting with a theatre producer who was eager to produce his play. All he needed was the funding and Russell knew he had that covered. He could finally quit his mind-numbing job as a drama teacher and live his dream of becoming a well-renowned playwright and theatre director.

Russell's grin dissipated as he turned onto the driveway and saw the young woman standing outside his front door, an impatient look on her young twenty-year-old face. It was Heather. She must have been waiting a while. Russell stared daggers at her as he switched off the engine and climbed out of the vehicle, slamming the door shut.

He approached her with menace hoping his demeanour would incentivise her to scarper before he did something rash, but she remained firm footed.

'What the hell are you doing here? I told you, it's over,' he said through gritted teeth.

'I need to talk to you,' Heather replied.

'My wife will be home soon.'

'It's important,' she urged him. Her stern look burned a hole in him and he couldn't remain strong.

'Five minutes,' he said with a sigh as he opened the front door.

They entered the stylishly decorated living room. Theatre posters on the walls mixed with various antiquities placed on shelves and mantles. A large book case stood at one end of the room filled with old leather bound tomes. Russell turned to Heather expectantly.

'Well?' he asked, trying to hurry her along.

'I'm pregnant.'

Russell's face dropped. He wasn't sure if he'd heard her correctly. He tried to speak, but no words would come. Heather waited for a reply, but could see none was forthcoming.

'I'm pregnant, with your baby,' she reiterated in case it wasn't clear.

Russell shook his head in disbelief. He began pacing up and down the room nervously.

'No. That's not possible. You're lying,' he told her.

Heather frowned at his insulting comment.

'I'm not lying. I took a test this morning. In fact, I took two, just to be sure,' she assured him. Russell was still unable to keep still. He didn't know where to look, whether to stand or sit. He had never been flustered like this before. He had always kept his calm in moments of distress.

'You need to get rid of it,' he replied finally.

'I'm not getting an abortion,' Heather shook her head so as to ensure he understood her. Russell furrowed his brow staring at her in bemusement.

'Why not?' he enquired. He felt his palms starting to sweat.

'I want to keep it.'

Russell had to keep himself from laughing. Was this girl serious?

'You can't keep it, Heather. You're too…'

'Young?' she said, cutting him off.

Russell shook his head.

'No, I…I just think you've got a lot to lose right now, being tied down with a baby.'

'You mean you've got a lot to lose if someone finds out,' she snapped back. Russell was beginning to lose patience with her.

'How do you know it's mine?' he enquired, trying to get out of this anyway he could. Heather stared at him in disgust.

'Are you implying there could be a wealth of candidates?' she asked, restraining herself from slapping him hard across the cheek. Russell merely lifted his eyebrows as if to reply to her question in the affirmative. 'You asshole! You're the only man I've ever been with and suggesting otherwise is incredibly insulting.'

'I'm sorry,' he said, shaking his head in shame. 'I just don't see how you can cope with a child. How are you going to afford it?' Heather hesitated. She stared at him and he knew exactly what she was thinking. He laughed incredulously. 'Me? You want me to pay for it?'

'I want ten thousand, just to get the essentials.'

'I'm not giving you ten thousand. I don't have that kind of money,' he protested.

'What about your wife's inheritance? That should cover it,' she suggested with a smarmy grin on her face. 'That's why you refused to leave her and end it with me, isn't it?'

'I'm not having this conversation again, Heather. You need to leave.'

Russell grabbed her arm and squeezed tight. He tried to pull her over to the door, but she planted her foot and looked deep into his eyes.

'If you don't give me the money, I'll tell her everything.' Her threatening tone surprised him. He didn't think she was the type. Clearly, he underestimated her.

'If I give you the money, she'll find out anyway,' he replied.

'Not if you're careful. I'll give you a day to think it over, and if I don't get the money, I'll make sure she hears all the filthy details.' Heather grinned devilishly. She pulled her arm from Russell's grip and stormed over to the front door. She yanked it open and stepped out, slamming it shut behind her.

Russell was scared and angry. He wasn't sure what to do. Could he get the money from his wife and pay off Heather without her finding out? It felt too risky. He needed a plan. He approached a drinks table and poured himself a large scotch downing it in one. He was about to pour another when his attention was caught by tyres screeching outside.

150

When Russell stepped outside the front door, he found a car parked next to his on the driveway at an odd angle. Tyre burn marks ran from the back of it onto the road. As he neared the scene, he found his wife, Wendy, crouched down by the front fender looking over the body of Heather. The young girl's bottom half was covered by the car and blood was pouring from her head.

'Oh my God, Wendy. What have you done?' he exclaimed.

Wendy stood up straight and turned to him with a distressed look upon her face.

'It was an accident. She came out of nowhere,' Wendy protested as she rubbed a palm across her cheek. 'She's dead.'

'Are you sure?' Russell tried to step forward to take a closer look, but Wendy blocked his path pushing him back.

'Yes, I'm sure. She's not breathing. What are we going to do?'

Russell was lost in thought for a moment and didn't fully register Wendy's question. He was still staring at Heather lying dead on the ground. It felt so strange, only a few moments ago she was alive and well.

'I guess we call an ambulance,' he finally said.

'No, we can't,' she replied without hesitation. 'They'll contact the police. I can't go to prison.'

'Nobody's going to prison. It was an accident,' he reassured her with a gentle placing of his hand on her shoulder.

'I've been drinking,' she replied with a restrained whisper. 'They'll arrest me. I'll lose everything.'

Russell gave this some thought. She was right. If the police came out, they would no doubt breathalyse Wendy and it would be a clear cut case of driving under the influence. The prosecution would have no trouble convicting.

'Help me. Help me get rid of her.' Wendy's interruption broke Russell from his train of thought. He looked at her in surprise.

'You can't be serious.'

'Who is she?' Wendy asked.

Russell was caught out by this question and almost slipped up. He had to think quick.

'I don't know. She came to the wrong house. She was looking for a friend,' he lied, hoping that would be an end to the questioning.

'So, no one knows she's here?'

'I guess not.' Russell didn't like where this was going.

'Okay, so if no one knows she's here, we could just get rid of her and pretend this never happened.' There it was, he was waiting for her to say it, but wasn't sure if she would. He tried to think it through, but she was already talking again. 'Nobody's going to come by asking about her. Please, Russell. After everything that's happened. I can't deal with going to prison. What about my inheritance?'

Of course, he thought. *The inheritance.* That would all disappear along with his dreams of quitting his job and doing what he always wanted. Maybe she had a point. Plus with Heather's news that she was pregnant this made his life much easier. If they called an ambulance it would mean no money, an autopsy revealing the baby and eventually it could lead back to him. He would be ruined. Wendy was right. If they disposed of the body all his problems would go away.

'Okay,' he said convinced. 'Let's get her inside the garage before someone sees. Then we can figure something out.'

Russell wasted no time grabbing Heather under the arms and dragging her from under the car.

'Be careful with her,' Wendy insisted.

They placed Heather's body in the middle of the garage floor. Russell could only stare down at the corpse, trying to come to terms with what happened. Wendy was rushing around rummaging through clutter as if searching for something. She stumbled upon an old rolled up rug tucked in the corner of the room.

'We'll wrap her in this,' she called out. Russell watched as his wife calmly unrolled the rug next to Heather. He didn't hear her at first when she asked him to help her, but snapped from his daydream when she called out his name.

'Russell!' she shouted, though restrained so as not to attract the attention of the neighbours. 'I need you to focus. Help me lift her onto it.'

Russell carefully lifted Heather by her arms, Wendy took both legs. They gently placed her onto the end of the rug. Wendy then rolled her up slowly.

It was getting dark as Russell reversed the car up to the open garage door. He popped open the boot and assisted Wendy in loading the rolled rug into the rear of the car. It was strange he thought. It felt lighter than he had expected.

'You'd better drive,' Wendy said as she made her way around to the passenger side of the car.

The car was parked in the middle of a dark gloomy wood. A thin mist sweeping through the headlights. Russell and Wendy were stood in the beam's focus carrying the rug over to a clear patch. Wendy carefully unrolled it and pushed Heather's body off the end.

'Maybe we should bury her?' Russell suggested, unsure of himself.

'Why? I thought you said you didn't know her.'

'I don't,' he replied.

'So, if anybody finds her they won't link it to us. Let's just go.'

Wendy made her way back to the car and climbed in slamming the door shut. Russell took one last glance at Heather's lifeless body. Her clothes soaking in the wet mud. He almost jumped from his skin when he heard the car horn behind him. He turned to see Wendy hanging out the passenger window.

'Don't forget to bring the rug,' she ordered. Russell rolled up the rug and carried it over to the car.

The journey home felt long. Russell was desperate to get home and have a drink. He needed to pinch himself every so often to convince himself this was all really happening. He glanced over at Wendy staring out the window, not looking well.

'Are you okay?' he asked.

Wendy turned to him.

'I'm fine, considering.'

'Why were you drinking anyway?' he asked, a critical tone in his voice. Wendy furrowed her brow, waiting for him to remember, but he said nothing.

'My father has not long died, Russell. Or did you forget?' She returned her focus to the passing scenery. 'I guess it just hit me hard today. It's not like I'm an alcoholic.'

Russell was about to reply, but thought better of it. There was a moment of silence between them until Wendy's voice piped up once more.

'We can't ever speak of this again. This never happened. We will take this to our graves. You understand that, right? Otherwise, I could lose everything.'

'Believe me, Wendy. I understand,' he answered assuredly maintaining his focus on the road.

The following morning, Russell poured himself a large mug of dark black coffee and took a swig. The warmth ran down his throat and he could feel the caffeine rushing to his head. He hadn't slept well during the night, visions of Heather's corpse had him waking in cold sweats regularly. The same couldn't be said for Wendy who somehow slept like a baby. The doorbell snapped Russell out of his train of thought. He listened as Wendy answered the door. He was curious who it could be at this time and ventured into the living room.

Wendy was escorting a young woman into the house as he appeared still sipping at his coffee. The woman was wearing a female suit and carrying a brown folder in her hand. She had permed brunette hair and thick glasses that sat on an unusually large nose. Wendy turned to Russell nervously.

'Russell, this is…'

Before Wendy could finish her sentence, the woman stepped toward Russell extending a hand to shake and interrupted, 'Detective

Mays,' she said with confidence, taking hold of Russell's hand and shaking it firmly.

'What's this about?' he asked, knowing full well why she was there.

'I'm investigating the disappearance of Heather Aimes. She didn't return home yesterday and her parents are worried something has happened to her,' the detective spoke with that clear police officer tone.

Mays flipped open the brown folder and took out a photograph passing it to Wendy. She took it and stared at the face of the happy young girl grinning back at her before shoving it toward Russell. As he looked at the picture, a part of him was glad to see Heather in better circumstances. Something to replace those memories of her dead body on his driveway. He returned the photo to Mays.

'I understand she's a student of yours, Mr Markham?' Mays asked inquisitively.

Russell glanced over at Wendy to find her staring daggers back at him.

'That is correct,' he replied, trying desperately to keep his nerve.

'We've spoken to some of her friends and they told us she comes by here often. Is that right?'

'I wouldn't say often. Every now and then if she wants clarification on an assignment or to proof read an essay,' he grinned trying to hide the guilt he felt creeping up his spine.

'So, you have a close relationship with her?' Mays pried.

Russell's eyes darted back over to Wendy again and found her subtly scowling, burning holes in him. He gulped.

'No closer than any of my other students.'

'Her friends did say she mentioned coming over here yesterday. Have you seen her at all recently?'

'No, not for a while.' Russell could feel his heartbeat quickening as Mays left a long drawn out silence in the air following his reply. Finally she broke it.

'Well, if you do hear from her, please get in touch.'

'Of course,' Russell nodded with a hint of a smile.

Mays thanked them for their time and was about to head for the front door when she suddenly stopped and turned to them.

'By the way, did someone have a car accident outside?' she asked.

Russell and Wendy glanced at each other before returning their focus to Mays trying to appear oblivious to her assumption.

'Excuse me?' said Russell.

'I ask because I noticed a couple of tyre marks running up the driveway. Seems like someone must have stopped abruptly.'

Wendy cut in quickly much to Russell's relief.

'Oh, that was me. Sometimes I approach the house a little too fast. I almost hit the garage door.'

'I'd be lying if I said I hadn't done that myself,' Mays nodded with a smile before opening the front door and leaving. Wendy rushed over to the door and pushed it shut and then spun around to glare at Russell.

'I thought you said you didn't know that girl.'

'You were hysterical, Wendy. I didn't want to make it worse,' he answered, angry at this second line of inquiry.

'You should have said you knew her. We acted under the impression she was a stranger and wouldn't be connected to us,' Wendy was fuming.

'You're the one who killed her, Wendy. Don't rest this blame on me,' he snapped back.

'Was there something going on between you two? Is that why you claimed not to know her?

'Don't be ridiculous. I'm not going to stand here and listen to this insanity. I'm going to work.'

Russell grabbed his coat by the door and after a cursory glance at Wendy, left the house slamming the door behind him.

Russell found it hard to concentrate during his class lecture on the Stanislavsky Method. Heather dead and the police investigating her disappearance. How did it come to this? He cursed his lack of control. Why did he have to start a relationship with one of his students? Whilst trying to focus on the sea of faces hanging on his every word, he was trying to conjure a plan in the back of his head. Could the police ever figure out what had happened or could this all blow over in a matter of days? But then there was still the issue of Wendy's suspicions. If she decided to divorce him he would never see a penny of her inheritance and that would mean the end of his play and more years of monotonous lecturing. He needed to assure her there was nothing between Heather and him, but how? At this moment he looked up at the class and his eye was immediately drawn toward the back of the room where Heather stood by the door smiling at him. He froze in fear. Was that really her? Or was he losing his mind? She seemed so real. She stepped out of the room pulling the door closed behind her. Russell looked at the students waiting for him to continue. He ordered them to read a paragraph from their text books, promising them he'll return before rushing toward the back of the room and stepping out into the corridor. He looked to the left to find it deathly quiet of any souls, then looked to the right to find Heather standing at the far end again smiling at him. She opened the main door of the building and stepped out. Russell sprinted down the corridor hoping to catch her, but as he burst through the door, he found himself in an empty courtyard and no Heather to be found. He must have been losing his mind. It couldn't have been her, she was dead.

Russell went home early citing illness, but he felt much worse when he stepped through the front door. Sitting across from each other sipping at a cup of coffee was Wendy and Detective Mays. It seemed they had been mid-conversation and Russell had just interrupted them. They both turned to him expectantly.

'Detective Mays. I'm afraid I still haven't heard from Heather,' he wasn't sure whether to smile or not as he spoke. His mind was constantly tackling the challenge of not looking guilty. He was cautious not to lean too far one way or the other.

'I'm afraid you won't be hearing from Heather. I'm sorry to say we found her body not long after I last saw you,' Mays replied forlornly. Again Russell contemplated his reaction. Seem surprised, but don't go overboard. 'We have a few questions we'd like to ask you, Mr Markham,' she continued.

'I'm not sure how much help I can be.'

Mays reached into her pocket and took out a notepad and pen as Russell sat down next to Wendy.

'Are you comfortable doing this in front of Mrs Markham?' Mays asked.

'Why? What is this about?' Wendy sat up curious as she spoke. Russell glanced at her and knew he had to take the risk.

'It's fine,' he said, slightly unsure of himself.

'We found diaries belonging to Heather. We've been looking through old entries and some are quite interesting. It seems several weeks ago Heather came by to enquire about extending a deadline. Is that true?' Mays began, reading from her notepad.

Russell took a moment to think and then shrugged his shoulders.

'I can't recall, but it's possible.'

'She claims that while she was here, you made a pass at her.'

'What?'

'When she refused your advances, you became quite violent and subsequently raped her.'

'That's outrageous,' Russell was shaking his head in disbelief.

'In several subsequent entries, she mentioned you stalked her and even threatened to kill her if she told anyone what happened.'

'Russell?' Wendy barked at Russell waiting for an explanation.

He jumped up from his seat shaking his head erratically.

'That's not true! That never happened!' he protested with fervour. Russell was desperate for his innocence to come through. Why would Heather write all those things? Why was she lying in her diary?

'Of course, we cannot take this evidence at face value, but one does wonder why she would lie in a private diary,' Mays explained.

'It's a lie. It's all a lie!' Russell shouted, pacing up and down the room.

'In her final entry, she said she was coming here to tell you she was going to the police,' Mays glanced up at Russell from her notepad waiting for his reply.

'I don't believe this,' was all he could muster.

Mays pocketed her notepad and stood up.

'We have a witness. They claim they saw you, Mr Markham, dumping what looked like a body in the very same spot we found Heather.'

'Oh my God, Russell!' Wendy screamed.

Russell felt his body seize up in fear. He could do nothing, but stare at Wendy. Should he tell Mays the truth, but then Wendy would go to prison and lose everything. He would still lose. But he couldn't go to prison either.

'I have no option but to arrest you Mr Markham on the suspicion of murdering Miss Heather Aimes,' Mays spoke with authority as she pulled out a set of handcuffs and slapped them on a bemused Russell.

'No, this isn't right. I didn't do anything. I didn't kill her. It was Wendy, she hit her with her car. I loved Heather. We had a relationship, it was consensual. She was carrying my baby, I would never kill her,' he cried as Mays tried to escort him to the front door.

Suddenly, Mays released her grip and unlocked the cuffs around his wrists. Russell paused and turned to her confused. He looked toward Wendy to find her grinning.

'What's going on?' he asked.

Detective Mays pulled off a wig to reveal long blonde hair. She slid off the thick glasses and ripped away the large prosthetic nose. It was Heather.

'Hello, Russell,' she said with a devilish grin.

'Heather? You're alive?' Russell couldn't believe his eyes as he looked her up and down.

'That's right. Alive and well,' she replied.

'I don't understand.' His brows were furrowed deep, his mind trying to comprehend this turn of events.

Wendy held up a Dictaphone and pressed play. The recording played back Russell's protests and confessions for his love of Heather and their baby.

'Thank you for that, Russell. My lawyer should have no trouble filing for divorce with that confession of infidelity,' Wendy said as she stopped the tape.

'How…' he spluttered before Wendy cut in.

'I already knew about your affair. Heather came to see me a few days ago. She explained how you'd promised to leave me and run away with her. But then you abruptly ended your affair, not long after I told you my father had left me a large inheritance. What a coincidence. We decided you needed to suffer a little. We arranged it all down to the last detail.'

Wendy regaled him the story of how the two women orchestrated everything. Wendy screeching the car up the driveway and Heather lying down in front of it and putting her dead acting skills to the test. Heather then sneaking away in the dark after they left her body there. She then took on the guise of Detective Mays to really turn the screw on Russell.

'It was really you at the school?' he asked Heather.

'Of course it was me. There's no such thing as ghosts, Russell,' she smirked.

Wendy stood and slowly approached Russell.

'I have to say, Heather is quite the actress. You must be a very good teacher.'

'I'll say. I wasn't sure he'd be convinced,' Heather remarked.

Wendy pushed her face into Russell's and scowled.

'You won't be getting a penny of my money, Russell. I should have divorced you years ago,' she snarled with venom.

'Why all this? If you knew, why didn't you just confront me?'

'Because I knew you'd lie and deny it. Claim Heather was delusional. I wanted an open and frank confession. And to have a little fun in the process. I must say, watching you squirm has been a real pleasure.'

Russell turned to Heather with puppy dog eyes.

'The baby?' he enquired.

Heather laughed.

'There is no baby, Russell. I just told you that so you'd be more inclined to go along with Wendy's plan.'

'And now, I think it's time you left. You can send someone to collect your things. I don't ever want to see you again,' Wendy said with relish, gesturing toward the front door.

'The same goes for me,' Heather interjected.

Russell looked at them both. He nodded and turned away in defeat ready to head to the door. However, before he made it there, he felt rage build up inside him. How did he let two women do this to him? What kind of a man was he that he fell for their pathetic ruse? He paused and clenched his fists. Suddenly, he turned back around and lunged at Wendy wrapping his hands around her throat. He pushed her back and she fell onto the sofa. He squeezed tight and she gasped for breath. At first, Heather could only look on in shock, but as she watched Wendy's face turn red, Heather acted without thinking. The young girl grabbed the nearest thing to her which happened to be a heavy stone ornament on the coffee table. She raised it high in the air and brought it down with force on Russell's head. She almost felt his skull crack upon contact.

Russell's hands loosened from Wendy's neck and she gasped for oxygen. His body collapsed to the floor and a pool of blood formed around his head. The two women looked down at his motionless body.

Wendy reached down placing a finger on his neck to check his pulse. Her eyes widened with worry. She looked up at Heather.

'He's dead,' she said through strained voice.

Heather stared back at Wendy in shock. She dropped the ornament on the floor and it hit the ground with a heavy thud.

To Kill For, To Die For

I sat at my usual table, a booth in the corner close enough to the bar to call for another drink, but hidden from the rest of the room. I sipped slowly from a small glass filled half way with whiskey, the strong tang keeping my eyes open and my mind awake. Unfortunately, alcohol seems to do nothing for depression other than make it disappear temporarily, but that was all I needed. When a police officer is suspended it's painful, it's like stripping him of his purpose. The very essence of his existence is deleted. I downed the rest of the glass, the burning felt good as it screamed down my throat. Slamming the glass down on the table, I attracted the attention of the barman and so called out for another. He didn't like my method, but then again nobody does. It was at this moment I noticed her sitting alone at the bar shaking with the cold, her eyes like a scared deer in the headlights of a car. I knew this girl was in trouble, this girl needed help, but I was the wrong man. She caught me staring at her so I smiled trying not to look like a pervert. It seemed to have worked, she slipped off the stool and straightened herself out. As she approached me, she smiled running her fingers through her thick brunette hair.

'May I?' she asked.

'Of course,' I replied. She sat down opposite, leaning in close. I looked into her eyes. They glistened like stars in the black night sky, hypnotising me.

'I caught you staring,' she said playfully.

'I'm sorry.'

'Oh, don't apologise. I like the attention of a handsome man.' She smiled again, her red luscious lips so smooth. I could have lunged forward and kissed her then, but I didn't. I smiled back at her and she leaned in close to speak. 'I'm surprised to see someone so handsome alone in such a place.'

'Well, maybe there's a reason I'm alone.'

'Is there?' she asked, desperate to know the answer.

'You'll have to find out,' I replied, clearly flirting. I'm not the type of man who likes flirting, but I'd had six whiskeys and I was interested to see how it would play out.

'Is that an invitation?' she asked. She knew it was and I knew it too.

Feeling her body close to mine, I kissed her soft delicate lips, I could taste the strawberry Chap Stick. I ran my hands over her glossy locks, it felt like silk between my fingers. It had been so long since I had been with a woman and had forgotten how good it could feel, so good it made me totally forget my dire situation. As we lay quietly in bed, the blankets draped loosely over us, I could feel her heart beating rapidly, her skin so warm close to mine.

'Protect me,' she whispered.

'From what?' I asked curiously.

'The big bad wolf,' she replied, fear in her voice. I had no idea what she was talking about. Was she delirious?

'My life is in danger,' she continued desperately.

'Why?' I asked, unsure if I wanted to know the answer.

'I'm due to testify against these men, they murdered my husband. They've hired people to kill me.'

I rolled her over to look into her eyes. I could almost see the fear running through them. Like I said, I could tell she needed help from the moment I saw her and that I wasn't the right man, but after our moment of intimacy, I felt like I had to oblige.

'I'll protect you,' I told her confidently.

'What if they try to kill me?'

'I'll kill them first.'

I climbed from the bed putting on my pants. I walked over to a dresser and pulled open the drawer. I reached in and took out my trusty old revolver, already loaded and ready to fire. I returned to the bed, she watched me as I did. I sat down on the edge and showed her the gun, its shiny silver reflected her sad eyes.

'You'd kill for me?' she asked nervously.

'If necessary,' I answered confidently.

She smiled as though she had already been saved and once again I felt I had a purpose in life. I stood and walked over to the window to look out at the lamp lit street. It had started raining, the heavy drops splashing in the puddles on the road. As I put on my vest, I watched as a man in a coat and trilby ran hastily across the street from his car. Maybe he should have parked a little closer.

I felt two arms reach around my waste and squeeze me tight. I turned in her arms to find she had the thin bed sheets wrapped around her like a makeshift dress. I moved my head closer to hers and kissed her lips. I could feel her heartbeat had slowed down. This girl trusted me, she had faith in my abilities.

I picked up the gun again and placed it against her back so she could feel the cold metal against her skin, the only thing that stood between her and death. Suddenly, there was a bang on the door. She looked up at me worried. I raised the gun aiming at the door, I held her close to me.

'It's open!' I called. The door creaked opened and the same man from the street stood at the threshold staring daggers across the room. I saw the gun in his hand by his side. Before he could raise it, I squeezed the trigger of mine. The gunshot echoed throughout the room, the man stumbled back slamming his body against the wall behind him. As I lowered the gun, his body slid down the wall leaving a bloody streak. She pulled from my embrace and moved slowly toward the door to get a better view of the downed killer. She turned to look at me and then smiled with relief. She ran toward me and wrapped her arms around me again.

'You saved my life,' she cried with relief.

Once again, her heart was beating rapidly close to mine.

I'm not a professional at disposing of corpses, but I've seen enough homicide cases to know the best way is to wrap it in black bin bags and strap it with duct tape. As I moved the body to pull on a bag at each end, I could feel the rigor mortis slowly coming. She sat there on the edge of the bed wearing my best nylon shirt, way too big for her. I wondered what she really thought of me, saviour or murderer? I knew this guy was going to kill her, the gun in his hand, the look in his eye. I did what needed to be done, no need to feel guilt or remorse, it was either him or her. I stood up tall and stared into her eyes as she sat looking at the body in front of her.

'Stay here,' I told her.

'Where are you going?' she asked me nervously.

'I have to get rid of the body.'

'Don't be long,' she pleaded.

I grabbed one end of the body and started dragging it along the floor, this guy was surprisingly light. I opened the door and got the body halfway out the door when I heard a voice behind me.

'What the...?'

I turned, stunned to see a man in a long black coat and slicked back hair standing on the stairs looking at me. He reached into his inside coat pocket, but I was faster drawing the gun from the top of my pants. I fired without hesitation. The red dot suddenly appeared on his forehead, the exaggerated look of shock on his face. He fell to his knees and slumped forward on his face cracking his chin on the step.

'What happened?' she called from inside the room.

'Nothing,' I replied, although after the noises she must have heard, clearly something did happen. All my neighbours must have heard too, but they know enough not to enquire when they hear gunshots. I dropped the bagged body, the thump echoed throughout the hallway. I jogged down the steps and checked he was dead. I picked up the wallet that fell from his coat and slipped it in my pants pocket. I grabbed underneath his arms and started to drag him up the stairs, this guy was heavy.

Outside in the alleyway the car was parked, I like to keep it here as the chances of it getting stolen reduce when not on show. The trunk of a 1940 Plymouth was a reasonable size, but I questioned whether I could fit two bodies inside. One was already in, pushed as far back as I could. As I forced him in, I swear I could hear a couple of bones crack, good job he's dead. I picked up the second and hung him over the edge of the trunk, then lifted his legs throwing them in the other side. I pushed firmly down squeezing him in, he fit, thank God. I shut the trunk and walked around to the drivers' side door and climbed in. I started the car and made my journey to the burial ground.

The docks were the perfect place to hide a body. As far as I know, nobody had ever been discovered here, so if anything is buried, it's buried for good. I grabbed the shovel from the back seat and picked my spot. I stabbed the ground and began the long backbreaking work. After about three feet, I took a breather and watched a tug boat as it drove by. It dawned on me I would either have to make it double the width or double the depth to fit two bodies in. I checked the time, two fifteen, and four hours till day break. I reckoned I could get it done in two. Two hours later and I had a hole I was happy with, deep enough and wide enough. I threw the shovel to the side and walked over to the trunk. I opened it and reached in. Grabbing the first guy, I pulled him out and dumped him on the soft mud. I dragged him over the hole and rolled him in. There's no sound like that of a lifeless body hitting the ground. I grabbed the second guy and threw him in after. The sound of a corpse hitting another was new to me. I picked up the shovel and started filling in the grave. Half an hour later, I was done. It was quicker filling in the hole than creating it. I threw the shovel in the trunk and closed it. I felt the wallet in my pocket and took it out. I flipped it open to check for cash and it was then I noticed the horrifying truth. The shine from the moonlight reflected in my eyes. Its sharp craftsmanship and quality detail. The letters 'FBI' printed clearly. He was a cop, they were both cops. I put the wallet back in my pocket and ran back to the car door and jumped in. I started the engine without hesitation and span the wheels kicking up dirt.

As I burst the door open she was standing there fully dressed leaning up against the dresser, a gun in her hand. She held my detective badge in the other.

'I didn't realise you were a cop. I guess I'm lucky, I thought you would have recognised a wanted fugitive,' she said coldly. I didn't know what to say, what could I say? This girl had played me, she had played me good.

She cocked the gun and rose to aim. I had time to move, but I didn't want to. A part of me wanted to feel that lead piercing my body, and the blood gushing. The gunshot echoed, it was like I'd been stabbed, my breathing started to speed up. I felt my shirt become soaked, a circle of red expanding on my chest. My vision became blurred, but I could see her walk toward me laughing. I fell to my knees, then onto my face. She stepped past my body and headed for the door. As I exhaled for the last time, the final thing I heard was the door shut.

The Gamekeeper

Autumn was his favourite season. The discoloured leaves emanating warmth against the brisk chill coursing through his body. Munroe traipsed across the rustling ground heading toward his first port of call. Lennox, his black Labrador retriever, had already excitedly run ahead and was now barking for his master's attention. He always found the quiet of the wood therapeutic in the morning, and now this infernal hound was breaking his calm. As he neared the tree by which Lennox was waiting, he was not prepared for the horrible scene he was about to witness. Foxes are often snared; it's Munroe's method of choice. He always carries his trusted CZ.222 rifle for the odd encounter with what he calls the "red devil", but the snare is the more successful. However, for this poor fox, the snare was only the start of its demise. As Munroe looked down, he could vaguely make out the various organs spread across a 50 centimetre radius. The death of the fox did not surprise him, however, the method about which it had happened did. What perplexed him more was the amount of meat remaining. Most predators would have picked it clean, as they would be unsure of where their next meal would come from, but this seemed like the animal was killed and then left. Normal procedure would be to bag the kill, tag it and record it, but Munroe decided to leave the mess for the birds to clear up. Despite the morbid nature, Munroe enjoyed his job. After a lifetime in the British Army and then the SAS, he was desperate to retire into a quiet job where he could be his own boss. He didn't have any friends; those he would have happily socialised with were taken from him during tours in the Falklands and the Gulf. However, living

168

alone in a small self-built shack with his faithful partner, Lennox, Munroe could honestly say he was happy. There was no stress, no worries and Mr McKendrick, the owner of the land, was an unobtrusive employer, trusting Munroe's instincts. Unfortunately, those instincts were to fail him.

She was lying unconscious blanketed by leaves, a pale looking woman in a tattered dress. Munroe stroked his thick beard as he examined her from afar, unsure if she was still alive. As he kicked the layer of leaves away from her face, he noticed her eyes twitch. He looked at Lennox who was sat by him panting, almost as if he was expecting advice from this four legged animal. Munroe removed his Westfield wax jacket and after brushing away the remaining leaves, draped it over her skinny frail body. Throwing the rifle strap over his shoulder, he bent down and slid his arms underneath her. She was so cold; the shock sent a shiver down his spine. Munroe lifted her with such ease he guessed she weighed no more than six or seven stone. A part of him wondered how this woman could still be alive.

Munroe's shack was not the ramshackle mess the word normally springs to mind. A skilled self-taught carpenter, it was carefully planned and constructed with extensive knowledge of structure and form. Granted it was basic, it was sturdy and had survived turbulent weather. Designed as one room, the bedroom, kitchenette/dining room and living room were separated by the furniture within. On the walls were many photos of Munroe with his battalion, the 40 Commando Royal Marines. During the Falklands, he was one of the first to land at San Carlos on Operation Corporate. Whilst defending the beach head, they were subject to air attacks the days that followed and shot down an Argentine Skyhawk with a machine gun. It was a moment Munroe would never let leave his memory.

As they entered the shack, Lennox headed straight for his basket and curled up, the cold was clearly too much for him. The shack was surprisingly warm, something Munroe insisted on during the design. An Edinburgh lad born and raised, he never liked the cold of Scotland, but he could never deny his homeland or the beauty it has to offer. Now that he was located further north in Fife at the Kirkwood Estate, he could swear the temperatures were always several degrees lower.

Munroe lowered the girl down on his bed, brushing the hair away from her face. Blood had dried around her mouth, most likely from a nosebleed or cut lip. As he moved her arm down by her side, he noticed black spots along the skin. They resembled cigarette burns. He approached the sink in the kitchen and ran a tap, soaking a flannel. The water came from a tank outside that collected rainwater. He was proud of his self-sufficient home. A wood burning fire provided heat and a solar panel provided what little electricity he needed.

He wiped away the dirt and blood from her face as she began to open her eyes. As he stared, she panicked, cramming herself into the corner where the bed met the wall.

"It's okay," he said softly in his thick accent. "I'm not going to hurt you." Her eyes darted around the room trying to understand where she was, pulling the duvet cover over for protection. "What's your name?" he asked. She looked at him hesitating for a moment.

"Sabina." She spoke with a thick eastern European accent.

"Where are you from?" he enquired curiously.

"Romania," she replied still confused as to where she was.

"You're a long way from home. How did you end up here?"

"Men, take me. I arrive in container. I am to work for them." As she spoke, the thought of what she was saying horrified Munroe. "But I escape," she added.

"Did they hurt you?" Munroe asked gesturing to the burns on her skin. She looked down at them and nodded.

"Don't worry. You'll be safe here," he said smiling sincerely.

"Thank you."

Munroe wasn't sure what he was going to do with her. A sucker for a damsel in distress, he was determined to help her, however, calling the police would surely result in her deportation and he wasn't sure how Mr McKendrick would react to the situation. Munroe reasoned that they had time, at least until she gained her strength and then they would decide on the next step.

Munroe was stirring a batch of homemade tomato soup, his favourite meal, especially on cold days like this. Sabina was still sat on the bed wrapped in the duvet watching him. As he raised the spoon to taste, the sound of voices could be heard outside. Munroe paused. Voices were unusual around here, this was private property and nobody should be trespassing. Sabina pulled the duvet tighter around her, frightened of who may be outside. Munroe put the spoon back in the saucepan and grabbed his rifle. He glanced out the window to see three men walking by the shack.

"Stay quiet," Munroe ordered. As he approached the door, Lennox stood to attention, ready to follow and, if necessary, protect his master. Munroe opened the door and stepped outside, the rifle lowered by his side. Lennox stepped up beside him. As the three men spoke, Munroe recognised the language immediately, it was one he was all too familiar with, Serbian. As a member of D Squadron of the 22 Special Air Service, he had taken part in Operation Picnic during the Kosovo War. Inserted into Kosovo in the early hours of 21st March 1999, their mission was to identify Serbian units, surface-to-air missile sites and supply lines and positions while remaining undetected. They also scouted possible invasion routes for NATO forces and collected photographic evidence of Serbian war crimes. On 25th March, his unit came across a mass grave in the small village of Bela Crkva, men, women and children all piled in together. The true capability of Serbians was etched into Munroe's mind, and ever since, he has held a dislike for the country and its people. To find three of them metres from his home did not sit well with him. The three men stopped in their tracks and turned to the armed man standing on the porch of his shack staring at them. The first to speak was stood in between the other two wearing an old 90s tracksuit jacket, his hair was greasy and the five o'clock shadow on his face gave an aura of intimidation.

"Hello, I'm sorry. I think we took wrong turning. We are lost," he said.

Munroe mustered up a sound of authority in his voice. "Aye, that you are. This is private property and you're trespassing. I suggest you turn around and head back the way you came," he replied.

"Thank you, we will do that." The three men began to turn around, but tracksuit stopped again and turned to Munroe. "You haven't seen a young girl come through here have you? She is our friend, we are looking for her," he asked politely.

"No, I haven't," Munroe answered trying to sound genuine. A moment of silence followed before a sound inside the shack alerted the three Serbians. They could see the discomfort on Munroe's face. Tracksuit smiled with a devilish grin.

"Give us the girl," he demanded. Munroe shook his head.

"There's no girl here," he replied trying to stay calm. Tracksuit was becoming impatient.

"Please, do not play with me. If you hand her over, you will never see us again. I promise." Munroe decided to give up the act and play it straight.

"I can't do that."

"Very well," Tracksuit said as he drew a Glock 19 Pistol from the back of his jeans and raised it ready to aim at Munroe. The gamekeeper was too quick though, lifting the rifle and firing a quick shot to disarm the Serb, severing off his ring finger in the process. He fell to his knees screaming in pain holding his injured hand as the blood dripped onto the leaves beneath him. His friend to the right wearing a leather jacket, with a shaved head and goatee making him look like some sort of nightclub bouncer, moved his arm around to the back of his trousers. Munroe fired a shot at the ground by his feet and Leather Jacket paused.

"Don't you even dare. Throw it away," Munroe ordered and Leather Jacket complied, slinging a Glock 19 several metres from him. Munroe then focused his attention to the Serb on the other side.

"You too," he told the man dressed in a denim jacket looking less tough than the other too.

"I have no gun," he replied lifting up his jacket to show Munroe nothing was tucked anywhere.

"You stupid asshole," Tracksuit piped up still squeezing his hand tightly to stem the flow of blood. "You do not understand."

"Oh, I understand fully. Now leave this land," Munroe ordered, this time with more force. Leather and Denim helped Tracksuit to his feet and they began to head off in the opposite direction, Munroe still with his rifle trained on them.

"We'll be back, and you'll be sorry," Tracksuit called out. Munroe waited for them to disappear within the trees then finally lowered his rifle. He re-entered the shack and looked over at Sabina who was still huddled in the corner, the blanket held up to her eyes.

"We need to leave," he suggested, placing the rifle up against the wall.

"I cannot," Sabina replied with fear in her voice.

"You have to." Munroe grabbed a large blanket and slung it over to Sabina. "This will keep you warm." Sabina lowered the duvet and grabbed the blanket throwing it around her shoulders. She pulled it over her head, and as she stood up, the end of the sheet reached down to the floor. She was completely covered. She looked up to Munroe.

"Okay, but where we go?" she asked.

"Somewhere safe," he answered as he grabbed a set of car keys off a hook by the door.

To say Munroe's Land Rover was old was an understatement. The 95 Defender model had seen a lot throughout its years and although a little rickety here and there, it churned up road like there was no tomorrow. Sabina was sat beside him still hidden within the blanket watching the trees whiz by. Lennox was in the back enjoying a trip in the car as he always did. Silence remained between them, nothing

173

but the ground crunching beneath. The main house of the estate was a couple of miles away from Munroe's shack. He wanted it to be located far enough that he wouldn't have to run into Mr McKendrick too often, or his guests, yet close enough that either man could easily visit the other. As the Land Rover pulled up outside the main doors of the house, Munroe jumped out onto the gravel driveway and ran to ring the bell, he then returned to the passenger side door and opened it helping Sabina out, the sharp gravel cutting into her bare feet. Lennox began barking as though asking when he would be let out.

"Stay boy, I'll be back soon," Munroe called to him. The door was opened by the main butler of the house, Wilson. Munroe knew him well, but did not like him and knew a petty argument would ensue between them about who the girl was, before he would allow entry. Munroe pushed Wilson aside and stepped in, much to the butler's protests. In a great ornate living room, Munroe and Sabina waited, Wilson standing by the door staring daggers at them. The fire was roaring and Sabina was sitting by it absorbing the heat. Munroe was pacing up and down near her as Mr McKendrick entered the room tying his dressing gown.

"Munroe, what is it?" McKendrick asked.

"Mr McKendrick, I'm sorry to barge in on you, but I need you to take care of this young woman," he told him. Mr McKendrick looked over at Sabina who seemed completely oblivious she was the subject of the conversation.

"Who is she?"

"I found her in the woods, several men are after her. She needs somewhere safe to stay, for the night at least."

"I don't know, Munroe. How can I trust her?"

"You don't need to leave her alone. Have Wilson watch her." Wilson was not happy to hear this suggestion.

"And where will you be?" he cried.

"Protecting my home."

"What do you mean?" McKendrick asked concerned.

"I'm sorry, Sir, but I have to go." Munroe rushed for the door.

"But Munroe," McKendrick turned to watch Munroe leave, confused by his haste. He then turned to Sabina who was still by the fire. "Wilson, ensure she behaves herself."

"Very well, Sir," Wilson replied begrudgingly. As Munroe drove back to the shack bouncing along the dirt road, he felt as if he was back in the Gulf War driving along the desert dunes to battle. He knew the Serbs would return and this time with more men and heavier fire power. Munroe would have to use every trick he had learnt from years under Her Majesty's service to protect himself and his home. Munroe searched the shack for anything he could find that would help hold off the inevitable siege. Along with snare wire, he gathered up every last round for his rifle and came across an old bear trap at the bottom of a wooden crate filled with farm relics. For a moment, as he stared at the rusty teeth, he felt it may be too much, but after his mind flashed back to that haunting mass grave, those doubts washed away. It didn't take long to plant everything. He knew they would attack from the same direction they originally came and so it was a simple case of creating a defensive line several metres from the shack. This would give enough time, for those that do get through, to pick them off with the rifle. Darkness was falling; this would work to Munroe's advantage hiding every trap from view. As much as he would want to fight alongside him, Munroe knew this was not Lennox's war and so shut him inside hoping the walls would stem the penetration of bullets and protect him from any harm. He was never one to put his fellow soldiers in danger, if it could be helped. Munroe perched himself on the roof of the shack in a prone position, rifle lined up. He used the scope to scan along the tree line looking for any movement. With no night vision to hand, he would have to rely mainly on sounds, something he was more than used to.

An hour went by and the temperature dropped several degrees. The lack of movement was making Munroe more and more cold. His hands were shaking and he was struggling to hold the rifle steady. He was starting to wonder if they would actually show up, would he have to stay here all night just in case? Suddenly, he heard the sound of a branch snap, and the rustling of leaves. Peeking through the sight he scanned the defensive line looking for any hint of motion. It was then he heard the sound of the bear trap snap shut and the blood curdling scream that followed. Denim's leg was in a helpless grip cutting into the flesh. He was crying in agony trying to pull his leg free, but each time he did, the teeth would drag more skin from the bone. He collapsed to the floor on the cusp of passing out. One of the Serbs dressed in a black hoody covering his head ran to the aid of Denim, but tripped on a cord made from the snare wire tied between too trees. He fell forward onto a set of carved wooded spikes protruding from the ground at a 45 degree angle. They penetrated his chest causing him to cough up blood. Munroe could not see what was happening, but the sounds of rustling neared every second. He was almost panicking trying to spot any sign of a human figure, but the darkness was concealing everything.

Leather Jacket, Tracksuit and a third man wearing a long winter coat were only a few metres from the shack. They each had AK47s and cocked them ready to fire. They created a line of fire as they cut up the shack's walls. Inside, Lennox was going berserk barking and bouncing up and down. The flashes from the muzzles lit up the faces of the three men alerting Munroe to their position. He lined up the sight and fired a shot taking out Long Coat, a perfect shot through the head. As he reloaded, Lennox had managed to get out the door and ran toward the two remaining men, barking loudly. He pounced at Leather Jacket sinking his teeth into his arm. As he roared in pain, he pulled a Glock 19 from his trousers and fired a shot. Lennox yelped collapsing to the ground. Just as Leather Jacket pulled himself to his feet, a shot echoed and he felt a piercing sting in his chest. He dropped to his knees falling forward taking a mouthful of dirt. With only Tracksuit left, he yanked back the trigger churning out round after round splitting the wood of the shack, splinters flying off in all directions. Munroe reloaded the rifle and trained his sight.

He fired, catching Tracksuit in the chest. He fell backwards casting the AK47 across the ground. Munroe waited several minutes scanning the tree line again, prepared for any more movements. He suspected they were all down and slowly crawled to the edge of the roof where he slipped off down to the ground. He reloaded the rifle and made his way over to Tracksuit who was panting. As Munroe looked down at him, he looked up.

"You fool. You do not understand. She must die. She is not human," he spoke under heavy breath. Munroe frowned at him, confused by these words.

"What do you mean?" he asked. Tracksuit gave his last breath and shut his eyes. Munroe looked over toward the main house. Munroe didn't hesitate to gather up Lennox and put him in the back of the Land Rover. He'd been shot, but Munroe suspected it wasn't anything too serious. The bullet was through and through, missing any vital organs. It was a simple case of stemming the blood flow until he could get him to a vet. But first he would need to stop by the house. As Lennox lay in the back of the car breathing slowly, but conscious, Munroe was still waiting by the door after having rung the doorbell several times. Past experiences told Munroe it didn't matter how late it was, someone would always answer the door. He decided he couldn't wait any longer and used all his strength to kick the door in. It slammed against the wall as it swung open. With rifle in hand, Munroe stepped into the quiet expecting someone to run in questioning the noise, but nothing. He made his way into the living room where the fire was still roaring, unattended.

"Hello?" he called out, expecting some sort of reply.

Climbing the stairs was something he had never done. The upstairs of the household was strictly off limits, but Munroe was becoming more and more concerned by the lack of presence in the home. He made his way across the large corridor of rooms, all with their doors open. Only one at the end was shut. He guessed this was Mr McKendrick's bedroom, and made his way toward it. He repeated the words of the track suited Serb in his head, "She's not human."

What did he mean by that? He reached out his hand and turned the door handle gently pushing it open. The hinges creaked, the light rushing into the dark room. As Munroe entered, he was greeted by a familiar scene. Lying on the bed was Mr McKendrick, not looking too dissimilar to the fox that he had discovered that morning. Blood was sprayed up the walls, the bed sheets were soaked. Limbs and organs spread all over. Mr McKendrick's severed head frozen with a face of pure shock that sent a chill down Munroe's spine. Down on the floor beside his feet was a crumpled up dress, the same one worn by Sabina. Behind him he could hear the sound of breathing. He carefully turned around and stared into the blackness in the corner of the room. Floating like two laser dots was a pair of red eyes staring at him. His heart began pounding faster than had ever before. She began to make a growling noise. Munroe slowly attempted to cock the rifle. The clicking noise startled her and she lunged out from the corner launching toward him. Munroe raised the rifle and fired a shot.

Birth Control

Annie sat with her feet up on the sofa scrolling through her social media feed on a tablet. Most of the posts were by protest groups asking for support in their cause. It had been two years since the Reproduction Act was passed into law and every male made reversibly infertile. They said it would curb teenage pregnancies, prevent children being born into poverty or to incapable parents and in time could reduce crime. Yet those who fell victim to this new policy were still fighting back in the hope it would be overturned. As she continued to browse, her eye was caught by a particular image of a new-born baby swaddled in blankets. A caption read, "Our beautiful new baby boy." She stared at the photograph longingly, a sadness forming on her round face. She gave a deep sigh and switched off the tablet. A knock at the door made her jump. She slid off the sofa to answer it.

Kim was standing at the front door with a bottle of wine clenched in her manicured fist. She raised it victoriously as a large grin showed off her bright white teeth.

'Time to celebrate!' she called with giddy excitement. Annie forced a smile from her thin lips and stepped aside to allow Kim entry.

Annie was back on the sofa waiting anxiously for Kim to return from the kitchen with two large glasses of red wine. Passing one to Annie, she wasted no time taking her first sip as Kim sat down next to her.

'Here's to your divorce. Good riddance to old rubbish,' Kim announced clinking her glass against Annie's without warning. Annie almost spilt hers on the cream velour beneath them. The thought of it made her heart jump. Kim could sense Annie was in no mood to celebrate. 'What's the matter?' she asked. 'You should be happy. You don't have to see that bastard ever again.'

Annie turned away and stared into her glass. She wasn't one to share her problems with the world, but needed to talk about it.

'I know, but I just keep thinking, the one thing I wanted, is now even more unlikely,' she replied with a sulky tone.

'You're talking about children?' Kim asked, already knowing the reply. Annie looked up at her and nodded subtly. 'Annie, you're thirty-one. You've got plenty of time to find someone and have children,' she assured her dismissively before taking a large sip of her drink.

'That's the problem. I don't want to find someone. I don't need a partner. I've done that and it didn't end well. I just want a child,' Annie claimed desperately, running her finger along the edge of the wine glass.

Kim didn't like these serious conversations, especially when wine was involved, but she knew she had to reiterate to her sister the disappointing truth. No matter how painful.

'Well, I'm afraid that's not going to happen by yourself. Unless you buy some guy's sperm off the black market,' Kim smirked, but as soon as she said the last sentence, she knew it wasn't wise to give Annie ideas. However, as Annie looked away shamefully, Kim felt it was too late, the seed had already been sewn. 'You haven't, have you?' Kim asked, not quite sure if she wanted to know the answer. Annie couldn't bring herself to make eye contact with her as she spoke.

'A colleague at work did it. She said it was easy. She offered to contact a dealer for me.'

Kim's eyes widened with shock before her brow furrowed with anger and frustration.

'Annie, are you crazy? Do you realise how much trouble you could get into if you're caught?' she barked, hoping her words would get through.

'Yes, but I'm willing to risk it.' Annie had now locked eyes with Kim, a steely determination in them.

Kim shook her head in disbelief. Was her quiet, reserved sibling really going to do this? She had to try and deter her. She placed her glass down on the nearby coffee table and took hold of Annie's hand.

'Annie, you're my sister and I love you, but right now you're being stupid. You need to think long and hard about this, don't rush into anything that you may regret. You will find someone, fall in love and have children. Have faith. Just promise me you won't do anything illegal,' Kim begged her as she looked deep into her sad eyes.

Annie felt backed into a corner. She was hoping for her sister's support and was hurt when it did not come. She looked away from Kim's intense stare, but she knew the gaze wouldn't end until the right answer had been heard. She returned her focus and smiled softly.

'Okay, I won't,' she said with very little conviction. Kim grinned with relief and wrapped her arms around Annie's neck pulling her in close, embracing her tightly.

'I know it seems impossible now, but just stay positive. Nobody knows what the future holds.'

Annie listened to the words, but they meant nothing to her. She just hoped Kim didn't realise she was lying.

Later that night, Annie was sat at her desk in the dark of the spare room. The glow of the computer screen lighting up her face as she leaned in close to read. She was on the website for the Family Planning Clinic. She shifted the cursor over to a link that read, "Apply for Fertility." She clicked it. An entry form appeared on the page with a set of terms and conditions written above. It read, "Before applying, please ensure you meet all necessary criteria." It then listed the bullet points required to be a successful applicant, they were:

- Applicants must be married for at least one year.

- One spouse must have an income of at least £15,000 pa. an extra £5,000 pa. per additional child.

- No criminal record.

- Acceptable housing fully paid for or mortgaged by applicants.

- Accommodation must be located in a high standard area (See map for details).

- A full clean bill of health.

Annie met all except one. She felt it unfair, why must she be married? She was perfectly capable of taking care of a child by herself. She would be the most wonderful mother a boy or girl could ever have. She would love them dearly and surely that was all that mattered. She was pulled from her daydream by an email alert in the corner of the screen. Annie brought up the received message and was taken aback by its contents. It read, "Your friend contacted me. If you're still interested, I have stock. Let me know." Annie couldn't believe it. Her colleague at work had come through and now she had the opportunity to make her dream come true. She stood up and paced around the room biting her nails. Her heart was racing with excitement, but what would Kim say? Oh, why did she have to visit today? Her mind was made up, but now Kim's words were running through her head. Could she really do this? Could she really break the law? Annie moved the mouse cursor over the delete button. She was about to click, but paused. She took a couple of deep breaths before moving the cursor over to the reply button and clicked. She composed a return message. It simply said. "I am interested." In no time at all, another email came through. She opened it, her hand shaking with nerves. "Meet me tomorrow at midnight, Old Street. Bring £2000 cash." Annie couldn't take the pounding of her heart in her chest. It felt like it was jumping around all over. She sent a message back. "I'll be there." She sat down to catch her breath, her hands still shaking.

The protesters were gathered outside the entrance of the Family Planning Clinic like cattle. They each had crudely made signs with slogans such as "Let God Decide", "We Have Rights" and "Children Of Oppression". Steven was watching them from the waiting room window. With his hands wedged in his trouser pockets, he was an air of calm as he observed the commotion outside. His wife, Felicity, was sat near him picking at her fingernails. She glanced over at him with an irritated look.

'Come away from the window, Steven and sit down. You're making me more nervous standing there,' she demanded with a slight strain in her voice.

Steven shifted his attention to her and smiled. He took a seat next to her and placed his hand gently on top of hers.

'There's no reason to be nervous. We tick all the boxes. This is merely a formality for us,' he assured her.

'They can still turn us down,' she snapped back.

'I doubt they will. Just relax,' he replied, rubbing her hand to calm her. At that moment, a door opened and Felicity felt her heartbeat quicken as she turned to see who would appear. A nurse stepped out and looked over at the couple.

'Mr and Mrs Marsh?' she called.

Steven and Felicity smiled as they stood.

Dr. Thompson was a short and jolly looking man with spectacles balanced on the end of his nose. He was sat at his desk reading a file whilst Steven and Felicity sat before him holding hands as they waited anxiously. Dr Thompson scratched his beard pensively and gave an impressed murmur. He looked up and smiled.

'I must say, I'm very impressed with your application. Excellent income. Mr Marsh, you're a teacher. Mrs Marsh, an environmental lawyer. You live in a wonderful area of the city. I don't think I've had a couple more qualified pass through this office,' he said with a bounce in his voice. Steven and Felicity looked at each other and smiled. 'I'm happy to say you've been granted fertility,' he added. Steven and Felicity embraced each other with relief as Dr. Thompson stamped their file with a large "Fertility Granted" stamp. Felicity was on the verge of tears, giddy with laughter.

'Thank you, doctor,' she said with relief.

The doctor gestured toward a table in the corner of the room.

'Steven, if you'd like to sit up on the examination table.'

Steven managed to pull himself from Felicity's grip and made his way over to the table. His tall height allowed him to hop onto it with ease. Doctor Thompson unlocked a drawer behind his desk and took out a small EpiPen like device wrapped in plastic. He tore it from its packaging and approached Steven as he rolled up his sleeve. Doctor Thompson placed the auto-injector on Steven's arm and pressed the button with his thumb. Steven winced briefly before the device was removed leaving a small needle sized dot on his arm. The doctor placed a ball of cotton on the tiny wound. 'Okay, all done.' Steven replaced the doctor's finger on the cotton. He glanced over at an excited Felicity and smiled lovingly as he slipped off the table and approached her. The doctor tossed the now empty injector into a secure refuse box. He retook his place behind the desk and sat down. 'Now, you'll need to wait twenty-four hours before having sexual intercourse. You'll be fertile for thirty days. If in that time you haven't been able to conceive, you may have another injection, but depending on circumstances it may require a small charge. Any questions?' The doctor waited, but merely received an excited shaking of the head from both of them. 'Excellent,' he added with relish.

'Thank you, doctor,' Steven said extending a hand to shake. The doctor reached out and reciprocated. Felicity stood and shook the doctor's hand with enthusiasm.

'Thank you so much, doctor,' she almost screamed with elation.

'Not at all. Good luck conceiving,' he replied with a large grin on his face.

Steven was now the nervous one pacing up and down the thick carpeted bedroom floor nibbling at his nails. Felicity was sat on a chair, hunched over, staring at a pregnancy test. Steven paused and glanced over at her.

'Well?' he asked impatiently.

'It takes a few minutes,' she replied. Steven sat down on the edge of the bed, his knee bobbing up and down. 'It's doing something!' Felicity called out. Steven was back on his feet and leaned over to see. 'Negative. False alarm,' she added with disappointment. Her head dropped as she closed her eyes wishing for a better outcome. Steven dropped to his knees before her and took her hand affectionately kissing it.

'Don't worry. It'll happen eventually. We have plenty of time,' he assured her.

Meanwhile, another pregnancy test was underway. Annie was sat on the toilet seat in her small bathroom. The plastic white stick perched on the side of the sink. Annie eyed it before looking at her watch. She stood up and closed her eyes.

'Please, God,' she whispered to herself.

Annie opened one eye and looked down at the display. A clear plus symbol. She opened the other eye and took a closer look to be sure she wasn't seeing things. She picked up the stick and reassured herself what she had seen was the truth. Her smile was ear to ear as she danced across the tiled floor. She couldn't contain herself and burst into happy tears. She wanted to scream in delight, but was reluctant to disturb her neighbours. Perhaps a glass of champagne would suffice? Before Annie could enjoy her news, a knock at the door startled her. She wasn't expecting anybody. Perhaps it was Kim coming to make sure she didn't go through with it. Now wouldn't be a good time to tell her.

Annie opened the front door to find a smart looking gentleman in a suit standing before her, a second man in a police uniform stood behind him.

'Mrs Williams?' the suited man asked.

'Yes,' she replied with hesitation. Annie could feel her heart rate increasing as the suited man held up a police detective badge for her to see.

'We'd like a word,' he said with authority.

Eight months had passed since Annie was convicted of illegal insemination and sentenced to one year in prison. The days had bled into one and she couldn't tell what time or day of the week it was. Mundane routine had dulled her senses and visits from friends and family were the only thing keeping her going. That and the child growing inside of her. Annie entered the visitors room and spotted Kim sat hopelessly toward the back of the room. She made her way over to her. They were forbidden from making physical contact and so quickly sat down before one of them felt the urge to lean in for a hug. Kim forced a reassuring smile and Annie threw one back in order to make her sister comfortable.

'How are you doing?' Kim asked, trying not to sound too cheerful.

'I'm not too bad. I may be in prison, but this little thing makes all that fade away,' Annie said as she looked down at the bump stroking it.

'It can't be long now,' Kim said with much needed optimism.

'One month,' Annie replied, matching Kim's tone, but her mood shifted as she continued. 'It's just upsetting I won't be able to keep him, but you'll take good care of him, won't you? And that way I can always visit,' she said hopefully.

Kim hesitated and this made Annie nervous. When the words finally came, Annie was reluctant to listen.

'Listen, Annie. I looked into the adoption process, and as much as I'd love to have him, they won't let me.'

'Why not?' Annie asked with desperation.

'Some bullshit law that prohibits children of convicted criminals being adopted by relatives. I guess they don't like the idea you could still see him.' It cut her up inside to shatter her sister's hopes. Before Kim finished her sentence, she could see the tears welling up in Annie's eyes. She had to do something and so risked placing a hand on Annie's and leaning in close to shield it from the observing prison guards. 'It's okay, we'll figure something out. Try and stay positive.'

Annie snatched her hand from under Kim's and placed it alongside the other on her belly in a protective manner.

'I won't let them take you away from me,' she said softly, then snapped her head up to look at Kim, a steely look in her eye. 'I won't let them,' she added with determination. Kim could only look back at Annie silently, hoping she didn't do anything else stupid.

Steven and Felicity found themselves back in Dr. Thompson's office for the tenth time. As Steven glanced around the room, he realised he had read nearly every poster on every wall. How many more times would they have to return? Felicity was sat next to him clutching his hand in hers on the verge of tears. It was starting to feel like torture. He didn't want to keep putting the woman he loved through this, but she was insistent. He felt a wave of pain rush over him as he stared at Felicity. Why couldn't he give her a child? Dr. Thompson lifted his head from reading a file and cut in breaking Steven from his daydream.

'I'm sorry to say this, but we've exhausted all avenues; 5 injections, plus I.V.F. At this stage, I'm afraid there's not much more we can do.' The doctor hated giving bad news like this. There was nothing worse than dashing someone's hopes, but it was all part of the job.

'There's not much more we can afford,' Steven quipped, before glancing over at Felicity praying she didn't see his remark as a joke at their expense. She remained silent, staring at the floor, a solitary tear running down her cheek.

'Of course, there are other options,' Thompson said, pulling a leaflet from his desk drawer.

'What kind of options?' Steven asked inquisitively. The doctor placed the leaflet on the desk in front of the couple. In large white letters on the cover was the word "Adoption". Steven picked it up for a closer look.

'There are many children out there looking for a loving family. I could submit a recommendation, possibly fast track you. You're beyond all qualifications, so I can't see it being a problem.' The doctor tried to make it sound as easy as possible, God knows these people have already been through enough stress. Felicity couldn't hold back any longer and burst into tears. Steven put the leaflet into his pocket and placed a hand on her shoulder to console her. 'Once again, I'm very sorry. I understand how you must feel.' The doctor wanted so badly to help this couple. He had spent so much time with them they had become almost friends.

'Thank you, Doctor. We'll consider it. Come on, honey. Let's go.' Steven gave a thankful smile and helped Felicity to her feet. They slowly made their way toward the door, Steven supporting the broken woman by his side.

She hadn't experienced pain like it. Annie writhed around on the bed screaming in shear agony. Her cuffed wrist pulling and scraping on the bed frame. A midwife was next to her mopping her sweating brow with a damp cloth. The doctor at the foot of the bed checking between her legs, reaching in without hesitation. A prison guard watched on from the corner of the room, a face of disgust trying to block out the incessant noise. Annie's screams stopped and they were followed by the cries of a baby as the doctor produced a small pink bundle in his arms. Annie caught her breath, watching as the doctor severed the umbilical cord and carried the blood stained infant over to a towel to clean him up. The midwife joined him and took over, wrapping the child in fresh linen. Annie reached out as best she could considering her wrists were bound.

'Let me see him,' she whispered weakly. The midwife heard Annie's request and looked over toward her sympathetically. For a moment it seemed she was going to appease the new mother, but instead she turned to the prison guard and passed the baby to him. 'No, don't take him. Let me see him. Please.' Annie leaned further forward, but the manacles yanked her back. The prison guard deaf to the woman's cries pushed open a door and stepped through. 'Please, don't take him away,' she called out, her voice strained. As the door closed shut, a weakened Annie slumped back on the bed and began to sob.

The church was packed full of people squashed into pews. Those who couldn't sit were stood along the sides and at the back. They had all come to listen to Father Michael Winfred speak. Annie slipped in through the open door and pushed her way through bodies to catch a glimpse of the man who owned the strong commanding voice echoing around the room. It had been several weeks since her release from incarceration. She looked tired and depressed, but Michael's words gave her energy and hope.

'Our God given right, taken away from us, why? Because some don't earn enough money, are considered too old or just made mistakes in our youth, like most people do.' He spoke with confidence and vigour, punctuating his words with erratic hand gestures. 'All we want is to be mothers and fathers, and for that we are arrested and imprisoned. I say this has gone too far and it's time for us to take a stand. Time for us to take back the human rights that have been denied us. Time for this government to yield to the will of God. We are his vessels of creation, the manufacturers of life. We decide. Not them.' He finished with a bang of his fist on the pulpit. The crowd stood up and clapped. Michael bowed gratefully before making his way to the side of the room as the noise simmered down. A woman stepped in his place and spoke to the crowd. As Michael shook hands with supporters he caught sight of Annie making her way toward him. Before he had a chance to greet her, she spoke with urgency.

'Did you find it?' she asked.

Michael nodded. He took Annie by the arm and led her toward the back of the church where it was quiet. He reached into his inside jacket pocket and took out a folded piece of paper. He held it up to Annie.

'This is everything I could find on the people who adopted your son,' he explained, but Annie had already snatched it from his hand. She unfolded it and perused the contents. 'Think long and hard about this. Once you cross that bridge, there'll be no going back,' he warned her, a stern look in his eye. Annie looked up at him, but his words were meaningless. She simply nodded and pocketed the document.

'Thank you,' she replied abruptly before turning and disappearing back into the crowd.

Felicity was enjoying her day home alone with her new son. She found it hard to tear herself away from him to do various chores. His cherub face melted her heart every time she looked at him. She had never been so happy. While he was sleeping, she took the opportunity to catch up on some laundry, but was interrupted by the doorbell. Annie was standing on the porch as Felicity pulled open the front door.

'Good afternoon, Mrs Marsh. My name is Rachel Smith, I'm from social services. I've just come to see how you're doing with the new addition to your family,' Annie said with conviction. She was wearing smart clothing and glasses. An ID badge was clipped to her collar and she held a clipboard in one hand.

'Oh yes, of course. They said someone would be coming. Please, do come in,' Felicity replied politely. She stepped aside and Annie cautiously entered the house. As she did so, she was already criticising in her mind the suitability of this house for raising a child. She found the decor disgusting and a putrid stench in the air.

'What a lovely home,' Annie lied.

Annie followed Felicity through into the large living room. Annie paused at the threshold when she saw the tiny baby sitting in a bouncer fast asleep.

'Here he is. Our little bundle of gorgeousness. This is George,' Felicity said as she approached the boy to check he was sleeping okay. 'Can I get you a tea or coffee?' Felicity asked with a smile, but received no answer. 'Miss Smith?' she called. Annie broke free from her mesmerised state and smiled back at Felicity.

'Oh yes, tea please,' she finally said, her heart racing. Once Felicity had left the room, Annie slowly approached the silent child and reached down. She carefully picked him up so as not to disturb his slumber and held him close. A tear ran down her cheek as she smiled at him with such affection she thought her heart would burst through her chest and explode with love.

Felicity was rushing around the kitchen filling two mugs with tea bags and milk as the kettle finished boiling. The noise loud enough to drown out all other sounds. She poured out the hot water, allowing the tea to brew before removing the bags and placing the mugs on a tray along with a plate of biscuits. She carried the tray through to the living room.

'I hope you don't mind soy milk…' she called out as she entered the room, but was cut off mid-sentence when she discovered the lady had disappeared and her son along with her. The tray slipped from her fingers and the mugs smashed to the floor spilling their contents across the carpet. Felicity rushed to the front door to find it still ajar. She stepped out into the quiet street looking up and down the road, but saw no sign of the woman or her child. Felicity screamed as the tears welled in her eyes.

The police arrived quickly, but not before Steven had rushed home from work. He was consoling his wife best he could as they sat close on the sofa. Two uniformed police officers were sat opposite, one of them scribbling in a small notebook.

'Had you seen the woman before?' the officer asked. Felicity was in a zombie-like state staring off into the distance. There was silence as everyone waited for an answer, but it did not come. 'Mrs Marsh? We could really do with a description of the woman,' the officer pushed, yet careful not to upset. Steven could see Felicity was struggling, but she needed to speak. He hoped she could give a good enough description to find this person. After all they had been through, this was terrible.

'Honey, please, tell them,' he said desperately, nudging her gently with his arm around her shoulder. Felicity slowly looked up and stared the police officer in the eye.

'Please, find my baby,' she begged.

In a quiet dense wood, a small campfire was burning brightly in the coming darkness. Annie was sat on the leaf covered ground staring into the flames, deep in thought. The cries of a baby snatched her back to reality. She stood and entered a small tent. Inside, bundled in blankets acting as a makeshift cot was George, stirring from his sleep. Annie knelt down next to him and gently lifted him up cradling him in her arms. She rocked him, humming sweetly to calm his screams.

'Shh. Mummy's here now. Everything's going to be just fine,' she promised.

The church was empty, almost eerie in its silence. Michael was stood at the pulpit editing a speech for that afternoon's sermon. He was a man of words and was blessed with the ability to inspire and encourage with his oratory skills. Putting pen to paper, however, was not something he had ever learned to love. As he struggled to form a sentence, his train of thought was interrupted by echoing footsteps approaching down the aisle. He glanced up to see two women marching toward him with authority. One tall and stick thin with exquisite posture, the other shorter and curvier with a permanent scowl. Both wore suits and stylish shoes with suitable heels causing the rhythmic tapping on the stone floor.

'Father Winfred?' the taller of the two asked.

'Yes,' Michael replied stepping out from behind the pulpit to greet his visitors at level height.

'Detectives Hart and Welch,' the taller said as they both presented their badges. 'We're investigating the kidnapping of George Marsh.'

By analysing their identification, Michael was able to learn the taller was Hart and the shorter, Welch.

'I see. Yes, that is a terrible affair. My thoughts are with the parents. What can *I* do for you?'

'We received an anonymous tip off that you purchased documents regarding the adoption of George by Steven and Felicity Marsh,' Welch said as she pocketed her badge.

'What? That's ridiculous. I did no such thing,' Michael said with a laughter of disbelief, hoping it would mask his deception.

'Can you explain why someone would accuse you?' Welch followed up with.

'Believe me, I have collected many enemies since I started speaking out against the system. I've had plenty of death threats and accusations, this does not surprise me in the least. Now, if you would excuse me, I have a large congregation coming any minute now and a sermon to complete.'

Michael turned his back on the two detectives with the intention of returning to his place behind the pulpit. He hoped this would be enough to end their line of inquiry, but they simply looked at each other with suspicion on their minds.

'Mr Winfred, I'm sure a man of religion, like yourself, can understand a serious crime has been committed and the victims are distraught. If you know anything, it is your duty as a Christian to help us,' Hart said.

She didn't like that she had to take advantage of someone's religious beliefs to force co-operation, but sometimes you have to use what you have.

Michael turned to face her with the intention of looking her in the eye to convince her of his story.

'I told you. I don't know anything.'

Welch stepped closer pushing her larger frame into his. Despite being several inches shorter, he found her very intimidating.

'Of course, there is some suspicion around your congregation as a whole. Especially the possible connection to the extremist group Manus Dei,' Welch said with an accusatory tone.

'They do not represent our movement,' he replied.

'They were started by followers of yours though, weren't they?'

Michael stared uncomfortably at Welch.

'Maybe we should look into your current members, search locations you're known to speak at. Perhaps we'll uncover evidence connected to the bombing of the fertility clinic,' Welch continued.

'We had nothing to do with that,' Michael insisted.

'I guess we'll find out,' Welch said before turning her back on him as if to leave.

'Alright, I will tell you what I know, but please leave my people out of this,' Michael blurted out before Welch could take a second step.

'Go on,' Hart encouraged.

'I purchased the documents for a friend.'

'Who?'

'Annie Williams. She is the birth mother of George Marsh. I had no idea she would take him. I just thought she wanted to see him, be sure he was with a happy, loving family.'

He was half expecting the two detectives to slap cuffs on him there and then, but they merely thanked him before heading back down the aisle.

'Please, be compassionate. She is a broken soul,' Michael called out to them before they stepped out of the church. He glanced over at the speech he was drafting. He snatched it from the pulpit and tore it up. All those words he planned to preach were now laced with hypocrisy.

A cold chill blew through the trees, the leaves swaying gently in the wind. Annie cradled George in her arms desperately trying to keep him warm. He was crying loudly, his voice no doubt carrying like some human alarm. She rocked him a little too quickly for comfort hoping the motion would silence him, but she knew he was hungry.

'Please, stop crying. I don't have any milk left. We need to wait, I can't go now. Please, stop!'

Her voice strained as she spoke, drowned out by the screaming child. She lay him down in a basket and started packing some things into a rucksack. She was going to have to risk it.

Kim was sat in a comfortable armchair, but comfort was hard to come by right now. She had a thousand yard stare out the window as her brain try to comprehend the news she had just been given.

'Mrs Barnes?' Hart called out from a nearby sofa. Welch was sat beside her with a pen and notepad at the ready.

Kim broke from her daydream and turned to the two detectives with a furrowed brow of disbelief. She shook her head erratically.

'I don't believe it. I can't believe it. Annie wouldn't do such a thing,' Kim protested as if trying to convince herself.

'We've checked the records. She is the birth mother of George Marsh, which means she has the motive. We also showed her photograph to Mrs Marsh who identified Annie as the woman who took George. We need to find her, before she does something rash,' Welch said.

'You think she'll hurt him?' Kim asked. 'She wouldn't hurt him. She's not capable of that.'

'And I'm sure you didn't believe she was capable of kidnapping. She has spent a year in prison and had her baby taken from her. Who knows what that could do to a person psychologically. Right now, we don't know what she's capable of. If you know where she could be, you need to tell us,' Hart leaned in and clasped her hands together clenching them tight as if praying.

'I don't know where she is.'

'You haven't heard from her?' Welch asked with pen prepared to write.

'No. I haven't spoken to her since she got out of prison. She's been something of a recluse.'

Kim thought back to that day she went to collect her dear sister from incarceration. She didn't speak a word on the car journey home. She was a different woman. As if the life had been sucked out of her.

Welch was now leaning forward with a hint of anger on her face. She didn't like it when people beat around the bush. She wanted answers and quickly. Time was of the essence.

'Kim, I don't need to remind you that if you know anything—'

'I don't know anything. If I did, I would tell you,' Kim declared.

Suddenly, a thought crossed her mind. It was fleeting and most likely irrelevant to their case, but she thought she had better mention it just in case.

'Wait, there is something,' Kim said. 'I don't know if it would help.'

The two detectives insisted she speak her mind. The smallest piece of information could help in large ways.

'She always said, if she ever had a child she would move out of the city, to a small town called Grey Heath. She might have gone there.'

Welch scribbled the name of the town down in her notepad. Finally something that could be of use. The two officers stood.

'Thank you, Kim. You have our number, if she gets in contact, let us know as soon as possible,' Hart said as Welch pocketed her notepad and pen.

Kim nodded with acknowledgement then returned her focus out the window as the detectives let themselves out. She wondered where Annie was and what it would mean when she got caught.

Annie bounced George up and down in her arms to keep him from screaming out again. She had managed to temper his cries, but he was a ticking time bomb. She was scanning the shelves of the shop looking for the right pack of baby milk formula. She was surprised at how many brands there were. She wasn't sure which to buy so had to take a guess selecting the nearest one to her. She took the formula over to the counter where a middle-aged shop clerk was casually perched on a stool reading a gossip magazine.

The clerk glanced up at Annie and smiled, but as she punched in the buttons on the till, her smile turned into a frown. There was something familiar about this woman. Where had she seen her before?

Annie was feeling anxious. She wanted to pay and get out of there as soon as possible. It was only a matter of time before her face was plastered all over the news and people would start recognising her and now it felt like this woman may know who she was. Annie slapped a few coins onto the counter and snatched up the formula. She hurried out of the shop still trying to keep George from crying.

After she had gone the clerk was still racking her brains as to where she had seen the woman's face before. Was it somewhere in the news? The clerk approached the rack of newspapers displaying that mornings headlines. One of which caught her eye. It read, "POLICE HUNT CHILD KIDNAPPER."

The clerk picked up the issue and there on the cover was a large image of Annie's mugshot. The clerk couldn't believe it. This was the first time anything related to a newspaper headline had entered her life. She rushed back behind the counter and picked up the phone.

George had exploded into a loud screeching cry as he begged to be fed. Annie had to take a seat on a park bench to quickly mix up a small batch of formula from a flask of hot water she had been carrying in her rucksack. A frail old woman sat beside her watching as she shook the mixture in a plastic bottle and then began feeding the small child.

'Oh, isn't he sweet?' the old woman commented. 'How old is he?'

'Three months,' Annie replied, trying not to let the old woman see her face.

'Aw, they're so innocent and pure at that age. Is he your first?'

The old woman shuffled along the bench to get closer to Annie and therefore a better view of George. Annie felt uncomfortable turning her head away.

'Yes, he is.'

'I'm sure you'll be trying for more one day.'

'I don't know. One is enough. I'm more than happy with just him.'

The old woman reached out a bony finger to stroke George on his cheek as he suckled at the milk.

'I suppose you should consider yourself lucky to have just one. So many people out there are not eligible to have that gift. Not like in my day.'

Annie smiled, but from the corner of her eye she saw a passing police car and her heart began pounding. She pulled the bottle from George's lips praying he didn't cry for more and packed her stuff away in her rucksack. She stood up slinging the bag over her shoulder and hastily carried George away. The old woman watched them leave wondering if it was something she had said.

She knew the effort he had put into cooking, but the food in front of her just looked so unappetising. Felicity stared at it trying to find the enthusiasm to eat, but she couldn't even bring herself to pick up the fork. She could hear Steven eating and wondered how he could do it. Did he not care?

'Please, honey. Try and eat something. You need to keep your strength up,' she heard him say.

'It's my fault. I should never have left him alone with her,' she replied not taking her eyes off the cold food.

Steven reached out a hand placing it on top of hers. She could feel the warmth, but it was not as comforting as she'd hoped.

'No, it's not your fault. You couldn't have known what she was going to do,' he assured her.

Felicity could no longer hold in the tears. There had not been a day in the last week she hadn't cried and wondered if there would be a day in the future when this pain would stop. Steven made his way around the table and wrapped his arms around her tightly.

'We'll find him. I promise.'

Felicity broke free from his embrace and jumped up from her seat. He watched her in agony as she stormed out of the room. He felt a failure. He could no longer comfort his wife in this time of distress. He prayed that their son would be returned soon and all this misery would be behind them.

Hart and Welch didn't spend much time at the shop. A uniformed officer already at the scene informed them of what the clerk had told him. That Annie Williams entered the shop with a baby looking rather distressed and then after leaving spent several minutes in the park before heading in the direction of the woods. Welch radioed in to the station and requested additional support to search the woods.

At first, Annie didn't hear the footsteps crunching through the fallen autumn leaves. She was sat in her small tent rocking George to sleep as she sang softly to him. As the crunching neared, they were joined by voices and Annie was forced to stop her singing in order to listen carefully. The voices were getting louder.

Annie placed George down on a blanket and loaded her rucksack with only the necessities; baby formula, blankets, nappies and threw it over her shoulders. She cautiously picked up the slumbering George and headed off deeper into the woods clutching him tightly. Hart and Welch pushed through some thick bushes and spotted the tent. A few feet in front walking away from them was Annie.

'There she is,' Hart said.

'Annie!' Welch called out.

Annie turned to see them and began running. The bouncing woke George and he began crying. Hart and Welch set off in pursuit with several uniformed officers in tow.

As Annie broke free from the shelter of the wood and felt the warm sunlight on her face, she had to stop herself before she almost tumbled over the edge of a large quarry. She was trapped, the only way was down. She peered over the cusp and felt queasy at the sight of the long drop into the water. She clutched the crying George tighter in her arms.

'Annie, step away from the edge,' Hart quietly said out of breath.

Annie turned around to find Hart and Welch standing before her, two uniformed police officers behind them.

'Please. It's very dangerous,' Hart said softly, extending a supportive hand.

'I won't let you take him from me again,' Annie said, tears running down her cheeks.

'Annie, if you fall, George will go as well. Surely you don't want that. So, come to us and we can talk,' Hart pleaded desperately.

'No, you're going to take him away,' Annie replied, shaking her head.

Annie squeezed George and the volume of his crying increased. She took a step back and several chunks of rock spilled off the edge plummeting into the abyss below.

'Annie! Don't move!' Hart screamed, reaching out a hand and taking a step forward. 'It's okay. We're not going to take him. He's yours, he belongs with you. We just want you both to be safe. Come away from the edge.'

'I don't believe you. Why should I?' Annie screamed back.

Welch was becoming impatient. 'How do you see this ending, Annie? You're a criminal. You can't keep him and you can't keep running. What kind of life is that for George? You need to stop being so selfish and think about what's best for your son,' she said with very little empathy.

Hart glanced over at Welch disgusted at her tact. Hart too was a single woman keen to raise children, but she didn't have the courage to do what Annie did. In some respects, she admired Annie for trying to live her life the way she wanted.

'He should be with me,' Annie cried.

'But they won't let that happen. Annie. I understand how you feel, but you must see, deep down inside, this is a lost cause. You need to hand him over, now,' Welch was keen for this to end, but her attitude was irritating Hart who sensed this method could escalate the situation.

'But, I'll never see him again,' Annie said glancing down at the screaming bundle in her arms.

'That's not necessarily true,' Hart said before Welch could continue her attempt. 'We can speak to the Marsh's. We can arrange visitation. You can still have a relationship with him, but not like this.' Hart felt bad for lying, but knew this was the only way to end this peacefully and ensure both survived.

Annie looked down at George with such affection and then back at Hart.

'Do you really think they would let me see him?' she asked like a hopeful child.

'I'm sure they would,' Hart reiterated as she took another step closer.

'Okay,' Annie whispered.

Annie passed George over to Hart, but as they exchanged the child between them, Annie looked into Hart's eyes and realised she wasn't willing to look at her. There was deception in her face.

'You're lying!' Annie screamed, shaking her head.

Annie tried to pull George back closer to her, but Hart had already snatched the child from her grip and was now cradling him in her own arms. Annie stepped forward to claim the child back, but Welch blocked her path.

'Give him back. You're lying,' Annie cried.

'I'm sorry, Annie, but you'll never see your son again,' Welch said without compassion.

Hart handed the baby to one of the uniformed officers who carried him back into the woods. Annie watched as her son disappeared again unable to reach him due to Welch's barricade. Welch took out a set of handcuffs and slapped them on Annie's wrists behind her. Annie dropped to her knees and burst into tears. Hart turned back placing a hand on Welch's shoulder.

'It's okay. I can take it from here,' Hart said. 'You make sure the child gets back to his family safe.'

Welch nodded and followed the uniformed officers into the wood, leaving Hart and Annie alone on the edge.

Hart crouched down beside the broken Annie.

'I'm sorry it ended this way, but there's no other option. Your son is with a good family, they will give him a good life. I hope you take comfort in that.'

Annie ignored her words, lost in her own pain. Hart helped her stand and was about to walk her back into the woods when Annie caught glimpse of a small teddy that had fallen from her rucksack.

'Could I have the teddy, please. To remember him by,' Annie whispered.

Hart was glad she could do something to comfort this woman. She bent down to collect the plush animal, but upon turning to Annie to hand her the item she saw the sorrowful woman tip over the edge. Hart rushed forward to try and grab her, but it was too late. She watched Annie's body slam into the water below.

It was a day she always hoped would come and now it was here. Felicity rushed out of the house in her bare feet. Not even the gravel of the driveway punching into her soles could stop her from taking custody of her child again. She almost snatched George from the police officer and pressed her face up against his, relieved to feel his warmth against hers. Steven was not far behind her and wasted no time embracing his family. It was over. Finally, it was over.

Annie's body was found the next day and a small funeral service was put on, very few attended. It seemed this incident would fade away into history, but for Michael and his followers, it was a spark. The priest felt guilty for giving up Annie to the police, knowing full well at the time how it would culminate, but using her proved its worth in the end. This was the catalyst they needed to strengthen their movement and force a change in the law. They would spend however long it took marching in the streets carrying signs that read, "JUSTICE FOR ANNIE." Kim was there alongside him hoping her sister's death would not be in vain.

Worst Laid Plan

The cigarette removed the taste of him from her mouth. It had been a sickening experience for Nadine, but she knew it would all be worth it soon. She pulled the soft hotel robe tighter around her voluptuous figure as she lounged on the king size bed. Her daydream was disturbed by a knocking at the door. She stubbed out the cigarette in an ashtray on the night-stand and slid off the bed, the robe riding up her body before falling back down as she stood up. Nadine cautiously approached the door.

'Who is it?' she called.

'It's Josh,' a deep voice replied from the other side.

Nadine smiled with excitement as she hastily pulled off the chain and unlocked the door. Josh pushed his way in and wrapped his arms around her. They kissed passionately, she running her fingers through his thick hair. He kicked the door shut behind him and reluctantly pulled from her embrace.

'How did it go?' he asked, taking hold of her hands and looking into her big blue eyes.

'As smooth as silk,' she said unable to resist his handsome face and leaned in for another kiss.

'Where is he?'

'On his way to the bank, withdrawing the money as we speak.'

Josh grinned. He planted another kiss on Nadine's lips then pulled her over to the bed. They perched themselves on the edge, hands still locked together.

'You followed the plan?'

'To the letter,' she replied a little insulted by his questioning.

'Tell me.'

'Why?'

'So I can be sure you didn't leave anything out,' he replied firmly. Nadine can be rather forgetful at the best of times and he remembered she was nervous before leaving the room. Nerves seemed to frazzle her brain beyond belief.

'Okay,' she complied. 'I went down to the hotel bar around nine…'

Nadine entered the extravagantly decorated bar wearing a slinky revealing dress. She was the most attractive woman in the room and everybody knew it. They watched as she glided across the floor to the bar and leaned up against it so her rear was protruding out. The male patrons found it difficult to look away, but their wives and girlfriends made sure of it.

Nadine ordered a drink and while the barman was pouring her a glass of white wine, she turned her attention to the far end of the bar where a heavily-built man with thinning hair and thick glasses was sat nursing a glass of scotch. She knew he was the man she was looking for, the hair loss and spectacles were a dead give-away but upon seeing him, she questioned whether she could go through with it. He gave her the creeps just looking at him and the thought of being up close and personal made her stomach turn.

He caught her staring at him, so she swallowed her pride and smiled with a playful wink. The idea of that cold hard cash filling her palms was enough to give her beer goggles for the night. And by the looks of it, it wasn't going to be difficult. She already had his attention as he smiled back at her with a devilish grin.

He made his way over and paid for her drink asking if she'd care to sit at a table. This was going to be the easiest money she'd ever made. He introduced himself as Gordon and Nadine was able to confirm she had the correct target.

They sat for a few hours deep in conversation. Gordon was surprised at how many interests they had in common, Nadine wasn't surprised at all. She kept him hanging on her every word, he was transfixed, watching her plump red lips. She knew as soon as she suggested the next step he would pounce on it like a dog with a tennis ball.

She leaned in close and whispered into his ear. His eyes lit up before nodding at her with the enthusiasm of a child on Christmas morning.

Nadine led Gordon down the corridor of the seventh floor of this four star hotel to room number 1101. When they reached the room, she could feel him shaking with excitement. It felt too easy. She could have led this man off a cliff. She unlocked the door with a key card and they both slipped inside.

Nadine flicked on the light and shut the door behind them. Before she could get into the room properly, Gordon was all over her like a lapdog pushing her up against the door and kissing her neck. His hands were mapping her body with haste and she felt smothered. Nadine broke free from his relentless affection and pushed him back. He tripped over his own foot and fell onto the bed. Gordon stared up at her slender body with anticipation as she slowly unzipped her dress.

Josh didn't care to hear all the details of the night. He held up a hand mid-sentence and encouraged Nadine to skip the dirty work and pick up from the morning.

Gordon's hairy body almost filled the entire bed, the silk sheets draped over him revealing every curve of his unappealing body. He stared up at the ceiling, a satisfied look upon his chubby face. Nadine was wrapping herself in a robe as she made her way over to a dresser at the end of the bed and removed a small camera hidden behind a lamp. She studied it with joy. Gordon caught sight of what was in her delicate fingers and sat up startled.

She explained how every filthy thing they had done that night had been captured on video. He was not happy. Gordon threw his half naked body out of the bed and charged over to her with anger. He snatched the camera from her hand and tossed it against the wall with such force it shattered into pieces on contact with the wallpapered surface.

Nadine broke the news to him that all the footage was automatically uploaded to a cell phone, so unfortunately his rash action had no impact on the situation. Gordon was distraught. He sat down on the bed with his head in his hands. Nadine went on to explain the footage would remain a secret provided a substantial cost was paid. Gordon would pay whatever it took.

Josh was so proud of her. She'd performed perfectly. Of course he didn't like the thought of the woman he loved lying with another man, but it wasn't for anything more than money and it was done with his consent.

'He headed out to the bank almost straight away,' she said.

'I can't believe this worked,' he replied shaking his head.

'She told us it would.'

Nadine kissed Josh, hoping they would have time to erase her memories of the night before, but they were interrupted by a knock at the door.

'Who is it?' she called.

'It's Gordon. Let me in.'

The couple looked at each other with concern. If Gordon caught Josh in the room, it could blow the whole plan.

'You should hide in the bathroom and be quiet,' she hastily suggested.

'You can do this,' he assured her with a quick kiss.

Josh made his way into the bathroom and quietly closed the door behind him. Nadine tightened her robe and took a deep breath before opening the door. A sulking Gordon shuffled in carrying a small duffel bag. He shut the door and put the chain lock on.

'So, did you get it?' she asked firmly.

Gordon put the bag down on the bed. He unzipped it and reached a hand inside. Nadine watched anxiously, desperate to set her eyes on the dollar bills wrapped in bundles. She was surprised however to see him pull a gun, complete with suppressor, from the bag and point it at her. She took a step back.

'Gordon, what are you doing?'

'I've changed my mind. I won't be giving you a penny. Instead, you're going to tell me who you sent the video to.'

Gordon was an accomplished businessman and a shrewd negotiator, but this was the first time he'd used a gun to conduct business.

'I can't do that, Gordon. Just get me the money and you won't have to worry about it.'

'If I were to give you the money, what's to stop you asking for more and turning me into a cash cow for the next six-months, holding that video over me?'

'It's not like that, Gordon. I just want what I asked for and then we'll delete the video,' Nadine said, her voice shaking.

'I don't trust you.'

'Please, Gordon. Can you stop pointing that gun at me and we can talk about this?'

Nadine could see the bathroom door behind Gordon opening slightly and Josh's eye peer through the crack. His brow furrowed upon seeing the gun pointed at his girlfriend.

'Tell me who has the video and I'll let you go,' Gordon said impatiently.

Josh was careful to pull the door fully open as quietly as possible. The last thing he needed was a creaking hinge and for Gordon to spin around startled, his trigger finger snapping back.

Nadine watched nervously as Josh lunged toward Gordon taking hold of his gun hand and desperately trying to wrestle the firearm from him. Gordon was reluctant to surrender and the two men struggled around the room fighting over the gun. Nadine was ducking and diving, avoiding the direction the gun was pointed.

The gun became pushed between the two men and a muffled shot caused them to pause. There was a moment of silence as Nadine looked on anxiously. Josh stumbled back and collapsed to the floor.

A blood stain was growing on his shirt. Nadine screamed and fell down to her knees next to him hoping she could help.

'Oh my God,' she cried. 'What have you done?'

Gordon looked down upon them, the gun still trained in their direction.

'I suppose you're Josh,' Gordon said.

'How do you know his name?' Nadine asked glancing up at him in surprise.

'You said it last night as we were screwing,' Gordon snapped back.

Nadine knew she needed to stem the flow of blood gushing from Josh's stomach. She needed a towel and was about to get up and head into the bathroom when Gordon shifted the gun over to her.

'Where are you going?' he asked.

'To get some towels. Before he bleeds to death. Is that okay?'

'Be quick.'

Nadine rushed into the bathroom. Gordon stared at Josh, the half dead man struggling to breathe. Nadine returned seconds later with towels and knelt down beside her lover. She wrapped the cotton blankets tight around his waist to apply pressure. He winced in pain, gritting his teeth.

'I'm sorry,' she whispered.

'It's okay,' he replied gasping for breath.

Nadine looked up at Gordon with puppy dog eyes.

'We need to call an ambulance,' she pleaded.

'Not until I get that video.'

'He's going to die if we don't get help.'

'You tell me where to find the cell phone with the video and you can call for help.'

'No way,' Josh struggled to say. 'That video is the only thing keeping you alive, Nadine. What's to say he won't shoot you when he has it?'

'We don't have a choice, Josh,' Nadine said on the verge of tears.

She turned to Gordon, the barrel of the gun still threatening her.

'It's in another room.'

'What number?'

'1104.'

'Key?' Gordon said holding out his palm.

Nadine reached into Josh's jacket and pulled a key card from the inside pocket. She slammed it into Gordon's palm.

'There, you have it. Now let us go.'

'I don't think so. You're coming with me, so I know you're not lying.'

'We're not lying. I wouldn't lie, not now. I just want to get him help.'

'Then I suggest we hurry, before he bleeds out.'

Nadine was about to stand when Josh grabbed her wrist and pulled her back down. He stared daggers at Gordon.

'No, she's not going anywhere with you,' Josh shouted.

'You didn't seem to have a problem with that last night,' Gordon smirked.

'That was before you introduced the gun.'

Nadine knew time was of the essence and any delay would surely mean death for Josh. She needed to hurry this along and two men fighting to be the alpha wasn't helping.

'It's okay, Josh. I'll be quick, and then I'll call an ambulance,' she whispered.

Nadine tried to stand and again Josh pulled her down. She looked into his seductive eyes as they glistened.

'Be careful,' he said.

'I will,' she assured him, though she wasn't feeling confident about that herself.

Nadine made her way over to the door with Gordon following close behind with the gun at her back. She opened the door and peered out to make sure no other guests were in the corridor. Once she was happy, they both slipped out. Josh didn't like the way this was heading. He tried to stand, but the pain was too much and he fell back down.

Nadine walked at a quick pace, her bare feet shuffling along the carpeted flooring. Gordon now had the gun wedged in his coat pocket in case anyone appeared from their rooms and questioned the situation. He'd already shot one man and he didn't want to have to shoot anyone else if he could help it.

'I suppose you do this thing all the time,' Gordon said.

'Actually, you're our first.'

'Maybe you should reconsider your career choice. You're clearly not good at it.'

'We just misjudged the target.'

'You certainly did,' he said with a grin.

They reached room number 1104. Nadine stopped and gestured toward it. Gordon took out the key card from his pocket and held it up to her. He ordered her to open it. She slipped the key card into the slot until the green light lit up. She pushed open the door and entered. Gordon stepped in after her and gave one last cursory glance up and down the corridor before closing the door behind them.

Gordon pulled the gun from his pocket and aimed it at Nadine. She stood in the middle of the room waiting.

'Well?' Gordon asked.

'I don't know where it is,' she said, shaking her head and shrugging her shoulders.

'Then hurry up and find it, before your boyfriend bites the dust.'

Nadine began to search the room. She opened drawers of the dresser, but found nothing. She opened the drawer of the night-stand on one side of the bed, nothing. Nadine was beginning to worry it wasn't actually here and Gordon would put a bullet in her brain. She crawled over the bed to the other night-stand and slid open the drawer. There it was. The cell phone sitting innocently next to the bible. She took it out and showed Gordon who was still standing by the door keeping guard of her only exit.

'Throw it onto the bed,' he ordered.

Nadine did as she was asked. The device landing softly on the cushioned surface of the duvet.

'The video is on there. You can leave and let me help my boyfriend.'

Gordon picked up the phone and unlocked it searching through the memory. Every so often he glanced up at Nadine to ensure she wasn't planning anything. She wasn't. The gun was still set on her, the blackness inside the barrel like a black hole keeping her in check.

'Not yet,' he replied, trying to concentrate on multiple things.

He found the video folder on the phones storage, but it was empty. His eyes darted up to Nadine, his brow furrowed.

'There's nothing on here. Where is it?'

Nadine bolted for the nearby bathroom. She ducked inside and slammed the door behind her, locking it, before Gordon could get to her. He tried to push it open, but it was sealed.

'Nadine! Open the door! Tell me where the video is!' he shouted.

He waited for an answer, but there was no reply.

'Nadine, if you don't open this door, I'm going back to the other room and I will shoot Josh in the head.'

Still nothing but silence.

'Fine!' he shouted.

Gordon turned and headed for the door.

Nadine was cowering in the bathroom, sat on the floor leaning up against the door. She didn't know what to do. She was panicking and no doubt making things worse. She was trying to plan in her head when she heard the room door open and slam shut. Now was her chance. She took a deep breath and cautiously opened the bathroom door peering out. It was eerily silent. She tiptoed across the room hoping to escape before Gordon returned, but it was too late. The large man appeared from around the corner where he had been hiding. He grabbed her arm and wrapped himself around her as she struggled. His grip was too tight and all she could do was scream.

Her body was squirming in fear and in the process, she threw her head back and smashed her skull into Gordon's nose. The pain was horrendous as he felt the cartilage snap. He released his grip on the girl and she swung her arms around to get away. Luck was on her

211

side again as she caught his hand and knocked the gun from his fingers. It was cast across the room.

Nadine ran for the door, but Gordon lunged and tackled her to the floor before she could reach freedom. He climbed on top of her, his body weight pressing down, pinning her to the floor. She felt like her body was going to collapse under his immense frame. That became the least of her worries however as he wrapped his chubby fingers around her slender neck and began to squeeze the life out of her. Her arms began to flail, she attempted to pull his hands from her throat, but he was too strong. She caught sight of his gun lying innocently on the carpet by her. She extended her arm as much as she could to reach it, her fingers just scraping the butt. She was becoming weak, her lungs giving in. She needed one last show of strength. She stretched and grabbed the gun. She brought it forward and pushed the barrel into Gordon's waist and pulled the trigger. Gordon winced, a sharp pain slicing through his guts, but he kept his grip around her neck unwilling to yield. Nadine's arm dropped, the gun spilling from her hand. Her eyes closed as she let out her final breath. Gordon felt her body relax under him and fell off of her. He looked down at his blood stained shirt.

He needed to leave, things had gotten completely out of hand. He used the bed to help him get to his feet and then stumbled into the bathroom leaving a bloody trail behind him. He grabbed a towel off the railing and used it to dress his wound.

He released the gun from Nadine's dead grip and left the room. The cell phone on the bed started ringing. It was Josh. He'd managed to pull the hotel phone from the night-stand and had the receiver up to his ear listening to the dialling tone. He was praying Nadine would answer. His eyes were drowsy. His skin pale. He'd lost a lot of blood and he didn't know how much longer he could hold on. Nadine didn't answer though and he couldn't hold on. His body slumped to the side and the receiver slipped from his hand.

The elevator doors opened with a ping and Gordon shuffled out clutching his side. As he made his way across the busy lobby, he spotted a face he knew. A face he was very surprised to see there. His wife, Darcey, was sat in a lounge chair sipping at a cup of coffee. It seemed as if she was waiting for someone. He approached and collapsed into the chair opposite her.

'Darcey? What are you doing here?' he asked.

He was expecting her to be just as surprised to see him, but she wasn't. She remained rather calm considering the circumstances.

'I understand you had an interesting night,' she replied with a grin.

'How did—' he tried to ask, but she cut him off before he could finish his question.

'How did I know you spent the night with another woman? Because I set it up. It was a honeytrap. I hired them to blackmail you. Although by the looks of it, it didn't quite go to plan.'

Darcey took out a cell phone from her bag. After a few button pressed, she held it up for Gordon to see the screen. There on the display was a graphic video of Gordon and Nadine in the throes of passion. Gordon couldn't believe it. Darcey put the phone away before the entire lobby became an unintended audience.

'You always brag to your investors you're an honest man. You don't look very honest there. I wonder how many will withdraw their money from your latest property development if this were to get out. It could be rather scandalous and potentially newsworthy,' she said with glee.

Gordon frowned with anger. He knew his wife could be vindictive and conniving, but this surpassed his expectations.

'Why?' he foolishly asked.

'Because I'm sick of your constant betrayal. I know she's not the first and chances are she won't be the last, so I want a divorce. Problem is that damned prenuptial agreement you insisted I sign means I won't get a penny. I suppose you knew all along this would happen eventually. Well, I needed to make sure I got something for my five years of suffering your shit.'

Gordon was struggling to maintain consciousness. A lot of his blood had been left behind in the corridors and elevator of the hotel and his heart was having difficulty keeping his large frame full of the stuff.

'Are you okay, Gordon? You don't look too good. You're looking very pale,' Darcey asked revelling in this moment.

Gordon lifted up his shirt to reveal the gunshot wound, but it could barely be seen for the amount of blood covering the area.

'Ouch, that looks nasty,' Darcey smirked. 'I guess things really got a little out of hand.'

'I don't suppose you could call me an ambulance?'

Darcey couldn't believe her luck. It was like all her Christmases were coming at once.

'I don't think so,' she said. 'This has actually turned out better than I planned. If you die, I get all your money.'

Darcey burst out laughing finding it hard to contain her delight at this turn of events. The laugh didn't last long, though. It was interrupted by a sharp pain in her chest. Her brand new white dress was turning red. Gordon had the gun tucked down by his side pointing at her, the barrel letting out a small plume of smoke. She dropped her head as Gordon closed his eyes.

Tom Batt has been writing since the tender age of fourteen trying his hand at a variety of different genres both as screenplays and prose. He has several short film credits to his name and found success in competitions. He began writing short stories as a hobby and felt now was the time to share them with the world. He currently resides in Milton Keynes, UK.

Read more of his short stories at
www.toms-tales.com